STARK REALITY

A NOVEL by DAVID POULOS

Library of Congress Control Number: 2024924937

ISBN
978-1-964488-40-0 (Paperback)
978-1-964488-41-7 (eBook)
978-1-964488-64-6 (Hardcover)

Dedication

This novel is dedicated to my wife, Holly, and family, without whose love and support I would not have been able to complete the work. Also, this is for Jay Schiavo, who, when he fired me, said I'd never master the English language. Thanks for giving me the motivation to make a handsome living writing, speaking, and assisting businesses with their marketing efforts.

Chapter 1

Fairfax, VA

What else could happen today? That's the question that I ask myself on many mornings when I first crack my eyes open. I'm not sure whether this is a reaction to all that has happened in the last six weeks, or whether I'm just surprised I'm still alive to be thinking anything at all and grateful that I *can* crack my eyes open.

The sun was trying to break through the seemingly constant cloud cover, and not doing a great job of it, as I rolled out of bed, stretched, dressed, and fixed some food on my way out the door. I had a "meeting" to attend—debriefing in official terms—at a certain government agency whose name I dare not mention in Langley, Virginia. Traffic in northern Virginia had been escalating in volume over the years to the point where most major roads were like exiting a rock concert parking lot, leading to an ever-expanding "rush hour" that had ballooned to nearly three hours on either end of the day.

As a result, my 10:00 a.m. meeting needed an hour advance departure, and I lived fourteen miles away. By nine ten I had only progressed three miles to the famous Beltway when my cell phone chirped.

My defacto boss, Dick Gray, was calling to be sure I was actually going to make it and in some sort of condition to function. Based on my status the last time I saw him, his fears were wholly justified. When last we met, I was flat on my back in a hospital bed, tubes and wires sprouting from what seemed like every orifice, swaddled in bandages, able to speak only in a hoarse whisper.

"Hey, Dick, top o' the morning."

"Enough of the fake Irish crap—you on your way?"

"Yes, and thank you for the thoughtful inquiries as to my health—I'm fine, thanks."

"Make sure you make it on time. The director doesn't like to be kept waiting," he barked.

"God forbid I keep the big man waiting in his comfortable, walnut-paneled office for more than a few seconds," I quipped.

"Drop the attitude, and I'll see you in the small conference room on the top floor outside the director's office at nine fifty-five," he replied, and I heard a faint click as he hung up.

I had worked at Langley for about a decade in the 80s as a field operative, gotten sick of it, and decided that I could do better as a contractor by having the ability to pick and choose the assignments I accepted. In financial terms, I had been absolutely right, and the ability to sell my specific skills and talents back to the government who developed them had allowed me a certain type of freedom and paid for a lifestyle that gave me little pause when making purchases of anything smaller than a vehicle. But there are other issues on the employment table beyond money, and I did enjoy a certain status as a contractor that allowed me to act and speak in a certain fashion without fear of reprisal from within—hence the comment about keeping the director waiting. I could speak to Dick that way about the director in complete privacy and confidence. I could make such comments knowing that, as a political appointee, the director could be gone in as little as three years and the Agency would just keep on ticking along, toppling governments, influencing elections, shifting the balance of power, and spending ungodly sums of money in the process of "keeping the world safe" for American democracy. As a career "analyst," Dick had his own issues with the director, but never voiced them, as his personality wouldn't allow him to commit what he perceived as career suicide. One of the reasons I'd bailed out at the end of the big hair decade was to avoid turning into a Dick-level bureaucrat, forever locked behind a desk, updating spreadsheets, writing and filing manpower reports, and putting together performance reviews while attempting to juggle the needs of the "new" agency against the available resources.

While I hacked my way through Fairfax traffic, my mind went over how I would relate the events of my last assignment, ordering the events and setting up a timeline in my head that at least sounded plausible and didn't reveal some crucial details I'd rather keep private. I needed to get paid for this one and needed to get hired for the next one, so some things were better left unsaid. Dick knew some of them, and that was his lever on me, having those less than ideal operational gems in his hip pocket was his way of keeping me in line. The director didn't, and I saw no reason to disabuse him of his sterling impression of me thus far.

It had been a complex six weeks leading up to this little gathering, and fortunately I had more than a few minutes of creeping along to get it to sound about right. In fact, upon contemplation, it had all started with a small meeting in that same conference room on the fourth floor. So much for auspicious beginnings.

Chapter 2

Six Weeks Ago

Initially Dick had called me, said he had a little job for me, and wanted to go over the particulars if I was available later that afternoon. I told him I was, and we agreed on a time later that day.

When I'd arrived at the entrance, I flashed my government contractor ID badge at the gate guard, expecting to be waved through with the usual desultory look at the name and photo. The guard, whom I didn't recognize, made a great show of examining the card on the end of the ubiquitous lanyard for far longer than usual, and checked his list several times, as if the spelling of my name would preclude me from entry, and finally, almost reluctantly, waved me by. Initially, I chalked it up to the new-on-the-job look about the guard and didn't think anything of it. Looking back, that lack of trust in my instincts probably set the tone for the whole assignment, a clear indication that all was not what it seemed, even for me.

I'd made my way, almost unmolested, to the top floor conference room, and my radar was up and running at top speed. This was a different-sounding part of the building, partly because of the added unseen physical security, but partly because far fewer people were inhabiting this portion of the office, quelling the sound level to a low hum, in stark contrast to the constant din of keys clacking, conversations, printers, and other office-related gear that emitted from the lower floors. But that wasn't what was setting the hairs on the back of my neck at attention. I couldn't put my finger on it at the time, but something was definitely off. I had arrived a few minutes late, more as a dig at Dick than for any physical reason, and the other players were already arranged around the small wooden government-issue conference table. Dick, of course, in his perpetually wrinkled, grey, institutional suit sat opposite the door, looking like he hadn't slept in a few days. To his left sat his administrative assistant, Stuart, looking as put together as ever, suit and shirt starched and pressed to within an inch of its life, silk tie perfectly picking up the hue of the chalk stripe in the pants, not a hair out of place, gleaming pen poised to take comprehensive and copious if unnecessary notes. Most of the conference rooms in the building were equipped with recording equipment, either just audio or audio and video, so his notes were not for official records, just to be sure he didn't miss any pertinent details in his endless, futile effort to keep a few steps ahead of Dick. Dick may look rumpled and half asleep, but he didn't miss a trick, ever, and had invented a few new ones in his time.

To Dick's right sat the director, having finally given up the advantage of affecting a grand entrance after making everyone wait five minutes. He was taller than most at 6'3", dressed the part of a senior government executive, down to the White House cufflinks, last year's tie, scuffed brogans, and slightly stooped demeanor, like the weight of the world was resting on his wide, bony shoulders. His face gave away nothing with a practiced ease, having held secrets and played the game for over a decade at the Agency—long enough to know that knowledge is power, and power unwielded is power banked for later. The only movement was a slight downward turn of the corners of his mouth to express his displeasure at my late appearance.

Standing in the corner was another man I didn't recognize from his face, but I'd seen his type before, and it was never good news. Short, slight, sort of bland grey, wearing gold-rimmed glasses and with an intense stare behind them that said, "I'm not the guy to fuck with if you want to keep working here." We shook hands all around, the director making the introductions without mentioning or making reference to the grey guy in the corner, which I found odd, but not unprecedented. I was sure his identity would be revealed when the director felt the appropriate time had been reached, and I'd learned a certain amount of patience for such things over the last few years of field work.

After a few moments of minor small talk and requests for coffee, we got down to brass tacks. Dick started with the usual run down of the current atmosphere in the Agency, budget cuts, personnel changes, shifts in priorities and policy since the last time I'd worked for them, mostly for my benefit as the only outsider.

Then he tossed it off to the director, who stood, cleared his throat, and began with the inevitable, "We have a little problem, and we'd like your help, Mike." At that point, I knew I was getting involved in something pretty sizeable, because for the director to actually admit that they didn't have the resources to meet the challenge, and to an outsider no less, was momentous and set the tone for the balance of the afternoon.

As it turned out, the "little problem" he referenced involved the international trafficking in automatic weapons to support third-world civil wars for the benefit of affecting the outcome in our favor. Apparently, the head of the largest syndicate of movers and shakers in that murky area of the world, Georgi "Big G" Papadapoulos, had disappeared from his mega yacht anchored off Crete under unusual circumstances. If he wasn't found, that would leave a void, creating a power vacuum that would be filled only after some rather ruthless infighting among some of the more individualistic contenders to the throne. Considering that throne was probably responsible for generating billions of dollars in tax-free revenue, I expected that the ruthlessness level would be cranked up a notch or two even beyond the normal psychotic situation. Hence the need for an outsider with my particular set of skills. They needed to find Papadapoulos, get him back in place in one piece or, barring that, for his successor to be pro-American and, therefore, controllable and predictable. They also needed deniability in case things got out of hand in a public way, to keep the agency's hands clean when it blew up on them. Enter me, their secret weapon. In government terms, I supplied "plausible deniability" to the agency.

The director got to his point while explaining their needs in his usual roundabout way and, at that point, introduced the grey man in the corner as Demetrius Ceros, liaison to the State Department from the Greek government, or so it said on his card. In reality, he worked for us as an undercover operative on the Mediterranean desk. Ceros had information that would prove invaluable to me in my efforts to find Papadopoulos, or so they told me. He would be accompanying me on the initial investigation into Big G's whereabouts.

I normally work alone, or at most with my own handpicked team, who work for and are paid by me, not the Agency. I've found that cash inspires greater loyalty than patriotism among a certain group of skilled individuals, and I wanted only the best watching my back—it's what kept me alive in uncertain territory. The addition of a State Department babysitter didn't sit well at all with me, and when I started to raise an objection, I was preempted by the director in no uncertain terms to cooperate to the fullest extent possible with Ceros, or payment would not be forthcoming.

Dick had stood by quietly for most of the meeting, knowing that once the director finished his presentation, it would be up to him to seal the deal and provide all the operational support and the details I'd need to get started.

Dick picked up the ball smoothly as ever and laid it all out for me—operational support available, need for secrecy, cover identity, deniability, schedule, compensation, blah, blah, blah. I was still mulling over the initial moves needed to lose Ceros so I could get to the serious stuff without "help." I think he sensed this because Ceros cleared his throat to politely interrupt Dick's recitation and made a short but effective statement:

"I won't be in your way, but I do need to know where you are and what you're up to, if for no other reason than to provide you adequate support, like evacuation transport. Not only that, I'll need to be able to prep my bosses with the proper, I think you call it 'spin,' so that they aren't taken by surprise if things become more public than we're comfortable with. I suspect we'll need to help clean up after you. I've seen your file, and there will undoubtedly be some 'collateral damage' that will need to be controlled. I won't interfere—just keep me informed, and don't be shy about asking for help or information."

He passed me a small folded piece of paper. "That's my cell number, not on the embassy list."

I liked him right away.

Dick dropped all the relevant documents on the table in front of me, as the director rose to leave, signaling the meeting was over. Time was of the essence, and I needed to huddle with Ceros, get more background on "Big G," and then head home to pack for Greece. By the time I got what I needed from him to hit the ground running, it was rush hour again. I hacked my way back through Tyson's Corner on Dolly Madison Drive, headed down the Beltway to Braddock Road to my little corner of the world. Twelve miles—fifty-five minutes. Greece was starting to sound pretty good.

On the way to Dulles Airport, I had sent text messages to the team members I'd likely need, just a couple of sentences, with no detail—they would know to call me immediately on the scrambled number to get flight information and a quick outline of the job. We'd take separate flights in, some arriving in a day or so, some on the one behind mine, to stagger the arrival both for security and need. Too many bodies arriving at one time with government contractor passports would send up a flag and make Ceros's cover job harder.

The flight left on time, after having been treated like a criminal at the security portal, as usual. I took my first-class seat after a surreptitious but thorough look around the cabin for familiar or suspicious faces, but saw nothing out of the ordinary. I settled in with my complimentary beverage and read the file three times, committing it to memory. I leaned back, closed my eyes, and for the next eight hours let my subconscious go to work on a plan to get the information I needed to find Big G, get him back on board his boat in one piece, and get him back in control of his dirty little empire, with our government's full backing.

Chapter 3

Athens, Greece

I was met at the airport outside of Athens by an anonymous sedan and its accompanying nondescript driver, Ceros's colleague. He spotted me from the description Ceros had given him and fell in beside me as we strolled through the airport to baggage claim, not saying a word. We pushed down the hallway among the turmoil that seems to always be in evidence in the Athens Airport, showed my passport to the relaxed-to-the-point-of-dozing immigration official, got my documents stamped without raising so much as a monobrow, and moved through the checkpoint to pick up my meager luggage. When I'm on assignment on foreign soil, I like to shop the local retailers for most everything, including clothes and shoes; it helps me blend in to the crowd better and gives me domestic labels if something needs to be cast off in a hurry and is later recovered by those by whom I'm trying to avoid detection.

We got through customs quickly and brushed our way out the doors into the blazing sunshine and moist heat of an Athens morning, the sun bouncing painfully off the concrete sidewalk and the sea of windshields in the pick-up lane. In the relative quiet of the outdoors, the exhortations of local cabbies, tour bus drivers, and other hawkers plying their trade were even more obvious after the relative silence of the plane. We walked across the landscaped island to a "locals only" parking lot and dumped my bag in the miniaturized trunk of his compact nondescript Ford sedan.

My new driver still hadn't said a word, just dropped into the front driver seat, flipped the key, popped the door locks, and waited for me to fold my 6'2" frame into the little car. I managed it, barely, after a quick scan of the horizon for 360 degrees, checking for folks loitering unaccountably, fixing things that didn't need fixing, or standing in places that didn't seem natural. I saw nothing out of the ordinary, but then again, they could have been there and I could have missed them—whoever "they" were. I couldn't shake the feeling of being watched, but no one but the driver and Ceros knew of my arrival, my real name, or my reason for visiting, so a tail indicated a leak in that tiny circle that would have to be plugged before anything further could be done. For the level of sophistication that Big G's operation had shown so far, a blatant tail seemed a bit out of character and sloppy to start with, and they had other, more subtle and reliable ways of gathering information and keeping track of us while we were in-country.

We pulled out of the lot without complication and headed into the city of Athens, working our way through light morning traffic toward the Athens Hilton. There were advantages to Uncle Sam picking up the tab for my expenses. The Hilton was large, and I could easily get lost among the tourists and business travelers among the six hundred or so guests and remain anonymous. I could stay here as long as I remained that way. Once someone from the wrong side of town knew I was here, I'd have to find different accommodations, but for now, this would make it easy to get anywhere on the mainland and most of the islands quickly, and make it comfortable while I made phone calls on the scrambled phone and used their in-room Wi-Fi.

I'd learned early on that sometimes in such situations, sleep was your best weapon and that the clarity that resulted from a good night's sleep often led to more forward progress than banging your head away at the problem for hours while fatigued and disoriented. I hit the "up" button on the lobby elevators and headed to my room for a few hours' shut-eye.

* * *

I awoke five hours later, rested and a bit time displaced, but ready to eat and get started with the evening's activities. I had an agenda, and the darkness made it much easier to accomplish. So I had some time to kill in a local restaurant refueling and getting used to the local patois. I jumped in the shower, dug some clean clothes out of my valise, put out the "Do Not Disturb" sign, and headed down the hall to the elevator, after putting some rudimentary but effective security devices in place— more as an indicator that someone had "visited" my room than to keep him out or capture him.

I'd been stationed in Greece a couple of decades prior for a brief period, not long enough to really learn the language, but long enough to pick up a few essential words and phrases that would let me blend in a bit if I applied the local accent well. I remembered a small café not far from the hotel that would provide a meal at this early hour without creating any suspicion, so I headed south into the city in search of some good Greek food and did some nondescript thinking.

First order of business after dinner was to do a little local shopping, to source some items I'd need before I got too deep into this little errand. I'd gotten quite a bit of usable intel from the file Dick had provided, and I wasn't scheduled to meet with Ceros again until the next morning. I had a pretty good idea of what I might be up against in the form of an unknown person or group who had the stones to kidnap one of the most powerful figures in the Mediterranean underworld. I wasn't going any further without procuring some reliable firepower, on the off chance that these folks weren't in it for the mah jong tiles. Chances were excellent these folks weren't going to be happy with me when I upset their applecart, and they didn't seem like the type to settle such affairs with a stern talking-to. That made the first order of business for the evening a trip to one of the less-than-desirable neighborhoods near the waterfront. I was looking for a tavern, not too seedy, but one that didn't cater to tourists but to fishermen, longshoremen, and other enterprising types—where a few drachmas in the right hands and a quick few words in the right ears would lead to a bit of information as to where an untraceable firearm might be found.

After half an hour of strolling somewhat purposefully along the quayside roads, I found just the type of place I needed. Stepping into the smoky room, it took a moment for my eyes to adjust to the low light and nearly opaque air. Apparently, the Greeks hadn't read the Surgeon General's report on smoking and cancer, and the air was blue and fragrant with a variety of tobacco products. The noise level was similar to those you'd hear in places of this type worldwide—that is to say, loud and getting louder as the stories unfolded and the level of inebriation rose.

Working men inhabited most of the seats accompanying the few tables in evidence and most of the stools at the bar. Most were drinking local beer or Ouzo. One group at the back seated around a larger table for eight was passing a large, raffia-covered bottle of local wine and swapping fishing stories at top volume. As expected, most heads turned in my direction and the noise level dropped quickly and alarmingly seconds after I crossed the threshold. I took two steps to the bar and ordered a beer in Greek. The heads returned to their original direction, and noise climbed back up after a beat or two. I'd been vetted as a nonthreatening entity, not a local cop anyway, and therefore not worth further notice. I mentally breathed a sigh of relief, found a small table in back, and sat down to get a better grasp of the local action.

It didn't take long to develop a mental list of likely candidates for my information needs. That list included the sort of down-at-the-heels, sketchy-looking character sitting in the back corner of the bar, making faces at the seasoned-looking barmaid. It also included the short, dark, unshaven chap in the black watch cap at the table next to mine, also by himself but clearly known to those seated around the room, based on the way they kept glancing at him as if waiting for him to do something unusual. That "something unusual" turned out to be him buying a round of drinks for everyone— after a rather long, loud rant that, based on my limited grasp of Greek, had something to do with how shaky the government was, how they had mistreated the commoners, and how the current administration had no hope of helping the working man make a living, as it was too busy with the local prostitutes and gambling. As a tribute to the last administration, who had apparently treated them all more kindly, he raised his glass and nodded at the barmaid, who promptly started filling glasses and shots and distributing them around the room. All glasses were raised, the toast concluded, and the short, slightly stocky figure sat down and went back to his business, muttering quietly.

That little performance, probably a nightly event here, made the sketchy guy in the corner my best candidate, so I sauntered by the short fellow's table to thank him for the drink and, after a brief exchange, changed direction toward the rear, as if heading to the facilities. I swung into the empty seat at the bar next to him without looking at him directly, got the barmaid's attention, ordered another beer, and waited for the right moment.

It came in about five minutes. I'd been keeping track of him for the last hour or so, and he'd ordered three beers in that time, which meant that there was a trip to the facilities in his near future. My plan was to wait until he headed that way, follow him in discreetly, and see if I could hit pay dirt with a couple of well-chosen questions and a noticeable wad of cash. It worked out about as I'd figured. He headed back toward the rear of the tavern and disappeared into the small door to the left of the back of the hallway. After a respectable wait, I followed, found him at the last of three bowls, just finishing his business. Perfect. I whispered a few words in Greek that I'd learned form a gunnery sergeant back in the day. He blanched a bit, frowned, and then grinned a shy smile and said the magic words, "How much you got?" Done deal. We haggled a bit, and he finally handed me a ragged business card with a phone number handwritten on one side and info for a nondescript garbage hauling company on the printed side.

"Call that number after eleven tonight. Instructions will follow," he breathed and walked back out into the bar.

After a few moments, I followed, but by the time I got back to my drink, he was gone.

I don't follow such information blind, no matter how much or little I paid for it. I had an hour or so before the call, so I headed back to the hotel. Nobody had disturbed my little tells, and I entered my room to find it expectedly empty. I pulled the satellite scrambler phone out of my pocket and dialed the number Ceros had given me from memory. He picked up after a few rings, awake but relaxed—I'd reached him at home with his family. He asked where I was and asked if he could call me back. Five minutes later, the little phone rang in my hand, and he sounded a bit more like I remembered, businesslike and alert.

"How can I help you, Mr. Stark?"

"I need the lowdown on a phone number," I replied. I read him the number, and he said to give him half an hour and he'd call me back. I disconnected and sat back on the bed to wait, thinking about what I needed to do later that evening.

There were only so many ways tonight's appointment could go. I could make the call, depending upon what Ceros came up with, set up a meet, and I could get what I needed and walk away unscathed. That's the best case scenario. Less than that created complications for everyone involved. It was possible my presence had been detected here, but after so short a time, not likely. If not, this could go down as a simple mugging—they get me in an out of the way spot, take my money, and walk away after a light beating to incapacitate me. Not likely, unless they brought quite a few colleagues and some impressive firepower, but possible. Another possibility would be that things could go really wrong, and they could be aware not only of my identity but purpose and would have considerably more preparation underlying a simple meeting for a transaction.

My thoughts were interrupted by the little phone buzzing in my pocket. I pulled it out—Ceros—and answered.

"Mr. Stark, the number you gave me is a cellular number registered to one Stavros Piriopolis of Athens, no wants and warrants current, short criminal history, including some burglary, modest property crimes, and some grand theft, one conviction for a two-year stretch, ending a year or so ago, probation still active for the next two years. Several known associates listed in the local police files, including some local thugs with B&E records, small time graft and theft. A fairly unsavory circle, if I do say so. What have you gotten yourself into so early after your arrival?"

"Nothing to worry about, just doing a little shopping," I responded. "I'd have come to you for some of the items I'll need, but I don't have two weeks for the paperwork to clear and all the information on the transaction to be recorded and filed for unveiling later at the appropriate time," I quipped.

"I understand, but please be extremely cautious around these fellows," he warned.

"The information to which I have access is official, but given the caliber of the average policeman, there could be much more of a backstory on any of these gentlemen than is recorded in their files."

"Most Greek men of a certain age have spent some time in the military, have been trained in rudimentary tactics, weapons use, and hand-to-hand engagement. These aren't going to be pushovers if it comes to physical interaction," he noted.

I reassured him that I could take care of myself in such a situation, but that I would be careful not to make the outcome troublesome for him. It seemed to placate him, and he wished me luck and rang off after confirming our appointment in the morning.

At about twenty minutes after eleven, I dialed the number, using the garbage hauler from the men's room as a reference. After a moment's hesitation, the man who had answered the phone handed it off to another, who started abruptly without introduction, "You want guns?"

I replied that was the case.

"How many? What kind you want?" he spat.

"I'll need two pistols, automatics, SIGs, Kimbers, Colt, something with some stopping power, 9 MM parabellum, or .45 ACP. Also a long gun, Remington M7, chambered .308 with a 7x scope, mounted and zeroed. Plus a case for the rifle and two hundred rounds of ammo for each."

"Big order for someone I never heard of," he replied.

"Big orders pay big money," I replied casually.

"Petros said he meet you in tavern—you look like American army. Why you not ask them for guns?" he asked.

"This isn't an official request, and I'm not in the army," I replied.

"Unofficial orders cost more," he quipped. "Bring $3000 American, cash, to this location at five this morning. I have what you want, or close to it," he said.

"That's a bit steep, but I'm in kind of a hurry. What's the address?" I asked.

He rattled off an address in the tougher part of downtown Athens, told me not to be late, and hung up. Total time of the exchange, about thirty seconds. Smart, untraceable, location of his choosing, he was feeling pretty secure about this whole thing at this point. If things didn't go as I wanted, that feeling would quickly evaporate.

I needed to get my body more aligned with the clock, so I lay down and slept after setting the alarm for four o'clock. I felt pretty secure as well, knowing that I knew more about them than they knew about me, despite the brief fishing expedition on the phone. I'd gone into more dangerous situations with less intel, and my gift for improvisation had carried the day. I had no doubt it would do so again, if necessary. I slept like a stone.

* * *

The alarm woke me at 4:00 a.m., and I popped up, fairly refreshed and ready for the coming day's activities. I dressed in the last clean clothes I had in my bag, dark slacks and a dark button-down shirt, and headed out the door after securing my tells, heading for the lobby and something to eat. I got online in the hotel lobby, which at that hour I had to myself, and found a reliable set of directions to the address they had given me. Now I knew the reason for the early meet time; the address was listed as Hellenic Bakery. They were doing a little business out of the back of the bakery and wanted to get it done before too many employees showed up, after having been up all night gathering the items I needed.

That was good for me since they'd be a little fatigued and off their game, while I was fully rested. Points in my favor.

I headed out of the hotel, following the directions for about two miles of progressively smaller, progressively poorer roads, until I got to the bakery about thirty minutes early. No life showed through the front window, but none was expected. I wandered around back to the alley behind the building, dead quiet except for the humming of air conditioning units on the roofs. I did a quick reconnaissance of the area, saw no visible watchers in place, at least that I could find. I took a seat on the concrete abutment lining the back of the alley and waited. Ten minutes before the appointed time, the end of the alley lit up with the headlights of a dark-colored, battered, 70s vintage van, rolling slowly but deliberately down the alley toward me. It rolled to a stop five feet from me, and three forms got out, leaving a driver behind the wheel, for a total of four. Four to one odds weren't as bad as they could have been, but I got a little shot of adrenaline as they approached. They walked up to within a foot of me, swaggering like they owned the place, slowly and confidently. The taller of the three, in the lead and from his clothes and demeanor, clearly the leader, said, "You here from Petros?"

I nodded, and he motioned me into a slightly recessed doorway, where he unlocked the door with a key and motioned us all inside. He flipped on the harsh overhead fluorescents as the door banged shut behind us and stepped into a small but surprisingly well-appointed commercial bakery. Ovens flanking the walls, racks on wheels with flour-stained trays of baking sheets and loaf pans scattered about, two large walk-in coolers at the back and a doorway opposite leading to the storefront facing the main street.

Stavros took a seat on a vanilla bucket behind a flour-covered nickel-topped table, but no one else made any moves to find a seat, standing in front of and behind me, alert but relaxed, like this sort of thing happened every day. Maybe it did for all I knew, but they didn't appear concerned about much of anything.

He was of average height, shorter than I was, stocky but not fat, maybe 205 lbs., about forty-five with dark hair, longish, receding, and slightly oily. Based on my olfactory senses, he hadn't showered before the meeting after doing some mildly heavy lifting during the night—a good sign. Stavros motioned to me to pull up a chair, a battered office version from the 40s tucked in a corner with a broken wheel.

He leaned forward over the table and quietly said to me, "Let me see cash."

I slowly reached into my pocket and pulled out a street roll, mostly ones on the inside, but outer wrapped with thirty $100 bills. I held it up just long enough for them to register the denomination on the top bill and the size of the roll and tucked it back in my pocket. Then I leaned forward and said, "Let's see the weapons." He nodded and motioned to the fellow behind me, who had a rather ugly scar running down the side of his face from his eyebrow to his jaw line. He turned, stuck his head out the door, and whistled. In a moment, the door reopened, and in walked another player, the driver of the van, carrying a large, apparently heavy, black cloth duffle bag, the type American kids carry ice hockey gear around in. He stepped up to the table and dropped the bag on the table with a slightly metallic thud.

Stavros casually opened the bag's zipper, reached in, and brought out the long gun first, handling it with a relaxed confidence that said that this was just another product to him, nothing special. His attitude betrayed little of the quality of his merchandise, like this was just a small taste of his whole line. The weapon was clearly used, but in very good condition from all appearances. He racked back the bolt to show an empty chamber and handed it to me for inspection. Everything appeared to be in great shape, well oiled and clean, functioning smoothly, optics in good shape. No way to tell function or accuracy without firing, but so far so good. I put the rifle down on the table and nodded. He reached in the bag and pulled out two small compact automatic pistols, racked the slides, and handed them over as well. SIG Sauer P250s, chambered in .45 ACP, short barrel, complete with LaserMax laser site device, compact, light, accurate to about 150 feet—perfect for my needs for the next few days.

Stavros reached in the bag yet again and brought out some boxes—ammo for both weapons.

Then he reached in one more time, brought out a long box, and laid it on the table. He looked me in the eye and said, "If this works out, there's more if you need it. I even include little gift," pulling a short, ugly, sawed-off, twelve-gauge tactical pump shotgun out of the box. Pumping the action twice, he handed me the empty weapon, saying, "I throw in five boxes of shells, too, keep you busy for a while." I nodded and smiled, set down the scattergun without really examining it, retrieved the roll from my pocket, and counted off the three grand quickly onto the tabletop. He nodded as I finished, and one of his henchmen stepped up, repacked the guns and ammo in the bag, held it out to me, and pointed at the door. I turned to leave with my prize as Stavros cleared his throat to get my attention. I turned to face him, and his face grew grave, losing his confident grin. He said in a low growl, "None of us was ever here, right?" I nodded and made it to the door in three strides, leaving them to their daily routine. I turned out of the alley onto the larger road, slung the bag over my shoulder, and started humping it along the edge of the road toward more hospitable sectors of Athens. I heard it before I turned; as I looked back, I saw the van pull out of the side street, heading my direction from behind, accelerating quickly. As they pulled even with me, one of Stavros's colleagues in the passenger seat rolled down the window, lifted a huge black pistol above the window sill so that I could clearly see it, tapped his temple with the barrel twice, raised an eyebrow at me, and the van sped off, warning delivered. Needless to say, with my attention focused on the van, I didn't pay any attention to the small nondescript sedan that pulled out of the alley a moment later and pulled into a parking spot on the other side of the street, the driver talking quietly into a small cell phone.

Once I got back to the larger road, I flagged a Mercedes cab, hopped in the back, and in broken Greek directed the driver to take me to the hotel. Despite the feeling that everyone had been moving in slow motion from cautious mistrust, the whole exchange had only taken twenty minutes, so I still had the early morning lobby to myself when I returned, with the exception of a small, neatly attired businessman reading the *Financial Times* in the corner. I headed straight to the elevator and back to my room by a more circuitous route, up one floor and back down the stairs to the opposite end of the hall, and from there to my room. Tells intact, I slid in the key card and stepped in, dropping the heavy bag on the bed. Mission One accomplished, now I could focus on what I came to do—find Big G.

Chapter 4

Oranjestad, Aruba

The room was practically dark, the only illumination coming from the glow of the multiple computer screens and a small desk lamp in the huge, ornate library/office. An unusually large man sat behind the desk, his attention focused in the middle distance while he listened to a caller on the other end of the phone. He listened silently for what seemed like several minutes, and a slow, careful smile spread across his face. He politely thanked the caller with a tone in his voice unmistakable to the caller that reminded him that he owed the large man a huge debt, and that this didn't quite clear it off his ledger but certainly helped it go in the right direction. The caller rang off, and the large man sat back in his chair, gold cufflinks gleaming in the subdued lighting, and let his mind reel out the possible outcomes that this new information portended. One of his contacts had called to tell him that an American had just emerged from a bakery in a shabby part of Athens carrying a sizeable, heavy-looking bag. Further, this stranger was followed a few moments later by four local men, one of whom looked like one of the big man's lower level salesmen, a man named Stavros. How he had found Stavros, what the American was doing in Athens and who he might be were still a mystery, but the big man made some educated guesses based on his watcher's descriptions and the timing of the meeting. He came to the conclusion that this might be more than a minor annoyance in the long term.

There were several paths that his plan could now traverse, but he carefully played each out in his mind, weighing the odds of each coming to pass, rejecting those where the parameters were too narrow for success or odds of a successful outcome for any reason were too low. That left him with just three possible outcomes. Based on his vast wealth, seemingly bottomless network of contacts, prepaid influence in the most useful places still intact, he could really dictate the outcome he chose. But he took it as a personal challenge to work with one path and see where it went, adjusting to the various uncontrolled variables, shifting time, resources, and focus to achieve his goal. Trapped in that bulky body was a first-class mind, and he had developed unparalleled skills at this particular type of strategic thinking—skills effective enough to catapult him to the lower rungs of the Forbes global wealth list, were he to be in a legitimate business.

But one didn't get to the top of that list without making at least a few enemies, and while he had not seen the need to gratify his own ego by going out of his way to make any, a few had been unavoidable, and one business relationship in particular had been ongoing and rancorous. Such arrangements could be useful under the right circumstances, but this one had been sapping his resources and mental energy for too long to be of use at this point, and he was taking steps to resolve the matter as he sat there.

The smile on his beefy, florid face widened, and he heaved his bulk up out of his chair, donned his suit coat and hat, and made his way down the hallway to the private elevator. He dropped slowly down to the private garage and made his way into the hand-built Rolls Royce Silver Cloud that waited there, driver behind the right-hand wheel, waiting patiently for his boss to force his nearly four-hundred-pound frame into the rear passenger compartment and settle before pulling out into the warm, humid Caribbean evening. Tomorrow, he would take the second step in his strategy, but until then, unless the situation changed drastically, he had the evening to himself. He mumbled a few words to the driver, raised the partition behind the driver, and sat back to let his superior strategic mind work through the possible scenarios again—searching for weakness, working the angles, determining the odds of success for each move, until the most likely path was revealed, clear and unwavering. The smile returned to his face, and he relaxed until he reached his destination.

Athens, Greece

My meeting with Ceros wasn't scheduled until 11:00 a.m., so I had a few hours to get organized. I needed to know some specific things before I got down to the job at hand. I needed to see his yacht, the last place he had been seen. I needed names and contact info for some of his close associates and employees; I needed to get inside this guy's life a little bit, see where he lived and how he thought, what he was up to. There had not been a ransom note delivered to any of his offices, nor to his boat, and no one had stepped forward claiming credit for the disappearance. I wanted to review the forensics reports the local police had compiled, and I needed a way to get around that was private—a powerful but low-key car with a capable driver would be helpful, especially one who spoke Greek fluently. The one Ceros assigned me might have fit the bill if he didn't work for the state department. I needed to compartmentalize who knew what I knew, and a mute driver exclusively in my employ would be the best option.

Two calls came in from my associates en route to Greece on the sat phone, updating their arrival schedules and asking about various items they might need once they arrived. I assured them I had secured a good local source for a variety of useful items under the radar. We arranged a place for them to stay near my hotel, as my own policy dictated that they not stay in the same hotel as me for a variety of reasons. I was to meet them there once they arrived, so there was no connection to my colleagues for anyone watching at the Hilton to observe. I called to arrange a cab to the embassy, got cleaned up after my little adventure that morning, and put my tells in place on my way out the door.

I arrived at the American Embassy in good time, a few minutes ahead of schedule, after we hacked our way through traffic that never seemed to abate in downtown Athens – shades of route 495 in Washington leapt to mind. I announced myself at the front desk, showed my "new" passport, and was instructed to take a seat. The embassy was nothing to write home about, similar to American missions in any number of second-tier countries, government-issue furniture, scrubby looking walls painted industrial beige, worn carpets in need of a good cleaning, but fairly quiet. The staff was polite to the point of being obsequious, asking if I wanted coffee, if I was comfortable, etc., in the five minutes it took for Ceros to make his way from a back office to the lobby after I was announced by the marine guard at the reception desk.

Ceros looked just as grey and stooped as he had in Virginia and looked like he could use a few extra hours of sleep. Surely the loss of one multibillionaire, more or less, couldn't be causing him any undue strain, could it? He crossed the lobby and shook my hand, and I trailed him through the warren of cubes back to his office. We entered his office and continued through it to an attached conference room, more standard government-issue, long, wooden table, eight chairs of indeterminate vintage, no windows, single centered light fixture, blue/pink fluorescents—altogether a typical if uninspired meeting room in a U.S. government facility. We sat, he offered me coffee, and we got to it right away.

"Mr. Stark, how can I aid you in your efforts? Please be candid. I've taken the liberty of disabling all recording devices."

"I need information, and I need access. I need to do some snooping on Big G's boat, assuming that it's vacant, which means I need access to it, an address of the slip, or a way to get out to it. I need a list of his known associates, his staff, his friends, his enemies, and the last known whereabouts for all of them. I need access to his private office, if there is such a thing, and I need a car at my disposal with a local driver, one I can pay directly, not embassy staff."

"How do you Americans say...you don't ask for much? That's a very involved, almost impossible request. I gave my word to cooperate fully, but I can only go so far with the staff and time I have. I assume time is of the essence?

"Can you prioritize your request so we can start on the most important work immediately?"

"I think I can make this easier on you. Give me the information on his boat first, and pass along the database work along to your pals in the states," I replied.

It would take me an afternoon to go through the boat if it was as big and opulent as described, and the Agency's computers could likely spit out the remainder of the information in just a few hours.

"I can do that now. The ship is anchored off the coast of Crete, on the southeast shore of the island. I know the local police captain. I can have a small launch waiting to take you to it, along with the access permits necessary to get on board. I can have him call ahead and relieve the staff, if they haven't left yet. You'll have the run of the ship, but not likely for very long," he replied.

"Why the rush?" I asked

"The local police captain was a personal friend of Big G's, and in my opinion, likely on his payroll as well in some capacity. He has to help in some way to put on a good show, but he's not happy about a stranger rooting through his friend's things unsupervised. He figures if he can limit your time there, you'll run out before you find anything incriminating," he said.

"I'll be quick, but I know what I'm looking for, and I'll either find it or not, regardless of what the local police captain thinks."

Ceros looked a bit concerned at this.

"Maybe I should turn my attentions to *him*, put him in an interrogation room, and ask him some rather pointed questions as part of my inquiries?"

Now he was really looking grey.

"Let me worry about him."

"While I have my doubts about his personal choice of colleagues, I do have to work with the man while I'm here, so if you could handle him a bit delicately, we may find he comes in handy upon occasion."

"No worries, I'll be tactful."

"I've arranged your flight to Crete and a car there to take you to the town closest to the ship," he replied, trying to keep things moving.

"How quickly can I be there, and how many others have been there ahead of me?"

"Your flight leaves in two hours, takes about thirty minutes door to door. Town is about forty-five more by car. It's nearly noon—you could be on the boat by cocktail hour."

"Same guy going to take me to the airport?"

"If he's available—problem?"

"No, he's just a bit chatty…

He smiled, finally. "Nickos doesn't say much, but he's very knowledgeable about the area and an excellent driver. He's also extremely capable in a number of other less marketable skills that have been known to come in handy when traveling with those in our profession."

"Could I keep him on Crete, and when I come back? Does he work for you directly, or is he State?"

"I pay him out of my general funds, but he's not a State Department employee. I put him on my household budget account—he's my wife's brother. I can arrange for him to accompany you and to drive you while you're here, if you'd like."

"Do you feel he can be trusted, counted on in a clutch?"

"Implicitly," he replied. I believed him.

"Good, make the arrangements. Tell him he's working strictly for me for the next two weeks and is to do as I ask, without any questions."

"I'll pass it along, but he's not a slave," he replied.

"I didn't mean it that way. I just wanted him to be aware that he didn't need to report to you—I'm trying to give you some deniability here, work with me…"

"I appreciate your concern. I'll let him know," he said with a slight grin. I was starting to warm up to this Ceros character.

"I do have a few things to pass on about Mr. Papadapoulos. I have had peripheral dealings with him from time to time, and I can assure you he's not your average industrialist. He is a truly formidable individual, and while most generous with those who can be of use to him, he can be harsh in the extreme with those who betray his trust or mean him harm. I have heard stories that would make even a man of your reputation blush. I urge you to use extreme caution when dealing with his associates, even his enemies. You'll not likely get a truthful piece of information from any of them, as Big G values his privacy above almost all else. A brief story to illustrate this in a way that will properly emphasize the point:

"At one time, years ago, when his empire was smaller but growing and his 'product line' was more limited to handheld devices, a gentleman and his 'entourage' called on one of Big G's offices, demanding to see him, saying they knew where he was and what he was up to and wanted to make a purchase. They burst through the door, terrorized his private secretary, creating chaos in the office, demanding to see Big G. It turned out their intelligence was, shall we say, flawed, as Big G was in another country at the time. The gang stayed in his office waiting for him to materialize, shouting to anyone that would listen that they wanted to make a good deal on some weapons and they needed to see him right away, and that he should come out of hiding and face them like a man. Such indiscretions are not tolerated by your average arms dealer, let alone someone of Big G's caliber and proclivities. When he returned to the city the following day and learned of these gentlemen's behavior, he was nearly beside himself. He made discrete inquiries and uncovered the identity of the whole group. Within three weeks, all of them disappeared, one by one, including their families. It seems a string of extremely bad luck befell them in serial fashion—car accidents, drownings and boat accidents, muggings gone bad, accidental electrical fires. In total, nineteen people gone in less than a month. The local police were completely baffled, and none of the deaths were ever connected directly to Big G, but the message was sent loudly and clearly to those in certain circles. Big G was not to be trifled with under any circumstances, or everyone you know and love would suffer."

"Which makes my job easier, because it must take a very capable person or group to abduct such a scary and dangerous individual—that narrows the field of suspects a bit, doesn't it?"

"I suppose it does, indeed," he replied ruefully.

"Anything else you can tell me?" I asked.

"There is much I can tell you about Big G, most of it not terribly relevant to the current situation," he replied. "I will tell you that despite his activities in certain business endeavors, he has built a reputation among some very powerful people as a generous, dedicated, and giving man, and his allies will defend him to the death. His enemies are a different story, but even *they* will admit a grudging respect for his acumen and methodologies in accumulating a vast fortune and tremendous political power in the international stage among legitimate business concerns. I understand you are a very capable man who gets things done in a rather direct fashion, often at the expense of some collateral damage. Tread lightly when making inquiries, but you must get him back in place at the first possible opportunity if you want to prevent a massive bloodletting among the international arms community. Few others could control such a community as Big G has, and the stability of this part of the world as we know it could depend on maintaining that control."

"I'll be gentle with the locals, not to worry, Ceros," I quipped.

His face fell, and he said tersely, "I'll have Nickos waiting outside your hotel in one hour. Here are your airline ticket, a local cell phone with my numbers programmed in, and $2000 in local currency. Sign this receipt, and you can be on your way. I'll expect to hear from you each evening on the number I gave you. Please let me know if you need anything else."

I shook his hand and headed back through the now quiet reception area, out the door to the street, and hailed a cab back to the hotel to await the silent Nickos.

Chapter 5

Mediterranean Sea

The first thing he noticed when he regained consciousness was the smell. A strong, oily, fishy, salty tang to the air told him he as somewhere near a commercial port. Then he noticed the vague, gentle movement of the floor and felt the slight vibration deep beneath him that told him he was aboard a ship, a large one at that, likely a tanker or containership by the condition of the floor, what he could see. His vision was somewhat hampered by the loosely woven cloth bag over his head.

The last thing he remembered was that he was in the pilothouse of his yacht talking to the captain, a trusted employee of many years, when the windscreen shattered and the captain slumped to the ground. He'd turned and run straight into a large, dark shape, and the last thing he saw was a white rag coming up over his nose and mouth, and then blackness as he lost consciousness. Now he was here, in the hold of a boat, tied and bagged, with no idea how long he had been there or, more importantly, who had arranged such a thing. His razor-sharp mind, dulled with the residuals of the drug they had used to subdue him, was starting to clear, and all the important questions were starting to fall into place. How had whoever it was gotten through his rather extensive security? Who of his detractors and competitors was responsible? What did they want from him? Was the plan to ransom for money or access or leverage for something else? He had surmised that they didn't want him dead; if they did, he wouldn't be here.

Then the less obvious but more personal questions started to surface. Who knows I'm gone? Is anyone coming to rescue me? What are they asking for my return? Who has to pay? He put many of those aside mentally and started taking inventory of his physical condition, his surroundings, and listing his resources that could be used for escape.

His pockets had been emptied, by the feel of it, although he carried little of value while on the yacht—he didn't need to; virtually everything he could possibly desire was on board at all times. He didn't even carry his wallet unless going ashore for some reason. The keys to the offices, cars, and such were kept in other places; the captain carried items related to the boat, so he had little to work with there. His Rolex Mariner wristwatch had a stainless steel case and band, but unless he could get the bindings close enough to rub the edges on, it wasn't much help. He was wearing boat shorts and a knit shirt, and sandals—no laces with tips to work with, no belt to use as any kind of rope or extension. He couldn't see well enough in a narrow field of vision through the bag to get any kind of comprehensive look at his surroundings, even to find the door, if there even was one.

He took a quick physical inventory, detected pain when he breathed lower than midline on his left side, a likely sign of a broken rib. His wrists and feet were bound tightly, and the circulation was not quite cut off but was certainly limited, making his hands tingly and weak, as were his ankles. His face felt stiff on one side, and as he rolled his head on the decking floor, he felt a lump on the right side of his head and felt swelling and pressure. None of these were disabling or even debilitating, but could hamper his efforts to escape when the time came, at least initially, especially the hands and feet. Inventory complete and found satisfactory, his mind moved on to his physical surroundings.

If, as he guessed, he was in the hold of a ship, then they may have lowered him down into it from the hatch above. If, as many of his own ships were, it was designed for grain or fluids, no lower door was necessary, as the cargo was either drained out a port in the lowest corner, only eight inches across, or pumped out the top via vacuum hose or conveyor. A physically fit six feet and powerful for sixty years old, he was nonetheless too large to fit through even a twelve-inch port, and unless he could fashion a thirty-foot rope, his chance of getting to the hatch were minimal. That made this a virtually escape-proof prison, a smart move on someone's part. They could see him, but he couldn't see them. They could speak to him through the hatch, drop or lower him food and fluids, and waste stayed with him and didn't spread to the rest of the ship. Soundproof and mobile, they could hold him here almost indefinitely with little risk of being seen or heard, and if they kept on the move, no one could ever find him.

A feeling of great hopelessness washed over him, but it only lasted for a moment. His early life, starting in the orphanage, had taught him to be patient and wait for opportunities—that no situation is truly hopeless. Many times in the past, lying there in the dark in that room full of older, larger, more physically able boys, he'd waited patiently for his opportunity to strike back at his antagonists. Then sure enough, something would present itself, and the bully would be temporarily vanquished, bringing him momentary peace. Now it was just waiting for time to pass, time to be patient and see what his captors had in store for him. If he kept his head, kept his eyes and ears open, and didn't force their hand, an opportunity would open, as luck favored the prepared mind.

Chapter 6

Lentas, Crete, Greece

Nikos and I had left the city on time, as expected, caught our Olympic flight to Crete, which was uneventful, and landed on the island on time and without incident. We made our way to the airport parking lot and found the car that Ceros had arranged. Thanks to Nikos's diplomatic status, we had put the hardware from my big duffle bag into a lead-lined case and whisked through airport security. This time he had changed the anonymous Ford for a more rugged and equally anonymous Mercedes sedan. The old, grey 300D was a little noisy, smelled faintly of diesel fuel, and had 200,000+ miles on the odometer. It was reliable, economical, strongly built, and well maintained. Its leather seats were shiny but in good shape, floor mats clean, and trunk empty except for a few little items I added, including the new case and my small valise sitting alongside Nikos's small overnight bag. The air-conditioning was a little anemic, but I rolled down the passenger window and let the cool, eucalyptus-and-creosote-scented air roll in. We headed south, down the perimeter road that ran along the southern coast of the island, past WWII gun emplacements, sites where bomb damage had not been completely repaired, through small fishing villages with tiny shops, inns, and supply stands tucked in between seafood restaurants and small houses.

Nickos handled the old car well, dodging the errant local drivers, livestock, and ubiquitous delivery trucks with ease. After an hour or so of this, we arrived in the town of Lentas, a small seaside collection of slightly ramshackle houses, shops, and a modest marina and boat yard. We rolled the car down to the furthest dry point in town, a spit of land fifty yards off the main road, onto an asphalt and crushed-shell parking pad. A hundred yards off shore, I could see a sizeable white yacht, gleaming in the late afternoon sun like a white jewel in a dark blue velvet-lined box. Antenna bristled above the forward standing bridge, the aft deck and seating area clean, neat and squared away, complete with small pool, swimming deck at the rear, small café-style eating area, and large glass panels leading to the salon on the main deck, under the bridge. Nickos had brought along a small but powerful pair of binoculars, which he handed me without a word once we had both climbed out of the car and stretched.

The boat looked deserted, nothing moving on deck or behind the glass, no shadows moving at the side portholes, mooring lines slack in the bottom of the tide cycle, a slight onshore breeze blowing at that time of day, freshening the air. I walked around to the back of the car, opened the trunk, and withdrew one of the SIGs and loaded a magazine with the standard thirteen rounds, inserted it in the handle, jacked the slide, and tucked the compact powerful pistol in the back of my waistband under my shirt. Then I went back to my observation post leaning on the hood of the car with the binoculars. While we were checking out the boat, I heard a car approach from behind us, tires crunching on the shells as it got closer. I turned and saw a small, square, white sedan with a round decal on the door, surely the local police captain coming to "oversee" our activities. He must have picked up our car with out of town ID plates as we drove through town, and realized that based on our arrival time and the car, that it must be his visitors from Athens.

He pulled up a few feet away and got out of the passenger seat, his driver staying in the car for the moment. He was a short, portly bowlegged gent around fifty-five, dark hair graying at the temples, thinning and slicked back over his skull. The buttons on his uniform shirt strained against his formidable belly, overhanging his belt, underneath which an ancient Sam Brown rode with a sizeable, possibly antique revolver slung to the side in a brown leather holster. He was wearing dark aviator sunglasses, dark uniform pants, and scuffed black leather-soled brogues—the picture of a small-town lawman who thinks he's got respect tied to the badge. It was all I could do not to snicker.

He approached us, hailing us, doing introductions as he walked, until he was within handshake distance, although none was offered. He stood silently, leaning slightly back on his heels in order to look straight at my face, and sized me up. His glance traveling from my rubber-soled work shoes to the points of my collared shirt, up to my experienced but youthful face, and connected directly with my baby blues as if to say, "I can handle you if need be, no matter if you're six inches taller and forty pounds heavier. This is *my* town, and you don't mess with me."

In reality, I had no intention of messing with him, but that kind of arrogant attitude just rubs me the wrong way, so I couldn't resist a bit of push back. It came in the form of me stepping forward, looking over his head, and letting my gaze travel down below level until it met his, and raising my eyebrows in surprise, as if I'd stumbled upon a mouse on the ground. Nickos was translating at this point, but the message was clear in any language—I won't be intimidated by anyone; this is *my* investigation, and I'll go where and when I wish, regardless of your relationship with the embassy in Athens.

Chest beating and posturing over, we walked over in front of the car, all looking out at the yacht, and the captain was complimenting the ship in almost flowery terms, so proud was he that such a vessel was docked near his town. I was busy checking his security measures, analyzing access points, water depth, room access, and vantage points. Based on what I saw, it would have been pretty tough to get aboard without anyone noticing, but at night, with scuba gear, and a silent method of subduing his guards and crew, it might be possible.

Fortunately, I could do it the easy way, and the police captain led us to a small skiff he had beached a few paces down the beach. He directed most of his comments on operating the boat to Nickos, and we climbed in, got the small motor started, and pushed off into the calm warm water toward the giant yacht. A few moments later, we pulled alongside and dropped anchor. I tossed a line to the top rail, raised a rope ladder up the side via the rope, and boarded the vessel.

I was immediately struck by how immaculate and orderly the boat was. Clearly, no expense had been spared to produce a craft of understated opulence, but I'd learned that having money didn't make you neat and tidy. Whoever ran this vessel, named the *Lady Elena*, was highly organized, disciplined to the point of obsession, and meticulous in attention to detail. Each line, fixture, artifact was carefully placed, hanging on a hook, placed in a cabinet—the words "squared away" came immediately to mind from my military days— not anything out of place, walkways and aisles clear and unobstructed. I stood on the fantail for a moment, getting my bearings and my sea legs, observing from the only first impression I would have, soaking it all in. The boat was eerily quiet; only the humming of the ice maker and the slight vibration of the small generator motor disturbed the silence. I wanted to be really sure that I had the place to myself before I proceeded further. Nickos had come aboard and was standing quietly a few feet away, and the police captain, whose name turned out to be Marko Mavroulis, had stayed in the skiff and decided to enjoy his lunch while we looked. Once the hierarchy had been established, his attitude had faded a bit, and he seemed almost uninterested in our activities, although it could have been an act. I was sure anything we found would be communicated to Ceros, but since I was going to tell him most everything anyway, I wasn't concerned.

I moved slowly through the large glass sliding doors into the main salon, observing the apparent wealth on display. High-end furniture and cabinetry abounded, including sumptuous Persian rugs of early vintage. Antiques and cultural artifacts of museum quality were tastefully sprinkled about in a cozy arrangement designed to take full advantage of the large glass wall behind me. I walked slowly forward, toward the stairs leading to the bridge level, and headed up to the bridge. There was a faintly acrid smell lingering in the stairway, and when I arrived at the upper level, the white tile floor contained recent black scuff marks in parallel, as if someone had been dragged down the hall and down the stairs. Tough to fake, so I started to feel better that at least the abduction did indeed occur and that Big G likely wasn't complicit in it. The crunch of glass underfoot confirmed it. The windows were intact, but the dark mastic around the rubber seal shone under the harsh sun, clearly brand new window sealer. It all added up to a distraction shot, a quick-acting chemical anesthetic, and an unconscious captive being dragged off the boat—kidnapping 101.

I scanned the controls, noting the position of dials and switches, and calculated that the ship had been at anchor when the last person left at least. The small generator was powering minor appliances, lights, and motor control but that the main diesel was off, the fuel tank half full, position log up to date, the radio, radar and sonar, GPS position-finding gear were all functioning properly. Everything looked as it was supposed to, like Big G had told the captain to pull into this little cove, drop anchor, shut it all down, and leave him alone for a while to enjoy his solitude.

I moved back down the companionway to the stairs, headed down to the salon and further down to the living quarters. The layout was straightforward—a galley on the left, small dinette on the right, two large berths forward, and another stairway down to more living quarters for crew below, along with a communications room, office, crew mess, recreation room/bar/lounge for the crew, and below to the engine room and bilge. I figured I'd start with the living quarters and work my way down to the engine room.

The master suite was quite large, decorated in a masculine style, lots of deep browns, blacks, and taupe with chrome accents, heavy drapes pulled back to reveal a spectacular view of the shoreline. A private bath with chrome fixtures, plenty of space, large jetted tub, shower, king-sized bed, and antiques tastefully mixed in. There was a photo on the nightstand, showing a sixtyish man, tan and fit, with his arm around an attractive young woman with long legs and long dark hair, round green eyes, aquiline nose, and strong brow, wearing a light green T-shirt dress with a short skirt and matching sandals—a well-put together lady if I ever saw one. I'd guess her age at around twenty-seven or twenty-eight, so it could be either girlfriend or daughter. On closer inspection of the face, I decided on daughter—something around the eyes looked very much like the father. I checked the back of the frame, and sure enough, it said, "Georgi and Elena, Daddy's little girl, 2004."

My search took me through the rest of the bedroom, closets and all. I located a safe in a closet, bolted to a steel hull member and peeking through the drywall behind a fake plumbing access panel. It took me a few minutes to work my way through the obvious combinations, using data I'd memorized in the file—birthdays and anniversaries, initials converted to numbers, special dates, Social Security numbers, and other more obvious possibilities. Finally, I sat back and looked around the room, and my eyes landed on the photo.

I picked up the frame and pried off the back. Some days I'm good, and some days I'm just lucky. Either way, there was a series of numbers tucked up in the edge of the frame under the cardboard, which, of course, opened the safe. Inside, the usual corporate paperwork, deeds, title to the yacht, some property leases in Spain, Sardinia, New York, Singapore, offices most likely, some deeds for condos in those cities and others, some car titles, and about $100,000 in cash, a small pencil sketch that said Dali in the corner, and a brown envelope, used and well fingered. In it was a simple composition book, like the one high schoolers bring on the first day of tenth grade. In it were pages of names, initials, amounts, other fragments of data, clearly a sales log book. Taped to the inside cover was a list of initials and phone numbers, customer IDs most likely. Jackpot. Anybody meaning him harm from a business standpoint would find such information priceless and invaluable. Whoever took him hadn't found it or hadn't needed it. Time would tell which.

I tucked the envelope under my shirt and kept looking through the rest of the boat, working my way down through the crew quarters all the way down to the engine room. Not much of note, except in the office, where other ledger books, bank statements, account records of various types, contracts, all for any of twenty legitimate businesses Georgi was involved in. That meant that the log I'd found was strictly for arms sales. I'd have to study it in more detail when I got back to Athens. I boxed up the records in a carton I found in the crew mess and headed back up through the main salon when I heard a motor approaching, larger than our skiff, coming fast. I hit the deck in time to see Nickos tucked away around the corner of the salon, out of sight to the occupants of the small launch. Markos was standing in the skiff, watching the small boat approach. I shot a look at the boat's passengers and stopped dead in my tracks. Behind the wheel was a man I'd never seen—short, dark, sunglasses, ball cap—a water taxi driver in Greece. What had made me stop was the other passenger. I stood stock still as the boat drew up the yacht's hull and a line was tossed over the rail. I watched silently as the launch maneuvered under our rope ladder, as a dark-haired head popped over the railing, and a long pair of legs scissored over the side. I was standing there face to face with Daddy's Little Girl—Elena had arrived, in the flesh.

Chapter 7

Oranjestad, Aruba

The large man was seated at the back of a café in the lobby of the main building of the largest mall on the island—a casino, restaurants, shops, and services all under one roof—a building he happened to own, unbeknownst to the many passersby. The café owner knew, however, and made it a point to stop by his table personally whenever he visited, which was just about daily when he was on the island. It was fairly peaceful here, and he could get good cell reception and speak softly and still be heard on the other end, a bonus on an island full of music and gossip, and noisy stalls full of trinkets with barkers drawing tourists right across the street.

Today he had ordered an espresso, and a small local pastry, and was doing more listening than talking, absorbing reports from various quarters of his enterprise via his stable of competent and more mobile lieutenants. Most were positive, as things in general were going well. One in particular, the one from a ship in the Mediterranean Sea, made him smile a little. The first domino in a series had been toppled, and soon the inevitable chain reaction would start, one action triggering another, and another, until his goal had been reached.

One call did cause him some consternation, one from a small town on the southern coast of Crete, where his source had noted some activity on and around a large yacht anchored off the coast. Not only was there "official" interest in the form of a local police captain, whom he knew to be corrupt, but more disturbing was the presence of an unknown American accompanied by a Greek bodyguard. More disturbing yet was the arrival of a new player to the party in the form of Big G's daughter Elena. He'd met Elena just once years ago when she was just a little girl of nine. Due to his distinctive appearance, she'd likely remember him, though not his role in her father's life. Once upon a time he'd been more active in Big G's life, although not more physically present. They'd met face to face only rarely, but exchanged correspondence on a covert network for nearly a decade and by message through couriers before that, all to protect each other's positions in the tightly knit underworld in this part of the globe. But while Big G had gotten bigger and therefore more visible in his covert and legitimate dealings, the big man had reduced his public profile in inverse proportion to the growth of his seemingly infinite wealth. He had no need of publicity; his ego was fed through other channels. His considered opinion was that Big G's ostentation and public activity was calling undue attention to himself and therefore his associates, and the big man couldn't tolerate that at any price.

His plan for Big G was simple—hold him until he was assumed to be irreversibly out of power in his own empire, and wait for the vultures to circle. Once the fighting over the carrion started, he'd swoop in and take over the operation when the dust settled, filling the void in the arms trade and cornering the market on supply for that part of the world at minimal cost and minimal exposure for him. Plus, the plan they had been building for the last several years could be put into place at his own discretion, with no interference from other sources, for his own purposes.

The only trouble on the horizon was that meddlesome group now actively searching the boat and the arrival of Elena, his only living link to Big G. That "living" portion would have to be remedied, and soon.

Lentas, Crete, Greece

Watching Elena exit the little launch/taxi was like watching the first act of a ballet. Each move was carefully, artfully, gracefully choreographed to allow her to exit the craft while showing off her lithe form to best advantage. Clearly, she'd seen us standing on the fantail watching her board none-too-surreptitiously and was putting on a show. I didn't mind; it was a good show. Her long legs dropped over the rail onto the deck, tipped in wholly inappropriate high heels, and she stalked across the wide teak deck toward us at a confident clip.

"You must be Mr. Stark," she purred, clearly but with a lilting Greek accent. "The local police captain informed me that someone was boarding my father's boat today, without my permission," she added, clearly a bit frosted at not being consulted, but showing some control.

She stepped back, looked me up and down, all six and a half feet of me—noting my shabby boots, the cut of my clothes, the width and strength of my shoulders, my work-toughened hands with just a hint of dirt under the nails, the lack of recent haircut, perhaps the scar under my left jaw from an unfortunate incident years ago—and immediately dismissed me mentally as a step above a tourist. To her I was a working guy with no class, nosing around where he didn't belong, not in her social class or circle, and therefore not worthy of her respect or time. That was her first mistake. One I wasn't going to disabuse her of for the moment, as it gave me a tactical advantage.

"Disappointed?" I quipped.

"From the police captain's description, I was picturing someone more formidable," she replied.

"Next time, I'll hit the gym for an hour before I board," I shot back.

Then she looked me square in the eye, and I could see her demeanor change slightly. Suddenly after a real look at me and after gauging my reaction to her challenge, I was a little more "formidable" than she expected. She gave a slight frown and replied, "Don't bother—there won't be a next time," and stalked into the forward salon through the glass doors. The police captain followed her like a puppy after its master, with Nickos and me bringing up the rear. Once in the salon, she went straight to the bar, stepped behind it to make herself a drink, and turned watching us as we found seats in the sumptuous surroundings. She didn't offer us anything, and I didn't expect an offer. Before I sat down, though, I quickly and quietly gave my little file box a shove with my foot behind a sofa to keep it out of her line of sight. No sense giving away our discoveries unless we had to. Markos broke the ice with a quick comment in Greek about how he had been asked by his friend at the consulate to cooperate with our investigation and that we were supposed to be here to help locate her father. She didn't seem too impressed by that, but didn't comment either. Nickos was sitting off to the side of me near the door, looking uncomfortable, as if the plush room was too nice for the likes of him to be spending any time in at all, unless being reprimanded by the boss. She hadn't asked us to leave yet, but was clearly upset at our presence, Markos or not, but I wanted to hear it from her that our time aboard was at an end.

Markos continued to explain to her about the evidence of a struggle he had found, or in some cases the lack thereof, and how he had deduced that her father had been taken against his will, probably at gunpoint, to parts unknown. She didn't seem impressed by this theory either and sipped her drink, alternating her gaze between Markos and me.

"My father is a very private, very powerful man, in many ways, and anyone attempting to board this yacht would have been repelled by his security team, who live here on board. I do not think any one of his associates is capable of simply boarding unannounced and dragging him away without serious opposition. Tell me, Mr. Stark, what is *your* theory as to where my father might have gone?"

"It's very early in my investigation to tell anything about where he might be. I just got here a few moments ago, and Captain Markos's efforts at clean-up here have muddied the waters quite a bit for me to make any definitive determination without much more analysis. I'll need to question the staff, interview the harbormaster and others who frequent the area, talk to some of your father's associates, previous guests who've been aboard recently. Please believe me when I tell you that I will be completely professional and thorough in all matters pertaining to finding your father, as my superiors want him back as badly as you do."

"Now that was the answer I was hoping for. Thank you, Mr. Stark, for your candor. Sometimes 'I don't know' is the best answer, and in this case, I believe it is the only answer."

"I noted that the domestic staff had been given the day off on that day and, in fact, have yet to return to duty," I said.

"When I heard about my father's disappearance, I called the captain, told him his services would not be needed for the immediate future, to rig the ship for long-term mooring here, and to go ashore until hearing further from me. He called the remainder of the nonsecurity staff and told them the same. I'll be happy to furnish you with their contact information if that would be of help to you," she replied.

"Let's talk about that security staff for a moment. How many men were there on your father's security team?" I asked.

"Usually he had six men on guard at all times, round the clock. They took six-hour shifts, for a total of twenty-four men all together—a large team, but one called upon to be constantly fresh and prepared for anything that could potentially harm my father. He had some powerful friends, and even more powerful enemies, so he hired only the best. I can give you their files as well. Once we return to his local office, I'll call his secretary in Athens and have them faxed down if that would be adequate."

"That would be fine, thank you," I replied.

"Anything else I can provide you with, Mr. Stark?" she asked a bit curtly.

"I'd like to ask you a few more questions about your father's habits, his mood leading up to three nights ago's disappearance, and about his activities leading up to that time."

"I'm afraid I won't be much use to you on that score, Mr. Stark. I haven't spoken to my father about business in months, and not very often before that. I've been traveling for my own business, and he's been cruising the world's oceans for the last half a year or so. Our paths only crossed occasionally in that time. As far as his activities go, I could only speculate, as he didn't discuss his business affairs with me beyond a very surface remark here or there. I think he did so to protect me in the event one of his enemies decided to kidnap me and use me as leverage against him. My father loved me very much, and I him, and that could be seen by his associates as a weakness to be exploited."

"I see. Well, I'll need to have some idea as to your whereabouts and how to contact you for the near future during our investigation, so I can keep you up to speed on our findings. Where are you staying for the next week or so?" I asked.

"Why, Mr. Stark, I'll be right here, aboard this vessel, easily reached by cell phone or radio," she replied as if it were obvious that she could stay nowhere else.

"Very well, then, my associate and I will take our leave for the moment, but we'll be in touch soon. Captain, thank you again for your assistance, would you care for a lift back to shore, or will you be staying aboard?"

The captain looked longingly at Elena, but nodded that he'd take us up on our offer. While his back was turned saying his good-byes to Elena, I bent behind the sofa and grabbed the file box, handed it to Nickos, and hustled him out the salon door ahead of me, blocking her view of his back as he exited. He crossed to the port rail and tossed the box into our little launch, and followed it closely behind down the ladder. I quickly followed with the captain reluctantly bringing up the rear.

We cast off the mooring line and turned the launch toward shore, arriving at the dock a few moments later. Once ashore, the captain quick-stepped it down the dock toward his car, while Nickos and I clambered out of the launch, retrieved the box full of files, and headed back to the Mercedes. I dropped the box into the trunk, along with a few choice pieces of hardware, and dropped in to the passenger seat.

"So, Nickos, what do you think of our little princess on the yacht?" I asked quietly.

Nickos made a face, thought for a moment, and said, "Hiding something."

"My thought exactly," I said.

Chapter 8

Athens, Greece

While Stark was checking out the boat, the support team had been making their way to the rendezvous hotel in Athens, on staggered flights to help reduce detection and for safety, airline travel being what it is these days. Each called in as they arrived in their rooms on the sat phone issued to each.

First to call, luckily, was the team's comm expert, Samantha Bellows. Sam had been with the team since Grenada, when they provided some tactical support for one of the rescue units from Australia. She was part of a naval detachment assigned to support Stark's contractors in the effort to secure the American military forces from the guerilla forces there. As a lieutenant and communications specialist, if it could be made to talk, transmit data, or connect with something else, she could design it, build it, take it apart, tweak it, fix it, and make it work to its full capability and then some, even under the most adverse conditions—like being shot at, for example. She had taken the Langley government-issue sat scrambler phones and "upgraded" them with mil spec parts from one of her suppliers, put in switchable masking software on the GPS chips, so that the bad guys couldn't track us, but we could switch it on in case we needed to be rescued for any reason. At 5'9", wiry and strong with a model's face, flaming red hair, and a jet pilot's attitude, she was both enticing and formidable, not someone to be messed with. A crack shot with multiple weapons and cool under fire, as well as a trained Corpsman, everyone was happy to have her watching his back under most any circumstances.

Sam had arrived without any problems, aside from a stir in the lobby by a group of Japanese gentlemen who swore she was the actress/model Angie Everhart. She checked into her room and proceeded to call Stark to check in and see what the situation looked like, so she would have some idea of what we'd need for the mission. She'd read the briefing documents, but by now they were three days old and were likely outdated and in need of revision, based on the intel gathered by Stark so far. Sam had learned through hard experience to plan from the most recent intel possible, due to the fluid nature of the missions they undertook. Sam needed to hear firsthand how things were shaping up, knowing that Stark's keen intellect and strategic brain would already be formulating a plan of action. Once she heard the outline of his thinking, she could set about procuring what they needed to keep their asses out of a sling.

"Hey, boss, how are things over the waves?"

"Hey, Sam, welcome to the Greek Isles. You all checked in?"

"Yeah, no worries, good flight, nobody paying any attention to me that I noticed."

"Good. Don't get too comfortable. I'm gonna need your unique skills here shortly. My contact at the embassy is a good guy. I'll call him and have him arrange for a car for you, bring you down for a little rendezvous. Gonna need some long-range surveillance to gather intel on a good-sized yacht from about a mile away across water, audio and video if possible. Needs to last about three to four days, before being retrieved, but provide data in real time so we can move quickly if need be."

"Sounds like you've got a plan in mind."

"Don't I always? Once I get eyes and ears on this boat, we'll know more, but I'm following a few things that may lead us to our boy, Big G."

"Anything else you can think of at the moment we might need? I looked up the town you're in, not much in the way of electronics sources down there. I'd like to do my shopping here in civilization before I join you."

"I think a Phase II kit and some extra ammo would probably be a good idea. Beyond that, we'll have to wing it. Sorry I can't give you more, but we don't have much to go on so far."

"Gotcha. See you tomorrow."

She hung up the sat phone, leaned back on the hotel bed, and let the slim specification he'd given her float through her thoughts, mentally creating a checklist of specific parts and items she'd need to accomplish the task at hand. Combing through her mental database, the checklist slowly assembled itself until she was confident that she had it covered. She reached for her Netbook in her luggage, logged on to the hotel's wi-fi, via a scrambled encrypted modem, and started sourcing the items she needed. Most could be had readily, especially through those suppliers in time zones behind her own, providing a cushion for the delivery—she could leave the hotel at eleven the following morning after the 10:00 a.m. DHL delivery and be fully equipped. God bless the Internet and overnight delivery. Once the ordering was done, she hopped in a blazing hot shower and dropped into bed, knowing it might be the last sleep she would get for a while. She needed to get her circadian rhythms back in sync what with the local time and be prepared for a long few days ahead. Despite it being two in the afternoon, she fell immediately into a deep, untroubled sleep.

While Sam was sleeping, two more members of the team were hitting the tarmac at the Eleftherios Venizelos Airport outside Athens. While they knew each other quite well, no words had been exchanged between them the entire trip. They had arrived at Dulles separately, had not openly acknowledged each other in the lounge at the gate, sat in separate sections of the plane, and kept themselves separate on the way to baggage claim, through customs and immigration, until they appeared to randomly meet in the taxi line outside the terminal. While only slightly remarkable looking when seen separately, together they made quite a couple.

Jimmy "Tang" Tanaka was a relatively short, tough wiry-looking Japanese ex-paratrooper. At 5'8", 155 lbs., he'd barely qualified for jump school, but had outshone his competition in the unit by the second day, showing steel nerve, cool thinking, and a capacity to learn and analyze information with lightning speed. A Berkeley graduate in engineering, a black belt at Tai Kwon Do, a top-level marksman with five years of Ranger experience, he was one of the younger team members, but one they depended on quite heavily, especially in some of the more recent missions.

As intel analyst and ops officer, his job was to take Stark's wild plans and ideas and work them into something feasible that wouldn't get any of the team hurt or killed, and still accomplish the mission on time and with a minimum of collateral damage. His engineering skills were crucial to success in areas like building access, explosive impact, and in the construction and fabrication of some of the more specialized gear the team occasionally needed for specific tasks. His analytic skills and logical thinking allowed him to set emotion aside, take the facts at hand and mold them into an operation plan, cover all the contingencies, create several back-up and redundant plans, using both the full team and with members missing. He'd kept the team together, alive, and unhurt for the most part for five years, and they trusted him implicitly.

The man standing behind him in line couldn't have looked and been more different. Where Tanaka was small and dark, William "BJ" Thompson was tall, beefy, and fair, a good 6' 4" in socks, over 240 lbs., built like a pro wrestler. A Purdue grad in biology on a full ride as a linebacker, he'd spent as much time in the weight room as he had at fraternity parties, resulting in a finely tuned body that could bench press over 500 lbs., and run a 5.1 forty-yard dash at age thirty-five. After college he'd banged around the Midwest doing odd jobs until an uncle had passed away unexpectedly. At the funeral, he'd run into a cousin, in full navy uniform, and gotten into a discussion of how the navy was treating him, how interesting his work was, and how much opportunity there was there. He was impressed enough to go straight to the recruiting office and sign up for the navy.

Two years of outstanding service later, he'd enrolled in the SEAL team school and found a home. Graduating at the top of his SEAL class, he'd been assigned to a team immediately and proved a capable warrior in his first few missions. Although a demolition and explosives expert, his role in saving his team from disaster during their extraction had more to do with some great shooting and a good old-fashioned body tackle at a critical moment, disabling one of the captors, and clearing an exit for the team. One of the team had been hit in the knee, and BJ had hoisted the team member up on his huge shoulders and carried him back to the extraction point, loaded him on a zodiac after swimming with the other man in tow for half a mile, and saved his life in the process.

He'd done well in the teams, but during some down time when the fighting shifted to the Middle East region, he'd grown bored with no real missions to run. When he'd been approached by one of Stark's team, he was receptive to a new challenge, and they'd sealed the deal the next afternoon. He'd resigned his commission and become an extremely valuable member of Stark's team. As the explosives and demolitions expert, he also doubled as the team's armorer and chief medical corpsman, based on his biology training.

Now, standing next to Tanaka in the taxi line, they looked like Mutt and Jeff, but two more capable men you would not easily find. In this instance, this impression served to make it less suspect that the two were acquainted, so they shared a cab to the hotel as any two tourists on a budget might have. They discussed the weather, the local roads, their flight, anything but the mission, just in case there were ears trained on them that weren't readily visible.

They arrived at the hotel without incident, checked into separate rooms without raising suspicion using different desk agents and, after dropping their bags, met in Tanaka's room to check in with the boss.

"Gentlemen, any problems getting in?" Stark asked.

"Absolutely none, smooth as silk, boss," Tanaka replied.

"BJ with you?" he asked.

"Yep, right here, raiding the minibar, as usual," Tanaka quipped.

"Okay, guys, here's the scoop. I'm in southern Crete. I've been on board the boat, discovered a few things, but need to keep surveillance on it, as our guy's daughter is staying on board. I need to know what she knows, see who she's in contact with, who comes and goes for the next few days. Sam's here, getting the toys together to do the job, but someone's got to get back on board, plant the devices, and get back with no one the wiser."

"Sounds like a piece of cake—what are we up against in terms of security?" he asked.

"Not much really, a few cameras, a skeleton staff, no armed professionals, but the daughter is aboard. We've got to get into some private and public spaces without her knowing we're there."

"Any chance of a distraction, a contrived reason for her to go ashore?" Tanaka brightly asked.

"Certainly a thought. We can devise a story, call the ship-to-shore, and see if we can get her to go shopping or come to the local harbormaster's office for an hour or so—is that enough?" he asked.

"Plenty, especially in the dark," he replied. "I'll just have brawny here swim out there and poke around, drop a few bugs, and hit the drink—back on the beach in thirty minutes or it's free, no sweat," Tanaka replied, grinning.

"Okay, I'll have my contact at the embassy arrange for a car and get you two down here ASAP. Be out front of the hotel at eleven thirty or so tomorrow morning. You've got a few hours to cobble together the things you'll need to get it done. I'd bring a little extra as well—never know where these things are going to go, and our boy hangs with some pretty heavy hitters, both as clients and competitors. So be ready for anything," he cautioned.

"Understood, boss. I'll send the big guy here out for a few dive items, and I'll see if I can hunt down some support supplies that should be adequate to the task. We'll get it together this evening and see you midday tomorrow," he replied.

"A-OK, out," he signed off.

"What do you think of the plan, BJ?" Tanaka asked. "We gonna be okay on this one?"

"I think I've got my work cut out for me on the procurement end, but the job itself is a piece of cake. I swim farther than that every morning for fun. With her off the boat, not much to it really," he noted confidently.

"I think we're only getting the surface of the story, and we'd better not take things at face value. I was a Boy Scout, remember, 'always be prepared' and all that. Keep your shit tight, my friend. There's more here than meets the eye—mark my words," Tanaka cautioned.

"Always do," he replied.

Chapter 9

Falls Church, Virginia

He'd gotten the call from Stark while on the seventh hole at Pinecrest golf course in Springfield, Virginia. He'd taken calls from Stark in stranger places, lord knows. This one was about as cryptic as could be, but the urgency of the message was clear. He had time to finish the front nine, make his excuses to his guests, pack his clubs, and scoot back to his home in Falls Church on Lake Barcroft. William "Stacks" Jones was the only black bachelor on Lake Barcroft, certainly the only one his size. At 6'6" and nearly three hundred pounds, he stood out among the other Washington bureaucrats and nonprofit managers that made up his neighbors. His house faced the lake, and his "honorarium" from Stark let him live well enough to have one of the largest boats on the lake, moored on his own dock at the bottom of the hill. When Stacks came down the boat ramp and dropped the 28' Donzi in the water, and he fired the twin 350s, the whole lake knew that he'd arrived.

Stacks had been a full-ride scholarship to Grambling as a tackle, where his size made him a fearsome opponent on a team full of fearsome men with something to prove. However, he'd also graduated at the top of his class in engineering, continuing to earn a master's in hydrodynamics. His maternal grandmother, who'd raised him from age two after losing his parents in a drive-by shooting in Richmond, had hammered into him the importance of getting an education, and that and her stern but loving demeanor had kept him out of trouble growing up in some of Richmond's tougher neighborhoods. He'd hit the books, gotten his scholarship, and gotten out of there, only to return after a short but distinguished career as a Marine MP, rising to the rank of captain. While stationed at the Pentagon as part of a marine security attachment to the joint chiefs' office, he'd come to the attention of certain people of Stark's acquaintance, and they'd steered him to Stark. When the offer came, he'd decided he'd seen enough of politics and wanted back in the action, and taken it on the spot. Of course, the money wasn't bad either, and as he was unattached, the move from Richmond to the Washington suburbs became permanent soon after.

While in the marines, he'd learned that he had other talents and skills that hadn't found an outlet on the football field or in the classroom. He discovered he had a knack for things mechanical, especially vehicles, boats, planes, and the like, as well as a distinct talent for hitting what he aimed at. After earning Marksman and Distinguished Marksman honors, as well as finishing top three in the All-Service rifle competition, besting snipers from the army, Gunner's Mates from the navy, and keen-eyed pilots from the air force, he felt confident in offering his skills in the field to Stark in addition to his engineering and mechanical skills.

Stacks got his nickname while at Grambling, where the training table was the only one not hurting for funds or supplies. He'd been seen polishing off his third stack of some of the fluffiest, tastiest hotcakes he'd ever had. On his way back to the chow line for a fourth, the coach had stopped him and recommended that he spend more time in the stacks in the library rather than the ones in front of him if he wanted to finish with his degree. He replied to the coach "Stacks here pays for stacks there," and sealed the name forever.

Stacks packed light, having been told that they'd only be in Greece a few days, and that his main job would be security and surveillance, along with some general stealth work with the rest of the team. On his way to the airport in the back of the Towncar Stark had sent, he smiled to himself, thinking of all the great beaches and beautiful Greek women who inhabited them.

American Embassy, Athens, Greece

Ceros hung up the phone gently, wondering what he had gotten himself into. His conversation with Stark had been cordial and friendly, but the seasoned diplomat could sense the underlying tension in Stark's voice. He'd asked for three cars, drivers for each, airline seats on the next day's flight to Crete, cars on Crete to carry his passengers, and a series of lead-lined, hardshell cases. All doable, all available within the building, usually after about five days of paperwork requests, interdepartmental wrangling, approvals, and budget reviews up and down the chain. He didn't have time for any of that, and now had to scramble to line up his "unofficial" sources for such things by tomorrow morning. He would manage it, if for no other reason than his own professionalism and pride in doing a good job. The fact that this clearly competent operative would owe him a favor or two didn't hurt either, especially in a country whose political stability, or lack thereof, made his job or at least this posting tenuous at best. He needed all the connections he could get, and this one looked like it would have some long-term value later on. So scramble he did.

Fortunately, reliable transportation was fairly easy, thanks to his brother-in-law's ownership of a used car lot in northern Athens. He ran a full-service operation and kept a few sturdy vehicles on the lot for use as loaners while long-term repairs were being made on special customers' cars. They could be put on a ferry tonight and be waiting at the airport in Crete by morning.

The plane tickets proved to be a little easier than anticipated, again, thanks to his extended family. His wife had a niece who worked in a travel agency and was able to scare up some remaindered unoccupied seats on tomorrow's flight to Crete with minimal fuss.

The lead-lined cases were another matter. Usually reserved for diplomatic couriers who needed to fly with a personal protection weapon, most were smaller than Stark had requested, but he knew of a place further downtown where such items might be procured, although not cheaply. Such things weren't advertised or sold to the public without first vetting the customer. He'd picked up a few items there in the past, and they knew him to be a reliable customer whose discretion could be counted upon. He'd stop by there on his way home this evening, after first calling and speaking with George, the proprietor, about his needs. He could drop them off at the hotel desk posing as an airline employee dropping off lost luggage, and no one would be the wiser. He'd figure out how to hide the expenditures in his operating budget later.

The toughest part of all of these requests was the human aspect. He needed to find three discrete, reliable, capable individuals to act as drivers, who could be trusted to do as they were asked with no questions and keep quiet about it afterward. His best example of this was already on the job with Stark—Nickos could be trusted with the lives of his children, let alone competent operatives, and could take care of himself pretty well when called upon, having grown up in a rough part of Athens. His roster of such individuals was regrettably short, but he had two or three who had served him well in the past and could be pressed into service once reminded of the debt they owed him, usually for expediting or "massaging" some diplomatic paperwork for work permits, immigration visas, or the like for family members. He spent the balance of the day making some calls, leaving cryptic messages, and fielding the returns until he filled the three slots to his satisfaction.

He wondered what the next call from Stark would bring. He'd mentioned briefly that he'd secured some critical intel from the boat, but wasn't specific. Stark wasn't shy about asking for help apparently; if he needed anything to do with what he'd found, Ceros was certain he'd ask without hesitation. He could only hope that his activities would not send up too many red flags with the locals, which would then put them on the federal law enforcement radar screen. There was only so much one lowly diplomat could do, after all.

Chapter 10

Crete, Greece

Nickos and I proceeded back to our hotel to get situated, set up a command post of sorts, and wait for the rest of my team to arrive in the morning. Once done, I had a few errands of my own, including finding a decent meal in this little seaside burg. I had to run through everything that I had learned today, and especially to have a look at those ledgers and files I'd liberated from the boat. I was sure there were lots of answers that would lead us to Big G's whereabouts hidden in those ledgers, if only I could figure them out and make some sense of them.

First thing's first, I always say. I asked Nickos to find us some acceptable grub in the neighborhood. He nodded and picked up the phone in his room, speaking quietly into the receiver, and in about ten minutes he nodded, and we headed out the door for dinner.

As it turned out, I'd picked the right man for that job. The restaurant was a quiet, elegant little bistro, tucked away in a semiresidential neighborhood off the main drag about three miles. It was family owned and operated—Dad and sons in the kitchen, Mom at the hostess station, daughter-in-law behind the register, daughter behind the bar. Not many patrons, which suited me fine. Mom seated us in the back, facing the door, as if she knew what we were up to. A lovely young waitress strolled up to the table a moment later, took our orders from Nickos, and disappeared into the kitchen. I took a moment to scan the place, discreetly checking out the other patrons, and who should my eyes slide across but our friend, the police captain, Markos, sitting in the corner with three other younger copper types. I wondered who was minding the store, as a town this size didn't really warrant a force larger than about four officers, and they were all here eating. I filed away that little fact for our night mission tomorrow night, figuring that at minimum their response times if called would be lengthened, just for having to track down a viable, sober officer. I managed to turn away without catching his eye and kept turned away the rest of the evening until I saw him shamble to the door an hour later, followed by his subordinates.

Dinner was nothing short of fantastic, the conversation minimal, as one might expect from the likes of Nickos. That suited me fine, as we settled into an easy silence and let me get the mental wheels turning on the problem at hand.

We finished dinner, coffee, Ouzo, and finally headed back to the hotel, a small pensione in the heart of town. Our rooms were sparse, but all the required conveniences were in place. It was private, and the guest register was on paper only, no chain hotel computer to tell the tale of our arrival to those on other continents. I'd booked enough for my team and their drivers here, giving me a monopoly on the hotel's room count. With a force of ten total, including myself and Nickos, I could handle a wide range of situations with aplomb, but it got tough to hide that many newcomers in a town this size, as they all had to be fed and housed, equipped, and moved through public spaces, occasionally in broad daylight. That would start the rumor mill turning at full speed in less than twenty-four hours from their arrival. Hopefully, forty-eight hours after that, they'd be on their way back to the United States with information in hand to analyze and a plan to form, leads to follow, and work to do.

Nickos settled in for the night, and I headed back to my room to review what was in those ledgers. Maybe it would provide some obvious clue as to who was behind Big G's disappearance. I started with the front-page phone list. Most appeared to be mobile numbers, in no particular order, and were only tagged with initials, no real names. The first thing I picked up was that most of the numbers were based on the exchanges, based in Central and Western Europe. Some Asian and US numbers, a Hong Kong and a Singapore, Chinese, and Australian numbers as well. Not much, these could be dealers in his network, who acted as wholesalers for his weapons business, both legitimate and otherwise. It was a little late, but I noticed a couple in the UK, and since they were a couple of hours behind us here, I gave it a try. The number went through, rang three times,

and then a strange tone emanated from the phone—
not a fax or computer data tone, but something else.
I tried again, same result. I killed the connection and
tried another, this one in Italy. Same result. Three more
numbers throughout the continent, same tone. Have to
mull that over for a bit to make any sense of it.

I turned to the interior pages of the ledger. Line
after line, each containing initials, time, dates, a series
of two- and three-digit numbers, and some large figures,
probably money, although there were no denominations
next to them. Most of the dates had passed, but there
were a few at the end that were scheduled for a week
or so hence, some as much as a month, and then they
stopped. Clearly this was a live ledger, his basic business-
recording device, one that no one could hack from a
distance, that no one could interpret easily, and that was
clearly worth kidnapping him to obtain. Their search
hadn't turned it up, which meant that they may not
have been professionals.

I didn't notice any item listings or product
descriptions, so even if we could decipher the list
of clients, we had no evidence as to what they were
buying if anything. This didn't provide too many clues
on its surface, but I decided some additional firepower
might turn something up—time to call home and
get some brains pointed at this ledger. I grabbed the
sat phone and called Langley, left a cryptic message
for Dick, and called Ceros, left a message for him,
asking for a local courier service to get these into the
diplomatic pouch back to Washington. I wasn't too

eager to try to find a place to scan and e-mail the pages to him in the middle of the night, and we already had a full plate for the next couple of days keeping the boat under surveillance.

I packed up the ledger and started working through the file box from the office. If I was an IRS auditor and this was America, this might have proven interesting. As it was, most of it held little of interest, except one thing. In one of the file folders, I came across a pile of deeds and purchase agreements for commercial containerships, among them one of Lebanese registry, along with a photo of the boat. While not huge, it was certainly competitive, at 630 feet long, 220,000 tons, christened *Ophelia*. It didn't look especially impressive, brick red and white with a low superstructure, rust streaking her flanks, waterline fouled with barnacles, gunwale ports irregularly worn from anchor and drag chains, cranes center and forward rigged for sail, looking greasy and poorly maintained. Built in Norfolk, Virginia in 1968, she had started life as a commercial fishing vessel and been converted to container holds in 1976. She'd seen five owners and had logged untold hours at sea, and looked it. Why would a guy rich enough to have anything he wanted buy this old tub, given the cost of insurance, chance of piracy, liability for crews and such, when he could ship his merchandise under the guise of being something innocuous on commercial freighters anywhere in the world? Cover for something else? Maybe things were not what the seemed, here. I'd have to look into this ship further when time allowed.

I finished with the file box, finding nothing much of interest, especially where finding Big G was concerned. The only other element of note was the fact that most of the records were dated from two years ago and back, nothing more recent than eighteen months. Computerized record conversion? I hadn't seen a computer on board, other than the navigation and ship controls. Laptop in an office? I'd have to get some local Langley folks to arrange for records subpoenas from his various offices, to see what was up there.

I got undressed, slipped beneath the bedcovers, and tried to sleep, visions of containerships and things nautical kicking around in my brain until I slipped mercifully into a deep sleep.

Chapter 11

Oranjestad, Aruba

While Stark's team was assembling in Crete, the large man settled in for an extensive dinner with his closest advisors and confidants, to plan the next few moves in their grand plan to hijack Big G's operation. With the boss out of the way temporarily, the first door had been opened, but several subsequent moves needed to be orchestrated meticulously before the prize was theirs. He'd spent the day fielding reports from various enterprises by cell phone, and things set in motion weeks ago seemed to be progressing as planned. That good news got him through the series of gourmet appetizers on the menu.

His advisors, while few in number, were each formidable individuals in their own right. His associates were by necessity extremely competent in their respective fields because he'd learned long ago that working with the best in any field paid dividends regardless of the upfront apparent price. To his left sat General Ivan Paskevich, head of the most recent action in Afghanistan, the final one that finally realized that there was no way to best the tenacious Afghans in their own hills. He'd been named after his great, great, great,

great uncle of the same name who had commanded Russia's elite troops as a field marshal under the tsars in the 1780s and 90s. His strategic pullout had saved the Russian Federation billions in potential expense and was handled, both from a military and public relations standpoint, with delicacy and fortitude not often seen in the military of any country.

That made him valuable to the large man, but what made him more valuable was his demonstrated loyalty and discretion regarding his less than legal operations to liquidate Afghan-used Russian military hardware without benefit of the state as an official partner. Paskevich had sold some of the most valuable weapons systems and platforms possible, right under the government's nose at great profit to himself, without any breach of privacy or security by even one of his customers. He'd managed to sell of one of the Russian versions of the Akula-class submarines for a considerable sum without anyone knowing it for months. That kind of security and loyalty was what put him in the inner circle.

To the big man's right sat the only westerner in the group, former MI6 operative Andrew Whitherspoon. Andy had been disgraced and ousted from MI6 under a scandalous cloud, suspected of working behind the scenes to facilitate the devastation of several villages in Somalia for a local oil baron who wanted to build a pipeline across the land they occupied at the time. It was his one mistake to trust one of the Somali warlords with his plan, which lead to a BBC reporter getting wind of his motivations and connections. The reporter put two and two together and worked it back to Witherspoon and blasted him on national television. His producer had sold photos from the video to the London tabloids, where the public outcry had virtually guaranteed Witherspoon's sacking in disgrace. He still had many valuable contacts in every part of the world, contacts who knew how the world worked and had remained loyal to him. Those and his strategic thinking are what made him valuable to the big man. His position as head of global operations put him in charge of the bigger picture in this particular adventure, and he was quite content with the progress made so far.

Across from him sat his personal security chief, Ahman Akbar. Akbar was a former bodyguard to Mohammad Omar, head of the Taliban, and one of the fiercest commandos on the planet. He'd saved Omar's life at the Battle of Jalalabad in '89, dragging the mullah to safety after he'd been injured and blinded in one eye under extensive fire by Russian sharpshooters. He and the general were, of course, sworn enemies in public, but each had earned the other's grudging respect over the years of working with the large man, learning tolerance and admiring the skills and mental toughness of the other. Physically one of the most robust individuals, certainly at this table, his skills included top marksmanship, mastery of four different martial arts disciplines, and the ruthlessness of a modern psychopath, remote, remorseless, and focused on his task of extracting information, much as a hog butcher approaches his work on a pork loin. He'd attended an American medical school in Lebanon, was well versed in human anatomy, and knew intimately how to inflict pain without making the subject pass out or killing him.

He'd been in charge of the kidnapping operation to snatch Big G, which went flawlessly as usual, and he had stationed his top lieutenant as a guard on the modest containership. He'd not missed the irony of imprisoning the arms dealer in his own containership, the big man's idea, and was impressed with the simplicity and elegance of using a ship hold as a prison cell, no matter how temporarily. No escape possible, no prying eyes for miles, mobility, availability day or night, difficult for anyone who might find out to rescue him from deep in the hold of the ship. They'd had to rig a special harness on the crane hook just to lower the unconscious Greek down into the hold without dropping him at the bottom or scraping him against the sides. With some additional decking plates, some soundproofing, and some creative use of black and grey paint, they'd created a false bottom for the hold, so that even if boarded by whatever authority happened to hold sway where they sailed, if they opened the hatch, they'd see a flat, black hold that appeared very deep indeed. Ventilation and feeding were accomplished by means of a sort of sliding chute, similar to those used to demolish the insides of old buildings, which could be removed quickly and easily by one person and later retrieved if need be. A lot of work in a short period of time, but the boss trusted him to do it and do it right, so he had, without question.

The final member of the little cadre was an Aruban local, Wesley Johnson. He served on the local island government in a law enforcement capacity. He was also one of the most ruthless criminals on the island, responsible for extortion, prostitution, gambling, and loan-sharking in an empire worth many millions. Aside from his criminal proclivities, his main value to the big man was his control of the local law enforcement and the ports. He was also able to supply the big man with reliable manpower for some of the more physical tasks associated with executing his plans.

This small cabal of international criminals constituted the big man's advisory board, and he'd called them together tonight to bring them up to speed on his latest efforts. He paid them well, fed them beyond their wildest expectations at these meetings, and expected absolute perfection in executing their assignments. There was no other option, and the penalty for failure was disappearance without warning or preamble.

The big man waited until the coffee and chocolates had been served to come to the business at hand. Several of the men leaned back, lit expensive cigars, and listened intently as their boss revealed his plan for controlling the entire global arms business and putting a virtual lock on any weapon, guidance system, or piece of hardware or ammunition being sold or purchased anywhere on the planet. They each understood their roles in his plan as explained, asked few questions, and after two hours, adjourned, leaving the building individually, blindfolded and bundled into private cars provided by the big man, so as to keep his location secret.

Chapter 12

Crete, Greece

The team converged on the little hotel one at a time, casually, not causing a big fuss, looking as much like tourists as such individuals could. Sam arrived last, having come close to missing her flight when the DHL truck was later than usual with her purchases. Everything she'd bought was legal to carry on board individually, so she just packed everything into a newly purchased suitcase and checked it through.

I met them in the lobby and we headed over to our new favorite restaurant, where Nickos had taken us last night. We got a large table in the back and asked the proprietor for some privacy, which he was glad to provide based on the apparent appetites of these particular guests.

I worked everyone through their orders, the drivers helping the team make selections, and the waiter discreetly scooted out the door, giving us some privacy to go over operational details of the coming efforts.

"We've got to gather some information about the comings and goings aboard that yacht in the harbor. I want to know who's visiting the daughter, what they talk about, and what they do while they're on board," I offered.

Tang Tanaka frowned a bit and then brightened, replying, "I think we can get some cameras and audio gear on board in some strategic locations. At this point, I'd send BJ and Sam over via scuba sled, sneak them on board while a diversion is underway on the other side of the boat, have them work their magic, and drop back over the side. We can monitor from a car or other structure on shore. Sam?"

"I brought some short-range, highly sensitive transmitters, night/day cameras, all with micro batteries and a range of about six hundred yards, good for about seventy-two hours before they need attention. I can fit them practically anywhere—they're tiny," she said.

"We can monitor on a laptop in a car from the back of that parking lot by the dock. I'd suggest some kind of reason to get Elena off the boat altogether, easier to control what she sees and hears, gives us more time," said Tang.

"I'll talk to the harbormaster this evening, see if we can come to an arrangement, maybe some type of slip renewal paperwork or some such bureaucratic nonsense. Keep her in there about twenty minutes—that enough time, Tang?"

Sam asked, "Do you have any pictures from the areas you'd like to get shots of?"

"You're in luck. I clicked off a few frames with my cell phone while I was wandering around in there. I'll shoot them to you—why?"

"I can create something that looks like it belongs in there to house the cameras, either replace something there, or come up with something similar that fits in the décor."

"Done. Next challenge, Tang?"

"We'll have to pull another job to go back and retrieve the gear," he said.

"I think I can arrange a longer diversion once we find out what we need—a gal's gotta eat, after all," I replied.

"I saw the file photos in the briefing documents Dick sent us. I wondered how long it would take you to notice the yacht's occupant," quipped BJ.

I saw Sam color a bit, as my gaze shifted away from the room and into memory. I knew she'd seen the photos of Elena as well and that she wasn't as impressed as the guys.

"I have a question," Stacks offered. "Where are you going to be while they're going for a swim?"

"I'll be on shore watching, and later in the car, monitoring the bugs, taking shifts with you and Tang," he replied. "I'll take the first shift, make sure bugs are working right, then Stacks in four hours, then Tang can finish up in the morning. We'll add Sam and BJ if we need them the next day, but we'll have to move the car so we don't draw any attention."

"Works for me. Do we have speed sleds for the dive, or are we doing this the hard way?" he asked.

Tang replied, "I've sourced some stuff from a local dive shop down the coast a bit, went out earlier, and picked up everything we need. Sleds, tanks, regulators, suits, the works."

"Sounds like we're a go for the evening," I said. "Let's finish up here and amble back to the hotel slowly and separately. Sam, you head back to your room, pick up what you need there, then you and BJ get with Tang, get the gear you need. We'll meet in the harbormaster's parking lot at nine o'clock. I'll head over to the harbormaster's shack and see if I can get Elena off the boat without her seeing me.

"Take care heading back, I don't think anyone knows we're here, but you can never be too careful," I cautioned. "See you in an hour."

I stayed 'til last, paid the bill, and chatted with the owner for a few moments, while my team left in ones and twos staggered by a few minutes and headed back to the hotel.

Later, Nickos and I wandered over to the harbormaster's shack, found him inside, watching soccer on a small black-and-white TV with lousy reception. A few well-selected words, translated by Nickos, and a few hundred dollars American, and the problem of getting Elena off the yacht was solved. The harbormaster readily agreed to give the yacht a call on the radio, under the guise of signing the slip rental renewal papers—he explained he would have called the captain about such a mundane detail, but as the captain had been killed in the abduction, he had no choice but to contact the boat owner. Elena fumbled a bit with the radio, but agreed to meet the harbormaster later that evening to sign the lease renewal. Diversion granted.

The team had gathered their required gear and had assembled themselves a few yards down the coast from the parking lot keeping out of sight of the lit asphalt. BJ and Sam were suited up in top-performing dry suits, large fins for easy stroking in the salty water, small air tanks, and regulators—the harbor wasn't deep, and after dark bubbles weren't a problem. They slipped into the water a few moments before Elena was due to come ashore. I heard the small launch motor fire up and watched from atop a small rise through binoculars as the launch driver steadied the boat against the hull of the yacht, like a whale calf nuzzling its mother. Elena came down the ladder striding confidently, still shod in heels and wearing a short green dress that showed off her legs to best advantage. She hit the floor of the launch, and the pilot revved the motor and headed toward shore.

With the sleds and the fins, BJ and Sam were almost as fast crossing the distance as the launch was, and they arrived shortly after the launch hit the stubby wooden dock. Elena mimed for the launch pilot to wait and strode toward the little shack. The divers' heads bobbed at the base of the yacht, BJ tossed a line toward the ladder, caught the lowest rung, and hauled himself up the side of the giant craft and dropped over the side, Sam close behind.

Once they were on the boat, I turned my attention to the shack on shore, alternating between watching the door and glancing at my watch. I'd promised them twenty minutes, and I wanted to be sure they had adequate time to find good locations for the cameras and bugs. Sam had hidden a microphone in a picture frame virtually identical to one sitting on Big G's desk and a camera in a clock that looked much like one hanging on the wall in the salon—pretty good considering she'd only had a couple of hours to put it together after seeing the pictures I'd taken. The other cameras and microphones they would hide in more common although tougher to detect places, air vents, ceiling fixtures, etc. With wireless technology, locations were much easier to find, and with cameras so small, they were easier to conceal compared to just five years ago.

While I was watching the guard shack, I saw the light inside get brighter as the door opened, and Elena came striding out the door, chatting with the harbormaster about something mundane. It had only been about fifteen minutes, and my team wasn't expecting her back so soon. If she came on board early and caught them, the whole evening was for naught. I pulled Stacks aside and asked him to quietly intercept Elena in the nicest way, using his charm and physical presence to engage her for a few minutes to give BJ and Sam time to finish the job and get off the boat. He trotted over on an intercept course with her, covering the distance with remarkable speed without appearing to be in a hurry. At ground level, there were a few buildings between her and our location, so she didn't have a direct line of sight to us and didn't see him approaching until he stepped out from in between two small buildings and seemingly randomly ran into her.

She was startled, as anyone would be if a six-and-a-half foot, 250-pound black man had stepped out an alley suddenly, but recovered quickly, as Stacks apparently reassured her that he intended no harm, but was looking for a pub some friends had told him about. He turned on the charm, she tossed her hair and laughed at something, and the two started strolling slowly back toward the launch dock. With Stacks controlling her speed by holding her arm in a gentlemanly fashion, the hundred-yard trip took a good ten minutes, during which time Sam and BJ had placed and tested all the bugs and cameras, making adjustments via earpiece radios with Tang onshore watching on the computer monitor. They packed up and quietly dropped over the off-side gunwale into the warm water and retrieved the sleds, pointing them back toward shore, about sixty seconds before the launch nudged the hull of the yacht.

In a few moments, they were back onshore stripping out of their dry suits as Stacks ambled up, having left Elena at the launch dock.

"Making time with the surveillance subject?" I asked jokingly.

"Just doing my job, boss," he replied, sporting a huge toothy grin.

"What did you tell her?" I asked.

"Just asked where a lonely single athlete might find a little action in this one-boat town," he quipped. "I think she enjoyed the company of someone large and in charge, and told me there was no action in this town except on her yacht. She invited me aboard for a drink tomorrow night, if you can believe it, her old man missing three days, and she's dating."

"I knew I'd sent the right guy. You stalled her just long enough without making her suspicious," I replied.

"Sam, BJ, any problems with the equipment?"

"No sweat, we're reading all the critical areas including the private areas, five by five."

"Tang, everything okay with the observation car—got the shifts worked out?"

"You're up now, then Stacks at two, and then me tomorrow at 6:00 a.m."

"Okay, everyone, those of you not on shift go get some rest. Tomorrow we may have to move quickly if we learn anything this evening," I said and headed off to the car in the parking lot with the laptop under my arm.

I got to the car, made myself comfortable, and settled in to watch and wait.

For the first hour or so, not much to hear, less to see. Nothing moving topside, Elena was in the salon having a drink and reading a book, but was anything but relaxed, fidgeting and getting up and pacing at the slightest provocation or noise. Expecting someone tonight?

Then about eleven forty-five or so, I heard a faint buzz, and as it grew louder, I recognized it was a small boat motor, attached to a Zodiac inflatable, black, similar to the ones the SEAL teams used for incursions. It was heading toward the yacht from up the coast, loosely hugging the shoreline about one hundred yards out. I hadn't heard it earlier as there was a spit of land that defined the harbor north of it, and the high cliffs had blocked the noise until it rounded the tip of the cove entrance.

As the small craft drew closer, I could make out two occupants, that soon resolved into two men—one larger, wearing traditional black loose-fitting Arab blouse and pants, the other smaller, more compact, wearing dark civilian Western trousers and a turtleneck. Just judging by the hour, their dress, and their vehicle, I'd say these two were likely up to no good. Now I had a problem. I was supposed to be surreptitiously watching the yacht and Elena to see if there was anything to be learned. Now I was in a position to protect her from possible harm, but if I did, I'd tip my hand to my presence. How to explain that I'd seen the Zodiac approach and just dropped in to see if everything was all right, at just the right moment. Not terribly believable given the hour. Sometimes it's better to wait and see. Something would come to me.

I hit the transmit button on the radio and connected with Stacks, back at the hotel, watching TV, such as it was. He knew only rudimentary Greek, but had found a BBC channel in English. I asked him to meet me at the car in fifteen minutes, attracting as little notice as possible on his way, and asked him to bring us a couple of automatic pistols, a tazer, some duct tape, and nylon cord, just in case.

I watched the Zodiac's approach, and as it drew nearer to the yacht, I watched Elena pick up the sound of the approaching motor on the video monitor. Tough to decipher whether that was anticipation or fear on her face as she headed up the companionway to the top deck for a better view of the fast-moving raft. The little craft nudged the hull of the yacht at the base of the ladder; the smaller man dropped a drift anchor overboard, tied the bowline to the bottom of the ladder, and headed up the side of the hull to the gunwale opening and onto the main deck, his Arab companion close behind. Neither said a word of greeting, or at least not that I could hear, and Elena's reaction to such an uninvited boarding showed they hadn't made an appointment. Elena headed down the short ladder from the upper deck to the main level and confronted the two men, shouting angrily at their intrusion. Clearly, these two weren't whom she was expecting—time to go. I saw Stacks ambling toward the car, carrying the duffle bag from the Mercedes' trunk. I got out of the car and motioned to him to join me on the dock.

We hustled over to the end of the pier, and I spotted a small motorboat tied up at the end, the kind used to bring back groceries when the big supply ships docked offshore. We jumped in, fired the little motor, and sped off toward the yacht with nary a word spoken between us. With Stacks at the helm, I was free to formulate some sort of plan. Since she'd met Stacks earlier in the evening, I figured she might be receptive to a little midnight visit if handled properly. I'd have

Stacks go quietly up the ladder the same way the other two had, coming in behind them onto the deck, while I took the boat around the other side. I'd toss up a line to the bow rail and climb up it to the other side and could just "appear" on the port companionway behind Elena, catching the two between us. That was the plan, anyway.

I had Stacks throttle back the motor as best he could as we neared the yacht, and he jumped off and caught the bottom rung of the ladder on our way by. I continued around the fantail toward the leeward side and shut it down, drifting toward the bow as quietly as possible. When I got close enough, I fished a long line out of the bag, tied a large, loose knot in the end, tossed it up over the bow railing, and slid it rearward until the knot got jammed in a trailing stanchion, and tugged, securing the rope firmly enough for it to bear my weight. Up I went, using the hull to walk on until I reached the railing and silently clambered over it to drop onto the deck, out of sight, their view of me blocked by the salon and the upper superstructure.

I heard Elena shouting and one of the men responding in more assuring, low tones. As I inched closer, I could hear them better and made out Elena asking them what they wanted, who they were, and why they felt they could just come aboard her boat unannounced. The bigger man responded that they were friends of her father's and had come to offer her any assistance she might need. They'd heard about the kidnapping and were here to help. Not a terribly credible story, given the hour and the advent of the plethora of communications devices available to contact the boat ahead of time. She didn't buy it either, but she kept at it for a moment or two, time enough for Stacks to get in position behind them, their arguing voices covering the sound of his approach.

I rounded the edge of the salon bulkhead, got Stacks's attention, and held up my hand with three fingers extended. He got it, and as my fingers counted down from three to one, on my signal we both stepped forward and announced ourselves, guns drawn and pointed one at each intruder. "Something we can help you gentlemen with?" I asked.

The smaller man looked like he'd seen a ghost, his face slack with surprise. The larger Arab man had no such trouble and reacted instantly, moving left and into a crouch simultaneously. He backed toward the front bulkhead doors of the salon, pulling a small pistol in the process, pointing it at Stacks. Stacks was too well trained to shoot just anybody, but he'd stayed alive up 'til this point by making quick, correct decisions. Stacks shot the larger Arab in the knee, hurting him and immobilizing him, but keeping him alive to be questioned later. He dropped to the deck like a string had been cut, losing the gun and grabbing his knee and screaming. I motioned with my gun for the smaller man to move over and join his friend up against the salon bulkhead. Elena meanwhile had scampered up the stairs to the upper deck, out of harm's way, once she saw Stacks with a gun. She was screaming at the two intruders, reviling them with curses normally reserved for seasoned merchant sailors of the male persuasion. I made sure Stacks had these two under control and headed up the steps toward her, making calming motions as I went. I got to the top, and she stopped screaming, stood there glaring at me for a moment, and then collapsed into my arms crying and sobbing, thanking me for keeping her safe. So much for staying under the radar.

While I tucked her away in her stateroom, Stacks dragged the wounded Arab down to the engine room, and on the way to join him, I tied up the smaller guy with the cap using some duct tape and cord, securing him to the base of one of the railing stanchions, cast steel with long bolts that should hold for a bit. I headed down to join Stacks below decks and watched as he carefully, almost delicately, tied the Arab to a mount for one of the two huge diesel engines, with his back to the churning diesel, at idle now, moving just enough to charge the batteries and keep the ship steerable, on autopilot. He started babbling in Arabic and shaking his head like he didn't understand what was going on. I'd heard the Arab speak English in his exchange with Elena, so that little ruse would be short-lived. I started right away with English, keeping my own language cards close to the chest. I speak at least nine languages passably, Arabic and Farsi among them, but this character was likely to slip and, thinking I couldn't understand him, let something go I could use.

"Who sent you?" I shot at him once I had his attention.

Silence.

"I'll give you a chance to save some painful moments—just tell me who you're working for," I cajoled.

Nothing.

I faced him squarely, bent down, and got close to his ear and whispered, "I know how to create so much pain for you, you'll give up your whole family before I'm done, and you'll go back to them unable to perform your most favorite thing ever again with your wife. All you have to do to avoid it is tell me who you work for and why you're here."

Silence.

I reached behind me to a worktable and picked up a good-sized pipe wrench, maybe 18" long and about 9 lbs of solid steel. Before he could see what was coming, I swung the wrench and crushed what was left of his shot-up knee. His screams could likely have been heard onshore, if it wasn't for all the heat insulation in the engine room and the noise of the diesels.

"That was a small taste, just a sneak preview…any thoughts on your employer?"

Silence, except some muted sobbing and heavy breathing.

I started to swing the wrench again, and he started babbling before the back swing was even complete.

"I don't know exactly who pays me. I get my money from someone else who also works for the big man."

"That's a start—any ideas about *his* name?"

"I just call him money guy," he whispered.

"How about a description, what direction he comes from, where do you meet to make the payment, how do you get in touch with him when the job's done—you know—details?" I hammered.

"I send text to a number they give me, use only prepaid cell phone," he offered. "I say where, they say when in their reply, we meet."

"How does he get to the meetings? I assume you walk, pick somewhere close or convenient," I asked, softening my voice.

"Last time was Athens, in café at bottom of the hill from Acropolis. He walks while I can see him, but he's never sweating or hot when he arrives," he offered, trying to save the last vestiges of his knee.

"What does he look like?" I pressed.

"He's very strong, like spends time in training for war," he said. "He's got Arab turban on when we meet, but no hair underneath, dark beard, trimmed neat, not as big as you but very fit. Eyes like a dragon, like he sees through you with little effort—very intimidating," he babbled.

"So I fill out a wanted sheet for Interpol. I'm looking for a bald, bearded, fitness guru with dragon eyes. Is that what you want me to do?"

"That's how I see him, could be disguise," he cowered.

"Not much to go on—give me a better reason to keep from throwing you overboard tied to the anchor…"

"He owes me for this job—if I can bring him proof of completion. I need the money, will have to fake something. If you help me, you can follow, get close to him," he said.

"What's the proof you usually give him on a job like this—I assume you were to kill Elena? Any reason given as to why?" I asked.

"He never tell me why, and I don't ask. I bring him little finger. He takes print and discards it," he explained.

"So now that it's pretty clear that you're not going to complete this task, what is your plan?"

"This is the first time anyone has come close to stopping me. I have to think of something…How did you know we were coming?"

"I ask the questions here. Don't get cocky," I replied. "Just remember how easily I stopped the two of you, and I'm not even breathing hard."

He was still bleeding pretty badly, and his complexion had gone from swarthy to grey in the last few moments as his blood pressure dropped and shock started to set in. No matter how tough you are, and how well trained you are, or how accustomed to pain you are, savage injury will trigger your body's natural survival mechanisms, and shock is one of them. It starts constricting the peripheral blood vessels, keeping blood closest to your heart and brain, attempts to keep you conscious and your blood pressure up. It's a short-term fix until you can get the bleeding stopped and get some IV fluids in you, and without it, you can easily die from blood loss and a host of other complications. I needed to either save this guy or send him overboard in the next ten minutes or so, or he would make the choice for me.

Although they could probably hear me onshore via the various microphones and video links we'd installed, I went up top and called Tang, woke him up, and apprised him of the situation. He said he'd get on to some databases, make a few calls to the states, and get back to me in a few minutes. I asked him what he thought we should do with the two assailants. His response was a reasonable, "Turn them or burn them—we don't need extra drag." Sounded like sage advice to me.

I returned below, passing the smaller of the two still secured to the railing on the way; he just looked up a glared as I passed but uttered nothing. He hadn't heard the shot or the blows and resulting screams over the engine noise and through the door, and was none the wiser as to his partner's fate. I figured I'd keep it that way for a bit, see what developed.

I got to the engine room, found our friend with the story passed out at the end of his restraints, heartbeat weak and thready but regular. I looked at Stacks questioningly, and he shrugged, as if to say, "What do you want from me? He passed out." I untied him and tried to revive him, after a more thorough search of his pockets and belongings turned up nothing of interest. If he didn't know who sent him and couldn't tell me more about who paid him, the trail was basically cold as far as he was concerned, making him of little use to me. I dragged him into an unused maintenance room below, bound up both knees tightly with some rags to stem the bleeding, resecured him to a sink drain, and went looking for his friend.

Stacks and I untied the smaller partner with the cap, dragged him down to the engine room, and cuffed him with the same cuffs in the same position as his friend had been. He got one look at all the blood on the floor and the bullet holes in the decking and started shaking. His larger, more capable friend had clearly succumbed to our charms and was not to be heard from again as far as he was concerned. This conclusion seemed to loosen his tongue and improve his English skills tremendously, and he started babbling about how he knew nothing, was just a farm boy in Iran, had been selected for army service, and had been asked to accompany his partner on a mission to kill an infidel who threatened Islam's peace and security. I suspected his knowledge of his real mission and the players in it was minimal, and after a few pointed questions and some mild but painful ministrations, was sure he would be of no help. I didn't necessarily believe his story was true and complete, but it would likely mirror the other one, and if the sight of his friend's obvious demise hadn't shaken anything loose, more pain wouldn't likely net us anything additional.

I left him cuffed to the engine for the moment and went in search of Elena. She was sitting on the bed in her stateroom, looking dazed and disoriented. She looked up slightly upon my entry and then went back to staring into space, seeking answers at a distance from a source I couldn't see. I knelt in front of her, got her attention, and started gently asking questions.

"Do you know who those two were?" I prodded.

"Never saw them before, but I know their kind, sloppy brutes," she responded.

"Any idea what they wanted or who sent them?" I continued.

"No, are they still here, on my ship?" she asked, with a little more heat.

"Yes," I replied, "but they're incapacitated."

"What are you going to do with them?" she asked pointedly. "I don't want to sound ungrateful, but how did you come to be here just after they arrived?" she continued.

"I couldn't sleep, was out for a walk along the pier to get some fresh air, and heard their boat approach," I answered.

"He not able to sleep either?" she asked, nodding to the lower stairway toward where I had left Stacks.

"He's a longtime friend I asked to come along in case I needed some assistance. His name is Stacks, and he's a very capable and helpful friend to have in such situations," I replied vaguely. She seemed to accept this, and just nodded and lowered her gaze. Her color was returning, and her breathing had slowed to a more normal rhythm.

"Do you have somewhere else you can stay near here?" I asked softly. I needed to get her to a place where we could secure her without her knowing she was being secured, but we could still see her and monitor her movements.

"I have a cousin that lives near Athens. They will probably let me stay for a little while," she answered.

"I tell you what—it's almost three a.m. Why don't you try to get some sleep for the next few hours and later this morning we'll take you to your cousin's and get you settled in there for a few days until we can make heads or tails of this little event," I cajoled.

She nodded and started to get up and get out of her robe. I discreetly turned my back and headed up to the main deck to meet up with Stacks and see if we could get ashore without swimming. We still needed to figure out what to do with the two assailants short term, but the wounded one had actually had a good idea when he suggested we let them go and follow them to the next meeting, but the way I had it figured out, the results would be far different than he expected.

Stacks and I worked out our next moves, and he went below to secure both of them in a way that would facilitate transport. I stuck my head in on Elena and told her we'd be back in the morning to get her, to be ready to move by 8:00 a.m. Then I rejoined Stacks on the main deck where he'd deposited our two charges. My plan was to take us ashore in their launch, deposit them at the nearest hospital after doping them into unconsciousness, and then have Stacks take the launch out and scuttle it, swim back, and join us. We'd be able to keep track of the two henchmen for a couple of days while they got patched up and use them to lead us to the next rung up the ladder. Checking them into the hospital under false names and having no ID or other documents on them to refute us would buy us a few days, and to the casual observer, they would have simply disappeared. Once they were tucked away, we could keep Elena safe and see what else developed, while we worked out the details of how we would release these two and how to approach their boss after they identified him.

Meantime, Tang filled us in by phone with his findings from his database searches and phone calls. He'd found through a CIA contact a marine major who'd just been rotated back to the States who had included a similar description in an After-Action report as a sergeant during his stint in Iraq during Desert Storm in '89. What caught his superior officer's eye was the description of the crazy-brave actions of his opponents during a firefight with some Russian-trained insurgents, particularly one rather large, bald individual who appeared not only fearless but impervious to pain as he took several rounds and kept going, unphased, toward a protected bunker with another soldier over his shoulder. The crazy savior was later identified as Ahman Akbar, head of Taliban Security and notorious bad guy. Tang figured the references and descriptions were too similar to be ignored as coincidence and recommended that we work under the premise that he was our paymaster. Akbar's current whereabouts were unknown to intelligence sources, but he was thought to be floating around the Middle East region at large.

That little tidbit certainly gave me some food for thought and set the tone for going forward as well. I'd have to be cautious when dealing with our friend Mr. Akbar; he sounded like a tough customer. Better not to underestimate him, I figured, but his training and toughness could be used against him as well. I filed it away and concentrated on getting these two into their launch without dropping and drowning them both, and headed back to shore just as dawn was breaking, just after 5:00 a.m.

Stacks and I tossed the conspirators in the back seat of the Mercedes and headed into town to locate the nearest medical facility, our injured guest moaning only occasionally but hanging in there, still shocky but relatively stable. The other stayed mute the entire time; he just kept looking at his partner's bloody knee and rocking back and forth in the seat. We located a small municipal hospital about fifteen miles out of town on the road on the way back to Athens, and pulled around the back to a small dirt lot. I hopped out, opened the trunk, and extracted a small Dopp kit. After some scratching around, I came up with a small syringe and some morphine ampules. I drew up a significant dose, which would both dull the pain and render them harmless for a few hours, opened the back door, administered it to them both, and with help from Stacks, quickly pulled them out of the car and duck-walked them into the back door of the hospital.

We'd changed clothes in the back of the car before we left the dock, and we were both wearing decent civilian clothes. I've learned that physical carriage and a confident walk would get you into and around a variety of places, and hospitals were no different. We acted like we owned the place, so passersby thought we did, and no one paid us any mind. We found the admissions desk, or what passed for it, one floor up and near the front. We located a couple of chairs, dropped our two charges into them as they were passing out, and turned to address the nurse behind the desk.

Clearly a veteran, we faced an older woman, maybe fifties, iron grey hair pulled back in a severe bun, a good-sized woman but not really fat, just substantial. The look on her face said, "I've seen the likes of you before—I don't want any trouble out of you," so I approached her as placidly and harmlessly as I could. I leaned over and announced that I needed to speak with her privately, in English if possible, about a delicate matter involving the son of a public official. Her expression turned from one of annoyance to one of a conspirator hiding a secret, and I knew I had her. We went with her to a small room off the lobby, and she shut the door behind us. It was a tiny administrative office, with only one chair, so we motioned for her to sit, and we stood there, towering over her trying not to look too menacing.

I leaned down to face her and explained that my associate and I were military policemen from the nearby American battleship, docked north of here. We'd been out on R & R and had run across a bar fight, in which the two gentlemen we had brought in had been involved. One had obviously been shot, and both were banged up and scared, most of the scuffle being over with by the time we arrived. We felt it our duty to render aid, and through some rudimentary questioning, discovered that the injured one was the son of a Saudi minister, one with a particular warm spot for affairs in Greek government, and a large contributor to the Papandreau campaign. We felt it in everyone's best interest that his identity not become public knowledge, but that he be taken care of as quickly and efficiently as possible using the utmost discretion. I suggested we admit them both under whatever names she might choose other than their real ones and that their stay last a few days in a shared private room. I asked that they not be permitted to leave or speak with anyone until I could contact their relatives and seek guidance on their wishes for transportation home.

The nurse looked at me like I had just given her the secret to the atom bomb. She replied that she understood completely, that her brother had worked in Greek government service, and that such things could be handled with great discretion, with proper consideration. I reached in my pocket and pulled out a good-sized wad of cash I had left over from my recent purchases in the bakery, and counted off a few hundred American dollars. The nurse made them disappear into her uniform pocket like she was performing a magic trick, and we exited to the lobby. She called for a couple of stretchers and an orderly to take these two gentlemen to a private room while she filled in paper forms at her desk with brisk efficiency. I noted the names she had chosen on the forms and told her we'd be back in a few days to retrieve them, and that the royal family would be most grateful for their tender and discrete care of their charges. She smiled at me, winked, and turned away to help the orderlies load them on the gurneys and push the two silent figures down the hall, without uttering a word.

"Man, you sure can sling the bullshit when you need to," noted Stacks, who hadn't said a word during the entire exchange.

"Trick of the trade, everybody likes to think they know something others don't—makes them a conspirator, brightens their dull, boring day," I replied lightly. "She'll likely squirrel those two away in a corner room and keep them sedated while they patch them up, and get a big kick out of telling her girlfriends that she has some celebrity patients that she can't talk about at work.

"Worst case, she doesn't sedate them, and they happen to find someone who speaks Arabic in the hospital, and they make a liar out of me. They won't say much since they're not supposed to be here anyway, can't prove who they are with no ID, and can't involve the authorities for the same reasons. We're in good shape for at least forty-eight hours before anyone gets a hint they're out of commission, and if they attack it through channels, their names won't appear since they've now got 'aliases.'"

I pointed the Mercedes back to the middle of town and our hotel. I needed a few hours of shuteye before making our next move. I checked in with Tang, BJ, and Sam and let them know we'd be meeting at nine o'clock that morning in the restaurant to regroup and revise the plan. I pushed my way in to my hotel room, shucked my clothes, and dropped into bed, after setting the alarm on my watch for eight thirty.

Next morning, gathered at our favorite table in the back of the restaurant, the group ate like the athletes they were, while I filled them all in on the previous night's events, and we kicked around some ideas about where to go next. They warmed to the idea that we needed to find who the paymaster for the two goons was and work our way up the chain from there to likely find Big G's kidnapper. BJ and Sam volunteered to go ahead of us and scout a place to set up a meet in Athens, taking Tang with them to coordinate logistics and act as communications hub; they figured a couple would attract less notice, looking like a couple of tourists.

Stacks and I would stay here, keep an eye on Elena, clean up after our little escapade, and ride herd on our two unconscious friends in the hospital. Tang was going to head back to the office to do some more extensive research and arrange for some more specialized gear. Our local security team would work with us to transport the two Arabs securely and act as local liaison. After breakfast, we would head out in pairs and threes and disperse to our various locations, keeping in touch by disposable cell phone. I needed to head out and pick up Elena, do some sniffing around locally, and see if we could backtrack some of the facts we knew about the original kidnapping. Stacks headed back to his room to get some sleep, after dropping Tang at the airport, so his local escort could stick around and provide back up for me. We needed to get to the bottom of this thing and fast. I could feel the time slipping away and knew that other operations were in the works and Big G's time was getting shorter by the minute.

Chapter 13

Oranjestadt, Aruba

The large man had been busy, arranging details for his next big move. He'd contacted a few of his colleagues, many of whom had expressed concern for the lack of communication from Big G regarding pending deals. The big man did nothing to reassure them—in fact, planting the seeds of doubt for a rewarding outcome for their purchases, offering to fill their orders were things to go awry. This was the tip of the iceberg in his widespread smear campaign, but the first few contacts were some of the largest arms purchasers on the globe, and they would spread the word quickly once some critical deadlines were missed. In a rogues' gallery of arms dealers, trust was a fragile thing, and missed appointments created problems down the supply chain that were often hard to rectify. Indeed, part of his plan involved making sure a few shipments that were already enroute never arrived, thus giving the appearance that Big G had engaged in some misappropriation of their purchase funds. Some of those moves had been activated, representatives dispatched to intercept shipments and not only prevent their arrival, but reroute them to the big man's warehouse on the island. This way not only was he able to fill the orders quickly with the correct merchandise, but at no cost to himself.

News of Elena's continuing existence had reached him from an agent in place on Crete, but he was unaware of the whereabouts of his two would-be assassins, and Akbar was out of touch temporarily. He was not disturbed by this news as much as surprised, as Akbar had proved to be a most effective agent, never having failed an assignment before. He had every confidence that once notified of their failure, Akbar would hunt down the two miscreants and mete out the proper punishment, as well as complete their assignment to his satisfaction. This merely delayed the outcome, maybe by only a few days.

The rest of his advisory board was unaware of that portion of his campaign and were all busy carrying out their assignments in various parts of the world.

The big man sat back in his dimly lit office, closed his eyes, and started an envisioning exercise taught to him in his distant past by a Zen master who had since risen to global prominence. He entered a series of corridors in his mind, passing door after door until he reached one at the end of the hallway, which stood open just a small crack. Opening that door revealed a darkened room, the only light coming from a small opening in the ceiling. Lying on the floor was Big G, handcuffed, gagged, disheveled, and disoriented, but without a trace of fear on his patrician face. The big man watched as the range of emotions crossed Big G's face rapidly in succession, like watching a movie in fast forward.

Concern, distain, hatred, anger, calculation, curiosity, to vengeful satisfaction crossed his countenance in the time it took to peel a banana, and the big man gained a new respect for his adversary, realizing that he'd arrived at some sort of plan to thwart his efforts. The large man now knew that he'd have to change his disposition from kidnapping to something more extreme if his plans were to come to fruition.

Mediterranean Sea

Big G had been in this hold for three days, plenty of time to thoroughly search his surroundings, at least as well as possible given his condition and circumstances. He'd crawled over the floor of the hold, determined its size and composition, construction and condition, and realized that all of the above were of sufficient quality to contain him, with no hope of an exploitable weakness. The upper hatch, however, held his interest, and it was there that he applied his considerable powers of analysis and deduction. The hatch opened regularly to admit new food, water, and to allow his captors, whom he still hadn't seen, to hook the latrine bucket and replace it with an empty one. However, they only came at night and were backlit by a search light on the top of the superstructure pointed at the deck, so all he saw were silhouettes hovering in the opening for a scant few seconds, long enough to lower one bundle, pick up another, and lower the replacement. Having no watch, his only means of telling the passing of time was to monitor the light direction coming in under the edges of the hatch.

If he could see light, he reasoned, the hatch didn't secure properly and was therefore a weakness. However, as it hovered forty feet over his head, he still needed to devise a way to get there in order to exploit it. The walls were smooth, no handholds existed, as the maintenance ladder along the nearest bulkhead to the hatch opening had been removed and the welds ground smooth where the rungs had been attached.

He knew his captors were keeping him alive to ransom him for something, whether it be money or information. That was his edge—being worth more alive than dead. His only hope was to find a way out of that hatch, and off the boat in one piece, and make contact with any one of a dozen associates scattered around the globe to get him a lift back to his nearest office. His best bet was up that food delivery rope, but he'd need to take everyone on deck by surprise in order for them not to let go of the rope before he'd reached the top, and he'd have to time it so that it worked correctly. He concentrated on conserving his strength, eating everything they gave him greedily, drinking the small cup dry, and moving only enough to maintain muscle tone and circulation but not sap his energy. He'd not let them see him move when they looked into the hatch, lulling them into a false sense of security, thinking he was unconscious most of the time.

He heard a loud bang in the hold one afternoon and heard shouting and feet running on the deck above. This happened twice in the last three days, most recently about two minutes ago. After the second one, he understood what was going on, and the glimmer of a plan began to take shape in his mind. All he needed to do was wait for the right time.

Chapter 14

Crete, Greece

I started by getting Elena settled and out of the picture for a while until I could gauge her level of safety. If I could get to the next link in the chain and stop Akbar, I'd sleep a whole lot better. In the meantime, I needed to get her out of this little town, preferably off Crete altogether and safely stashed at her relatives' house, owned under a different name. Her cousin lived in a small village up the coast, as it turned out, and after ferrying out to the yacht and climbing aboard, Nickos stayed in the launch while I climbed aboard the now all too familiar yacht. I found her below decks filling a modest bag with clothes and personal items for the trip.

"I see you pack light," I quipped.

"Yes, my father got us used to traveling frequently, and we learned to take only what we would absolutely need and that which could not be replaced wherever we were going," she replied.

"Finish up and meet me on the deck. I'll take you breakfast on the way to your cousins'," I said.

"I'll only be a moment. How long do you think I'll be gone?" she asked.

"I hope to have this wrapped up and taken care of in a few days. If I can track down whoever sent those guys to get rid of you, I can find who's behind all this and find out where they're holding your father," I replied.

I headed up the companionway, and sure enough she followed a few minutes later. We hopped over the rail, down the ladder to the waiting launch, and headed for the dock. She had secured the yacht as best she could, shutting everything down cold, leaving emergency power only to run a few running lights and the bow and stern lights, securing the hatches and bulkhead doors, double-checking the anchor. She seemed comfortable doing all this, like it was a normal, repetitive chore that she'd performed hundreds of times. Perhaps she had.

We loaded her bags in the car and headed up the coast of Crete, Nickos driving silently and agilely up the winding little roads. On the way, she chatted amiably if a little reservedly about her father, her family, and her plans once he was safely home. I was trying to ascertain through some gentle probing how much she knew about her father's business and his associates. Based on her answers, which appeared to be genuine and authentic without a hint of guile, I could tell her knowledge was fairly limited. She knew he bought and sold weapons of various types, which, to her, justified all the last minute travel. She didn't seem the least bit bothered by the moral aspects of his business, saying that he worked closely with foreign governments to supply them with items they couldn't get on their own. To hear her describe it, he could be buying and selling uniform buttons, not subnuclear missiles and handheld rocket-propelled grenades. He must have soft-pedaled and rationalized his involvement and deeper purpose of his transactions for so long that it was now her reality, her truth about his business dealings. As it turned out, this would bode well for her survival in future. The less she knew, the fewer reasons there were for her father's competitors to want her dead.

We stopped for a little breakfast at a small, roadside café about halfway back up the coast. The service was excellent, even solicitous, and as usual, it was a family-run operation. The food arrived and I continued to probe her about specifics about her father's business, both the transactions themselves and his associates, hoping to tease out some clue as to who might be behind this abduction scheme. She was mildly adamant that she knew nothing about either one, but with some gentle prodding, she admitted that she had deliberately distanced herself from his business, concentrating on running her own boutique and keeping within her own social circle. She did remember some men who had at various times stopped by his office or been guests on the various yachts over the years, but most had been years ago when she was just a girl, with even less interest in their adult affairs than she had now.

We finished our meal, paid, and got back in the car after exchanging pleasantries with the owner and speculating about the tourist season's volume and how nobody had any respect anymore. On the way toward the airport, we chatted amiably, got to know each other a bit, and I discovered that she was a more substantial woman than she had first appeared. She ran a successful business, one she was thinking of expanding, had a strong group of friends, and kept in touch with relatives routinely, including her mother, who had left her father when she was very small, resulting in a nasty custody battle so her father could retain custody. As a result of an ironclad and legally groundbreaking prenuptial agreement, Big G paid neither child support nor alimony, and thus was able to show that her mother was unable to support the child and provide adequately for her well-being, thus gaining full custody. I had new respect for Big G's legal and business acumen after hearing this—apparently the crafty old guy had more on the ball than just missiles and tanks.

We got to the airport, located three tickets to Athens on Olympic, and settled in for the short flight to the capital. Elena's cousins lived an hour or so outside the city, and before we'd left Lentas, I'd had Tang run a full check on them, just to be on the safe side. They were as distant from the current situation as could be, clean as the proverbial whistle, with no obvious connection to Elena aside from the familial one; they were married daughters of one of her mother's sisters. She would be as safe there as anywhere.

The plane landed, we deplaned and, with no checked baggage, headed for the car Nickos had left there on his way to Crete. Knowing the difficulty of transporting weapons on local or international flights, Nickos had thoughtfully left a couple of pistols in the glove box of the Athens car, a slightly less battered Mercedes 300S, with what sounded like a highly modified gas engine transplanted into it. I had packed my big black duffel and shipped it back to the hotel that morning before we left; it would catch up to us tomorrow. All I had to do was get her to her cousins' house and get back to Athens without getting into further trouble—normally a simple proposition, but I was starting to doubt that anything involved with this project was simple.

As it turned out, we made it out to the suburbs without incident, dropped Elena off into the waiting arms of her cousins, hopped back in the Mercedes after receiving some admiring but guarded looks from her hosts, and headed back to the Athens Hilton. On the way back, I worked the phone, getting updates from my far-flung team. BJ and Sam had found a good spot to set up the meet with the paymaster. Tang had a comm net set up, including some hidden throat mikes for us to use on the sting, and the local boys back on Crete had been keeping an eye on our two guests with Stacks as a coordinator. The plan was for them to gather at the airport with our two guests in tow, under the guise of transporting gravely ill hospital patients to a treatment facility in Athens. They would be traveling on stretchers, unconscious, hooked to fluid IVs, and masked to prevent recognition. Once we got them on the ground in Athens, we'd hired a private ambulance to get them back to the hotel, where I'd secured some additional rooms. We'd bring them back to consciousness, get them to contact the paymaster, and set up the meet where BJ and Sam had scouted. We'd be set up well in advance of the meet time, and once the paymaster made an appearance, we'd let the meeting get started and then surround him, pop him into the same ambulance, and spirit him away for further questioning under more controlled circumstances.

It sounded good on paper, and I knew that Tang had a remarkable ability to pull together such things using whatever resources he could scrounge and make it happen smoothly and successfully, with a minimum of collateral damage or attention from the locals. I had every confidence that he could pull off a simple entrap and abduct in broad daylight in the middle of a tourist attraction without attracting attention. Tough assignment on a good day, but my team had a level of skills that I had no worries as to the successful conclusion of this portion of the job.

We gathered at a ramshackle warehouse not far from the base of the Acropolis, in sight of one of the most iconic structures in world history. Sam and BJ distributed gear, went over various aspects and fine details, comm protocols with everyone, Nickos quietly translating for the locals whom we'd included as some much-needed manpower. They seemed up for the challenge, quietly nodding, asking insightful and well thought out questions, refining the plan and their role like the professionals I suspected they were. The plan was to set up a loose net around the lower plaza of the Acropolis, near the entrance to the old theater ruins. We had brought the unconscious thugs back to life and gotten them on the phone, set up the meeting for the tourist signpost at the head of the path into the theater for six hours from now, after the last tourist bus had left but before the park closed. There would be enough visitors around to provide cover but not enough to get in the way or add to the collateral damage if things went bad.

Among the special gear Sam and Tang had dreamed up was some special ammunition for the Sig Sauer .45 pistols we were using that substituted dart heads for lead slugs, allowing us to deliver a variety of liquid compounds to anywhere we could see quickly and quietly. We planned to use them to knock down the paymaster and his colleagues, using one that mimicked a heart attack for him and simple nerve toxin for the remainder. The latter was a quick-acting and short-lived compound that paralyzed its victims almost instantly and completely, but only lasted a few moments, allowing them to return to a state of activity including breathing normally in time not to kill them. We'd hit the guards first, while they were seated, locking them in place without attracting attention. Then after the paymaster was grouped with the thugs, but before they could warn him, knock him down, and then "come to his aid," hustle him into the waiting ambulance under the watchful eyes of a group of tourists while his guards looked on helplessly. It would only work if executed perfectly with exquisite timing and optimal efficiency. The two thugs had been briefed extensively on the consequences of tipping off Akbar, and we'd have Stacks and BJ suitably equipped to silence them from a conceivable distance if we saw any indication of a signal or suspicious movement. Either way, they had served their purpose and were expendable, and they knew it.

We left the warehouse in twos and threes, fanning out to climb the mountain from different directions, setting up our net. Once everyone one was in position, including Stacks and BJ on higher-level escarpments overlooking the theater entrance, we settled in to wait. For untrained amateurs, this is the toughest part, the waiting. My team was extensively trained, seasoned veterans all, and had no trouble sitting still or looking unobtrusive for long periods. The anxiety level only climbed slightly twenty minutes before the appointed meet time when Stacks noted that the knot of tourists at base of the Acropolis was thinning out, but that there were several "un-touristy" looking individuals seated on benches as if waiting for a bus, but that the last bus had left fifteen minutes ago. Clearly, the advance team was in place, and we all took pains to identify and verify each one with the rest of the team, making sure we were all on the same page with who was involved in our little soirée.

It worked perfectly, almost. Suddenly Akbar appeared as if by magic, approaching the signpost on schedule, and our thugs started to saunter over toward him to make the meet, or as close as they could manage with one's shattered knee in a brace and the other's bandaged face. They resembled the famous image of the wounded revolutionary soldiers returning from the battle of Valley Forge. Akbar looked askance at their appearance, but let them get close enough to do the job. I signaled the outer team to lock up the watchers on the perimeter and told BJ to let fly with a dart round at Akbar. Like clockwork, small popping sounds from the base perimeter signaled that the locals had done their job, but the sound carried in a funny way through the ancient theater, much louder than anticipated, even with subsonic rounds and sound suppressors on the weapons. Akbar turned sharply at the sound and dropped into a crouch, and the normally accurate BJ missed his neck and hit his hand, trying to follow him down and overcompensated.

The dart hit, but went through the fleshy part between the thumb and fingers with the needle sticking out the other side, injecting the chemical harmlessly into the air. Akbar yelped, but kept his head, dropped down, and rolled under a small ledge of rock at the edge of the trail. The comm net came alive with positions and instructions as the team reacted. I had Stacks and BJ pack up and head down the hill and had Sam and Tang close in on Akbar with a couple of the locals heading up the trail to close off his escape that way. We'd lost the element of surprise, but he still didn't know who the enemy was or what they wanted, just that they wanted him down.

Akbar popped up and started sprinting back down the trail, expecting his minions to cover his back. In the space of the few seconds all this had taken, his guards were still immobile, so he was on his own. He ran straight into our local support guys, who looked like the locals they were and he didn't even see them until it was too late. The larger of the two, Stavros, executed a tackle that an NFL defensive back would envy, leveling Akbar and burying him under 220+ lbs. of tough Greek peasant. His partner piled on, locked both Akbar's wrists behind his back, cuffed him with zip-ties, and flipped him over and started lightly compressing his chest, still trying to convey the impression that Akbar had suffered a natural mishap, not professionally leveled. I had to admire that kind of quick improvisation and made a mental note to thank Ceros and Nickos for locating this group of guys.

The team converged on Akbar's prone form from above and below, including the ambulance team, lead by Stacks with a stretcher thrown over his shoulder. They loaded him onto the stretcher without revealing the zip-ties, restrained him, humped him down the trail to the waiting ambulance, popped him inside with a minimum of fuss, and whisked him away to the Hilton's underground parking garage. Once in the ambulance, Stacks injected him with a powerful sedative that would keep him incommunicado for many hours. The rest of my team wrangled the two thugs and our gear down the trail as casually and quickly as they could, as the guards regained mobility and, realizing that their boss was gone to parts unknown, scattered in multiple directions.

My team minus Stacks, the locals, Nickos, and myself all headed back to the hotel, mostly in pairs catching local cabs. We met up in a restaurant around the corner, a space-age modern café with sleek European furniture and young, inexperienced help behind the counter. We headed toward the back, near the floor to ceiling windows overlooking the main drag through Athens, traffic passing as if it was a normal day, which to everyone but Akbar, it was. We ordered huge quantities of food, hungry and working off the adrenaline from a successful mission.

Once everyone's food arrived, there were a few moments of silence while we dug into the food, and then the conversation started in earnest, blowing off steam as men of such action will after a mission. Sam joined in and held her own as usual. At one point, Stacks had joined us, intimidating the restaurant help, as a large, muscular black man dressed in commando gear in the middle of the daytime will do. He assured us that he had Akbar on ice, and we commenced to finish off the food, winding down to quiet, comfortable shorthand conversations.

Aside from returning Elena to her natural environment, our job in Greece was largely done. We had gathered all the intelligence we could on a local level, and we had a lead to the person or group behind the kidnapping and Elena's attempted murder. We knew they operated internationally, so they could be located anywhere on the planet and send Akbar to do their bidding. I congratulated everyone for their exemplary performance, including BJ, despite the missed shot, an extremely difficult feat under the best of circumstances.

He apologized to the team for the error and humbly accepted our accolades, along with some light-hearted ribbing about heading back to the rifle range at sniper school for a refresher. We agreed to do what was needed to get Akbar back to the United States for some stern conversation under circumstances we could tightly control. Sam agreed to run travel and gear logistics. Tang promised to stay behind and do some clean-up, pay the locals, return the ambulance, run interference with the press before the story surfaced, and some other details before joining us in Virginia in a couple of days. I called Langley and had them pull everything they had on Akbar. I'd need it to do a thorough job of questioning him later. I'd get Elena and deposit her safely on the yacht, and then join them in the office after catching the first available flight out. As the sun dropped behind the hill, we casually migrated to the local tavern for a drink or two before retiring in our hotel rooms for some well-earned rest.

The next morning, Nickos and I headed out for the suburbs, while the rest of the team headed for the commercial aviation section of the airport in Athens. We pulled up outside the small house where Elena's cousins lived, Nickos stayed in the car, and I headed up to knock on the door. She had it open before my knuckles hit the rough wood. Clearly glad to see me, and even more pleased that the threat on her life had been erased, however temporarily. Relief flooded her face, and she fired questions at me before I got a chance to sit down. Once she fully understood where things stood, she relaxed a bit, and we chatted like we'd known each other for years, comfortably and easily, for a few moments. Her guard had dropped, and I got a glimpse of the girl/woman that her father had cherished.

We headed out to the car, hopped in, and headed toward the airport. She was flying back to Crete, and I was heading to the States. I would have Nickos drive her to the dock and take her out to the yacht, make sure she was alone, safe, and settled. We talked amiably for a while and settled into a comfortable silence. I was running all sorts of scenarios in my head to make our parting at the airport longer and less awkward, but nothing was working. It was like my brain was running at half speed through a fog. Eventually I gave up and figured things would play out naturally and I'd think of something. Clearly, this had gone beyond "work" into the realm of "personal," and that normally isn't something I have an issue with. All of a sudden, I was concerned with something other than getting the job done, finding Big G, and getting him back in one piece. I had to get past this so I could function, or it could be the end of me.

We got to Heraklion in record time thanks to Nickos's skill behind the wheel and headed straight for the departure lounge. Nickos went to check us into our respective flights, with departure desks conveniently located right across the concourse from each other, while Elena and I headed to the little café upstairs to get something to eat before the flight. Over a helping of sloppy mousaka and some potato soup, we chatted and made plans to get together for dinner once her father was home safely. She was still gravely concerned for his well-being, but clearly had faith in my abilities after watching me with my team in action the last two days. She had warmed up to me considerably since our first meeting, just seventy-two hours ago.

As her flight was called, she leaned over the table and gave me a slow and seemingly meaningful kiss, pulled back, and said, "Call me first when my father is safe. I trust you to bring him back to me."

I mumbled something like an addled schoolboy and watched as she strode confidently toward the gate, Nickos in tow, and got on the plane back to Crete, her yacht, her life.

An hour or so later, I boarded the flight to New York, via London, and settled back to think, alone for the first time in nearly a week. So many things were tumbling through my head it was hard to make any sense of it. I'm a big believer in a couple of simple concepts, one of which is that sleep is one of a soldier's best weapons. A rested warrior is the prepared warrior. The other is that our subconscious is an underused tool when trying to solve puzzles, and I've had many a breakthrough by taking a long sleep and letting it do its work on the problem while I focused on resting. I settled in and slept until the wheels hit the ground at Heathrow. I woke, shuffled my way to the connecting flight to LaGuardia, and sacked out in my new seat within minutes of the doors closing.

Upon arrival in New York, I awoke surprisingly refreshed, with some interesting angles on things and some ideas to pursue to gather some much-needed information. I needed to prepare for my interrogation of Akbar, and I needed to get another look at what our cipher section had made of the ledger and those phone numbers.

I headed to the ground transport section after picking up my bags. Tang had shipped our special equipment ahead to the office in Virginia, so I was unarmed and felt a little naked. I rented a car one way at the local Hertz office, picked up the car, an underpowered, midsized, generic Ford sedan, and headed out of the city. I called in to let the office know where I was, and after some chit-chat with Dick Grey, with the promise I would update him fully upon arrival, I got connected to the CIA cipher section and spoke to the analyst handling the ledger I'd sent via diplomatic pouch. He told me that he'd uncovered some interesting angles on the numbers, but couldn't discuss it over the phone, and that he'd see me when I got into the office and fill me in.

My thoughts returned to Akbar, so I called Stacks, who happened to live fairly close to me, and asked where they had stashed Akbar.

"Stacks, did you get back on the ground okay—everything copacetic with our passenger?"

"No worries, Boss, I've got him stashed in a safehouse in Arlington, the one behind the Catholic school. Ironic for a Muslim, no?" he replied.

"What kind of shape is he in at the moment? I need him coherent but not ambitious," I replied.

"I tucked him in to the special room in the basement, no windows, no clocks, music piped in constantly. I picked a few selections off the metal collection in the den—Drowning Pool, Saliva, Metallica, Iron Dragon, the usual. I also left his morphine drip on an injector module about half open, so he should be pretty pliable, but not in any danger of getting up the gumption to get up and explore the neighborhood. I locked him in, left instructions for him to be fed every six hours approximately, but to vary the times by an hour either way to help randomize the feeding times. I left a couple of local guys we've used before babysitting in case he pulls something fancy, but my guess is they're bored already. I'd planned to get there an hour or so before you arrive and get him prepped. What time you planning on hitting the threshold?"

"If I get lucky and work around the Route 66 traffic, I can be in Arlington in ninety minutes or so. Better leave two hours from now, about midnight should do it," I replied.

In most cities in the United States, nobody would be worried about traffic on a six-lane thoroughfare at eleven thirty at night, except maybe Los Angeles, but Washington, DC, metro and particularly Northern Virginia experience traffic virtually 24/7 in some spots, and the local branch of Route 66 heading both directions was one of them. All it took was a small event in the city, a concert at Nissan Pavilion, a long train at Haymarket or Gainsville, or a truck tipped over on the Beltway, and that road turns into a parking lot. Knowing this odd circumstance, I pulled off Route 95 at Baltimore/Washington Parkway and headed through the city—not a car moving at this hour on a Saturday, I had the road to myself. I cut across the district and over what used to be called the Roosevelt Bridge to Arlington and headed north and east on Route 50. I pulled off 50 and wound my way through Clarendon on Wilson out into the suburbs and pulled into the driveway of the safehouse at just about eleven forty-five.

I walked into the living room of the small ranch house to find two rather large, well-armed, middle-aged gentlemen sitting at the dining room table playing cribbage, the TV on in the living room. A laptop open between them showed camera views of the approaching road, the driveway, the backyard, and the lower detainment cell on one screen. They'd seen me coming a block away and had been briefed by Stacks upon his arrival. They nodded and calmly went back to their game, but I noticed that their cards were held in their left hands, with their right hands tucked in to their jackets, resting lightly on the butts of their respective weapons hidden in shoulder holsters there. Alert, but relaxed, professionals, just another day at the office. Perfect.

I noticed Stacks huge form shadowing the view of the cell on the laptop screen and headed down the stairs. The first landing looked like a normal Arlington basement, linoleum tile, knotty pine paneling, washer and dryer, small non-egress windows set high in the walls, which were 75 percent below grade. Over in the corner, where a small powder room would normally be was a door leading down to the subbasement, a full level below the existing floor that had been dug at great expense and effort so as not to attract attention from the neighbors or the local permit office. The door looked like a standard paneled door, but when I opened it, I could feel the added weight of armor plating sandwiched between the outer skins, and the heavy duty hinges moved smoothly and silently. I headed down the stairs.

Chapter 15

Oranjstadt, Aruba

The big man sat behind his desk in a darkened office on the upper floor of his estate, having just finished a gourmet meal that would have fed half a nearby small village up the coast of the island. He was mentally agitated, but gave no outward sign of it, sitting quietly, cup of rich dark roast coffee at his elbow, the only light emanating from a single bankers lamp on his desk. His minions had brought him the news not only of the failed meeting between Akbar and his associates, but Akbar's abduction. He marveled at the skill of the team who had taken on such a fearsome enemy in Akbar, and the brazen daylight kidnapping of so capable and careful an operative. Akbar had never failed, and yet against these people, he had failed not once but twice. Not having received any ransom demands in exchange for returning Akbar unharmed, he feared for the man's life. He knew that no matter how much duress they created for him, the Arab was as loyal and as stoic as it was possible for a human being to be. He had withstood immense amounts of pain and discomfort in the past and never revealed a jot of useful information—indeed he was rather skilled at extracting it from others.

He had also been made aware of quiet inquiries being made among the diplomatic community regarding his activities and whereabouts of late. While he had made strong efforts to cover his tracks, no amount of subterfuge was going to cover the billions of dollars, euros, drachmas, rubles, wan, or yen he had moved around the globe after receiving it from grateful customers. He'd made strides in reassuring Big G's customers that the flow of armaments, ammunition, and technology would not cease in his absence, but merely be redirected through him. But he wasn't entirely confident that it would be enough to help him maintain his position when the dust settled. He'd already heard of two smaller dealers who had died in a bloody gun battle over the business of supplying a small cadre of loosely woven insurgents in Iraq. The fragmented Somali pirates that Big G had been supplying for years had threatened to pay him a visit on land if they ever discerned his location—such was their anger at the thought of losing or diminishing their supply of small but increasingly larger arms with which to ply their growing trade. The Afghan rebels had agreed to work with him, but they couldn't be trusted as far as the next hill, so he discounted their business almost outright, knowing they would try to cheat him, refuse payment altogether, or kill him outright and keep the funds he expected as payment.

He had arranged several meetings, one-on-one chats with the largest of his competition in an attempt to create a sort of coalition of dealers, of which he would be the head, consolidating power and cornering supply in one move. The lower echelon of dealers, the midlevel, distributors, were extremely loyal to Big G, and he was having trouble influencing them, per his master plan. He'd had to adapt to this unforeseen circumstance, but once the higher-level importers' and manufacturers' reps either warred among themselves or fell into line in his coalition, the distributors and wholesalers would follow suit, he felt sure. As long as there was the possibility that Big G was still alive, however, there would be chaos, and he'd have to move quickly to capitalize on it to cement his own position of power and influence.

Luckily, he had a couple of major sales approaching closure—a shipment of Stinger Type II missiles, which would be distributed throughout the Middle East in support of the Taliban, and a set of guidance systems and radar guided antiaircraft guns to supplement Korean border troops—a particularly difficult order to fill, which he had promised by day after tomorrow, pending payment in gold bullion. At this level, he didn't actually go with the delivery and make the exchange; he had representatives for that, whom he trusted and held enough information on to feel confident they would perform. He always maintained at least three layers of separation from the actual deal, keeping in the background, moving the pieces around the globe like the chess master that he was. Those two deals would not only do wonders to fill his coffers, but solidify his position among the buying community as a reliable, dependable supplier under difficult circumstances. He also had a line on a post-cold war Russian Explorer class submarine that a Russian general in a far-flung province had "liberated" and who was looking to build his retirement fund with some quick cash. The bullion from the Korean border contingent would likely be diverted toward that deal, which he would consummate for pennies on the dollar, and flip to a Mexican drug lord for transporting heroin and laborers across the border up the Baja peninsula, in mere weeks for a tidy profit.

All he needed to do was raise his profile on the backs of such activity, and the smaller dealers would fall in line behind him, secure in the knowledge they could offer their customers virtually anything and he could deliver it. The only fly in the ointment was the continuing existence of Big G and his daughter, Elena. The positive side was that Big G was showing no sign of causing problems, staying virtually comatose in the hold of his own ship for the last seventy-two hours. When the proper time arrived, he would make a public statement with the remains of Big G, but for now he was a good bargaining chip to keep in his back pocket until such time as it was needed. He knew that the operatives who had saved Elena were working for the American government intelligence services, based on the weapons they used, the tactics they employed, and the level of expertise and training exhibited in the most recent actions against him. That would have to be factored into his equations going forward. His most important consideration was why would the American government want to protect an international illegal arms dealer who was often supplying their enemies with weapons and ammunition? Something to ponder as he worked his way through his ruminations and planning for the evening while he awaited word of his latest dealings.

The Mediterranean Sea

Big G now had a plan and was patiently waiting for the right time to put it into action. The muffled bump he'd heard earlier was a small launch bringing food and supplies to the larger boat where he was being held. He'd been able to detect four distinct voices among his captors when they opened the hatch over his head to lower to food tray, and he noticed they rotated who was responsible for feeding him, so he'd only seen a couple of them twice. He could tell they were speaking Arabic but, despite his reasonable knowledge of that language, was unable to make out what they were saying. Between the echo from the ship's metal walls and the strange dialect they were using, it all sounded jumbled and impossible to decipher except when the hatch was open and they were speaking down into the hold. He also could hear four sets of footsteps moving toward the side of the ship where the launch and ladder was located immediately after the "bump" noise occurred. He deduced that all four were involved in unloading supplies from the launch, including food for themselves, his rations, fresh water, and cigarettes, based on the odors he detected coming through the hatch when it opened.

If he could catch them while they were occupied with the supply boat on the other side of this ship, with the hatch even partially open, he might be able to get enough leverage on the rope to climb up and out of the hatch unnoticed for a few moments. A lot of "ifs" he knew, but he was out of options at the moment and knew his days here were numbered. As soon as they got what they wanted from whomever they had sent the ransom note to, he would either be returned or killed, depending on how that arrangement went.

Once out of the hold, he didn't have any illusions about his ability to best four armed men, however unprofessional they might be. His early service in the Greek army as a paratrooper had trained him to realistically assess such odds and try to swing them in his favor, rather than blindly proceeding in face of insurmountable opposition. Heroes were usually dead, and Big G had no desire to join them. The plan was to jump overboard, hope that ship he was on was moored near a major shipping lane, and hope to get picked up before he died of exposure or the sharks got him. Long odds in any case. He knew tactics and particularly weapons well, but his options here were limited, and he didn't really have any weapons.

He'd had plenty of time to think while being held here and had a pretty good idea who was behind his abduction. An old nemesis had arisen from his past to come back and bite him, as they often do. He'd mentally reviewed the list of those who would like to see him dead, or at least disappeared for a while, for either personal or business reasons. Many of the individuals on the resulting list were either dead themselves by now or didn't have the resources necessary to implement such an action against him. As he ticked them off one by one, for various reasons, he was left with only one name—Koenraad DeGroot.

Big G had first met DeGroot at a munitions tradeshow in Dusseldorf, Germany, in the go-go eighties. Big G had been a broker on a few smaller deals but was working his way up the food chain and needed a few solid suppliers to give him some working credit and some access so he could start filling larger orders. His offer was simple: he'd take remaindered or expired merchandise off their hands and sell it only in countries where they had no representation, so as not to compete directly with them. This accomplished a number of things, including moving some older merchandise that was stillusable but not fashionable in first-world nations. The manufacturers got to liquidate some otherwise useless assets that were taking up warehouse space and turn it into capital, and Big G got a ready supply of items he could move on the open market in third world countries at an affordable price and still make a tidy profit for himself.

This was a good plan, and Big G had come to Dusseldorf to present the same offer to a few of the less prominent arms manufacturers, hoping to broaden his inventory, include a few more sought-after items, and make some key contacts. DeGroot was a factory rep for Heckler & Koch, a German manufacturer of small arms that were extremely reliable and popular in many nations worldwide. DeGroot had the Northern Europe territory including Sweden, Norway, the Nederland's, Holland, Greenland, Iceland, and Switzerland, but had been called in to work the booth that weekend from his native Holland.

DeGroot had a greedy streak a mile wide and saw the potential in Big G's proposal right away, but he added his own twist to it. DeGroot figured he would move not only older merchandise, but include some of the off-standard rejects that routinely ended up in the factory bins after failing QC for some minor flaw. Since the weapons were being sold where H&K didn't normally do business, the reputation that would suffer would be G's, not H&K's. These were under the table cash sales to buyers who were unlikely to complain to the manufacturer about anything. They would only know H&K from the secondary market and know of its reputation for quality, and think they were getting a bargain. If a few blew up in the user's face, they could only blame Big G for selling them shoddy stuff because those weapons purchased from anyone else would be perfect. G'd take all the risk, his territory of H&K would book profits, and his bosses would be proud of him and promote him to a more lucrative territory.

This might have worked, too, if DeGroot had sold them to anyone else. Weeks later after weeks of meetings, wining and dining Big G, visiting each other at home for meals, and other social events, when the first order was placed, the two met to make final arrangements on delivery and payment. Big G had been in the business long enough to know that on first orders from any new supplier, no matter how friendly, he had to scrutinize the merchandise carefully. Big G agreed to only a small down payment until the weapons had been test fired. DeGroot acted offended, but eventually agreed, fortunately for Big G.

He'd been burned earlier in his career by a Chinese maker of knock-off Russian AK-47s, who had tried to sell him forty crates of rifles with short firing pins. The few on the top of the boxes worked fine, but the bulk of the shipment was unusable. Fortunately, he'd taken a case back to his small warehouse on Corfu and examined them carefully. His military training had come in handy then, too, and he had test fired every rifle in the box and realized that only three of the twenty actually fired. He had disassembled one of the malfunctioning weapons and figured out the problem pretty quickly. Ten minutes with a set of calipers and he knew he'd been had. He quickly called his shipper and put the crates on hold, called the buyer, and explained that he needed more time due to a dock-worker's strike, common at the time in Greece. His next call had been to a local factory owner he had befriended over a glass of Ouzo one night. His factory assembled automotive subassemblies for a local importer of Saabs and Volvos to make them compliant with local registration and import laws. His workers were fast, accurate, and he had the room and time to perform the tasks needed. Big G asked him to take the cases of guns, disassemble each weapon, take out the firing pins and discard them, and insert a new one he would supply, reassemble the weapons, and put them back in the crates. The factory owner agreed to do the job for a piece fee of $5 per weapon and assembled a few of his better workers on a Saturday to push the job out in one day.

Big G called another friend of his who worked at a low-level assembly job at the Kalashnikov works in Russia who owed him a big favor for helping his brother-in-law find a job in the merchant marine. He asked the Russian to send him a box of AK-47 firing pins as quickly as he could. This was prior to the import ban, and the Kalashnikovs were churning out AKs for about $150 a piece wholesale. Boxes of parts were only loosely cataloged, so putting a box of $.20 pins in his pocket on the way home wasn't much of a trick. The box arrived in two days on a private fishing boat, and Big G delivered it to the factory the next afternoon. By the following evening, his fifty crates of guns all worked, and he got them to the buyer in time to meet their new deadline and keep the customer happy, at an only slightly reduced profit.

Needless to say, although he had salvaged the Chinese debacle, he was extremely cautious when working with new suppliers and scrupulously checked ALL the merchandise on the first and second order before reselling it. Big G had test-fired the crates of H&K HK417s from DeGroot, and out of the first fifty, he only found one that jammed slightly at the end of a long burst. On the next fifty, however, firing results were considerably more dismal, with nine either jamming or the magazines getting stuck due to a slightly misaligned guide in the receiver block. He, too, knew H&K's reputation for quality and immediately understood that these were not their standard retail product. With a failure rate of nearly 50 percent by the time he got to the end of the stack of crates, these couldn't be retail-grade products. He'd been burned again, but had found out before he tried to resell them to a valued customer. And he knew just whom to speak with about it.

He'd called DeGroot at home, demanded a meeting to show him the defects, and said he'd only be satisfied with replacements for the defective units or a full refund of his down payment. DeGroot, not one to part easily with a buck, or a Kruggerand, offered to replace the bad rifles with new ones at the same price. He eventually did exactly that, but the whole affair left Big G with a bad taste in his mouth for DeGroot, and he knew just what to do about it.

Several months later, Big G had quietly let it slip that DeGroot had been doing business with some rather unsavory characters in the Ukraine, selling their defective Soviet factory seconds to rebels in Sierra Leone and Croatia. As he knew it would, word got back to one Oleksandr Zhukov, a rising superstar in the Ukrainian underworld with ties to another suspected arms dealer, Leonid Minin. Minin could do without the competition, and Zhukov didn't like word of his dealings with DeGroot being made public—the simple answer was to remove DeGroot from the picture. Zhukov sent a pair of locals to "retrieve" DeGroot, and they kept him in a small cell in the basement of an abandoned Ukranian government building for four days of rather intense conversation with Zhukov. DeGroot managed to convince Zhukov that he was more valuable alive than dead, but not before several key portions of his anatomy were irreversibly and permanently damaged. He had spent the better part of the next two years in a prison cell, recovering, as the guest of the Croatian government after they discovered the swindle. He could never prove it, and no one had told him directly, but DeGroot knew in his heart that Big G had been the root cause of his misfortune and spent two years letting his anger simmer and then harden into a small, white-hot kernel of hate in his gut, swearing vengeance against the traitorous competitor.

Over the years, the two had crossed paths indirectly, occasionally filling orders for the same buyer. But the relationship was one of wary distance, not camaraderie, and as Big G's high quality control and sense of business ethics elevated him to the top of the arms-dealer heap, DeGroot languished in this portion of his endeavors, frequently losing bid contests to Big G, not on price but on delivery terms or quality guarantee. Big G's arms business grew, and DeGroot was forced to augment his business activities to include factory seconds, stolen or purloined merchandise, stock swindles, land grabs, oil flimflams, and other shady dealings at which he was quite adept. In the intervening twenty years, Big G had created a global enterprise of modest size, generating enough revenue to keep him happy and wealthy for the remainder of his life. DeGroot had amassed vast wealth, most of it illegally obtained, and had generated a list of nefarious colleagues on par with the likes of Mohomar Khadaffi, Idi Amin, and Manuel Noriega.

This abduction was the final act of DeGroot's imagined mental play that had been fomenting in his mind for over two decades. It was payback for that indiscretion twenty years ago, and the subsequent erosion of his reputation, or at least it seemed that way to DeGroot's twisted mind.

Sitting in the sweltering, fetid hold of the giant ship, Big G came to the conclusion that DeGroot was likely behind his abduction and that there had not been a ransom note to anybody. DeGroot wanted his business, but wanted to obtain it in a way that created results a simple killing didn't offer. He wanted Big G alive but on ice, so he could steal his customers, build his empire, extend and expand his power base, and denigrate Big G in the process, all things he couldn't do through legitimate means under normal circumstances, and all while Big G was around to watch his own demise. All this was gruesome enough, but it still seemed an unlikely reason for the abduction, if only for the simple fact that it could have been done other ways, simpler and less expensive, that would have accomplished the goal more quickly. But was there more to be gained, some subplot Big G couldn't conceive of? All he really knew was that he had to get out of here to find out, so he concentrated on that and that alone—for the moment.

Chapter 16

Arlington, Virginia

The interview with Akbar started slowly with the usual interrogator's dance, the "getting to know" you part. Stacks had picked up his entire file at Langley and brought it along, and as soon as I had entered the anteroom outside the actual cell, he handed me the file, saying, "Hope you're up for a long night—looks like this guy's seen the likes of you before."

I breezed through the file the first time, scanning for useful and relevant information that I could use to not only trip him up, but also make it appear that I knew more than I did about his current operation. Some of the information was familiar from my reading in Greece before we left, and some was new, but not terribly useful in the current circumstances. I did take note of the family information, a sister in Bagdad, and a living mother in a small mountain town in Kazakhstan. Akbar worked for the Taliban, but was a Saudi national and was Persian by birth. I noted the foreign education in things medical, noted his use of arcane interrogation and pain infliction techniques, and decided that I was indeed in for a long night. The standard fare not only wouldn't work on this particular subject, but was also too benign compared to the pain and agony he'd forced others to endure, usually at his own hand. No, this would require something special, but I had to get started and produce results quickly—Big G's life was likely hanging in the balance, and the clock was ticking.

I unlocked the door and entered the cell confidently to find Akbar secured to a metal chair with military-grade handcuffs, the chair bolted to the concrete floor with some pretty substantial fasteners. He had a black cloth hood over his head to limit light and increase the disorientation. I stepped up to him, removed the hood, and stared directly into the face of the only thing standing between me and the release of Big G. Under other circumstances, I'd have called it a handsome, rugged Persian face. Now it just looked rough and angry. His broad brow, heavy beard, and large hooked nose combined to make a hawkish, fearsome countenance that would have struck fear in the hearts of the Arabian Knights a few centuries ago. There was a crescent of scar tissue behind his left eye starting on his forehead and proceeding around the eye to his cheek. His eyes had a light to them I wouldn't have expected, based on what I knew was the narcotic dose he was being subjected to, and I wondered if he had taken something to counteract the drugs. The drip seemed correctly installed and working fine, and his muscle tone was as relaxed as I could imagine it being, given his conditioning. Something about the eye, though, made me pause. I stepped back, out of contact range of his long legs and strong teeth, and looked him over, not saying a thing, just observing.

He knew the game well and just stared back at me, eyes blazing, half in anger and embarrassment at being captured, half in hatred and scorn for his captors.

We sat quietly for a couple of minutes, and I addressed him in Farsi, saying, "I can make this easy on you, but I know you wouldn't appreciate it. I can make it quick if you cooperate, out of professional courtesy, and you might even make it out alive if you're helpful, but the next few hours will be extremely unpleasant if you don't help me with my little problem."

He just looked at me, and his face changed slightly, showing only a little surprise and some minor dawning of the reality of his predicament. He now knew that he was dealing with professionals, who spoke his language, who were seasoned and understood the Arab mindset and sensibilities, that to die here was more honorable than to be released an injured traitor. The light in his eyes dimmed a bit, but wasn't totally extinguished.

"I have nothing to say, nor would it help you if I did," he replied. "I don't know who you are or what your problem you're talking about, but to kidnap me and then demand answers to questions I can't answer seems foolish," he continued.

"I quite agree, but here we are," I answered. "I promise to ask only questions you can answer from now on, but if I suspect you can answer them but won't, your situation will deteriorate rapidly," I continued, a slight edge added to my voice.

He looked only slightly surprised at this, but said nothing.

"Who hired you to abduct Big G Papadopoulos?" I asked straight out.

"Who?"

"Bad start, Akbar. If you continue in this vein, there will be significant pain in your future," I replied.

"I don't know what you're talking about," he maintained.

"You were at the Acropolis to meet two gentlemen, and I use the term loosely," I continued.

Their job was to remove Elena Papadopoulos from this mortal coil. I stopped them. Now I'm going to stop you from killing her father, one way or the other," I said.

"Women, useless creatures, most not worth the air they breathe," he scoffed.

"Personal feelings aside, you don't deny you were there to meet her killers to pay them and receive their report?" I asked.

"I was simply touring the monuments, meeting with friends," he replied.

"You really expect me to believe you're a tourist, Akbar, armed with sophisticated and concealed weaponry, guarded by three of your chums with more weapons, half an hour before the place was going to close for the day?" I quipped incredulously.

"I don't care what you believe. I was merely viewing the antiquities," he smiled slightly in reply.

"You have no idea how badly this is going to go for you if you keep up this pretense, Akbar," I chided.

"So be it," he replied.

Maybe a little taste of things to come will soften him up, I thought. I stepped out of the cell without saying a word, closed the door behind me, and faced Stacks, who had been waiting in the anteroom.

"What have we got lying around that looks scary but won't do any permanent damage," I asked him, grinning slightly.

"My first thought would be an acetylene torch—there's a gas bottle laying upstairs in the corner where a plumber was sweating a new pipe on the kitchen sink last week," he replied with a grin of his own.

"Okay, that's a good bit of intelligence, but I think we need something a little more theatrical, and effective. This guy's practically impervious to pain, according to his file," I said. "How about a big syringe, a real horse needle? A little air in the wrist joint will usually loosen folks up pretty good, very painful, no permanent marks, no real damage," I said. "He'll know that too, has some knowledge of anatomy. He sees that ten gauge needle coming at his cuffed wrist, he'll know what we're up to—even better," I continued.

"I'll see what I can find in the medical kit upstairs—might be one in there for adrenaline shots for overdose cases," he replied.

While he was upstairs looking, I reread the file again, to see if there was something I could use to jar him a bit, get him off balance.

I didn't find much; the file was not as complete as I'd have liked, at least in the personal history section—the later stuff was largely public knowledge, as his group took credit for their actions to further the terror angle of the result. Car bombings, IEDs, kidnappings, assassinations, all littering the Mid East like a stain, with no real discernable pattern that I could see aside from random violence and death. Except for one year, there was a full range of activity for nearly two decades. I wondered what had happened in that one missing year. Maybe that was the place to start—2003 didn't seem like a great year for much of anything on a global scale. The US economy going great guns, Iraq war not yet started, Desert Storm and Shield apparently a weak and fading memory, and a lot of quiet from Akbar. What was he doing for a year? Where had he been? I wondered. Planning? Training? Building an organization? Maybe that was a good place to start my questions, but like most good interrogators, I needed to know the answers before I asked him the questions.

I stuck my head out the door and called to Stacks, "Is there a computer here with Internet access?"

"Upstairs, wireless laptop, with a secured cell card," he replied back quietly.

I headed up the stairs, hoping the answers would come quickly so I could begin my conversation with Akbar. He could cool his heels for a while down there, build some anticipation, and break him down a bit, but I was on a deadline and needed answers quickly if I was going to save Big G's skin.

After some research on the Internet that turned up virtually nothing on the whereabouts of a certain Akbar in 2003, I called into my research contact at Langley, Alan

Sherman. Alan was what you'd expect for a government researcher—slight, balding, paunchy, about fifty, curly hair sprinkled with grey, small half glasses perched on a rather prominent nose, but despite physical appearances, there was none better at finding out obscure factoids and tracking people's activities than Alan. He had some sort of sixth sense and knew how to make it work for him, knew the right places to look, how to piece little bits of information together into a plausible scenario, and then where to dig deeper to back it up. I don't know why I hadn't called him earlier, but I'd been distracted by Elena and her father's safety and hadn't been looking at this like a standard terrorist-tracking assignment.

I got Alan on the line and explained what I needed and briefly why and how soon. He listened patiently, saying little, until I'd reached the end of the story. He asked a couple of questions, asked for a fax number or e-mail account where he could send the information, and promised me a quick surface rundown on Akbar in a few hours.

With my own research yielding little and a few hours to kill before Alan got back to me, I figured I'd better get started with the dance moves that Akbar would expect, the "get to know you" phase that most interrogations take in the beginning. Maybe I could crowbar loose a few facts from Akbar while Alan was busy. I headed past Stacks standing in the kitchen, picked up the big syringe he'd had found off the countertop, and headed back downstairs to the cell with what I hoped would be a determined look on my face.

Chapter 17

Oranjstadt, Aruba

Aruba has a median temperature of seventy-nine degrees, but today was about three standard deviations away, upwards of ninety-four, and humid, even more so than usual, with minimal wind to circulate any air at all. As DeGroot walked out of his building and across the street to the vendor's stalls to find some lunch and check in with his local contacts, he started sweating through his French blue dress shirt under the cream silk suit jacket. His local bodyguards followed at a discreet distance, but weren't expecting anything untoward to happen to their boss today, didn't sense any unusual threat lurking in the dusty, crowded back streets near the dockside. A cruise ship had recently pulled into the harbor further up the main drag, and the stall vendors were busy bargaining and kibitzing with the tourists, eating lunch in the back of their stalls, and pushing merchandise out the front.

DeGroot had long ago recruited a few select vendors in the row to keep their eyes and ears peeled for any unusual activity, anyone who looked out of place or asked unusual questions about him or his operations. He had many such sources, and he kept them honest and productive by variously paying them well and occasionally arranging for a rough encounter with Akbar if they chose to be less than forthright. This carrot and stick method made him one of the most known, feared, and respected men on the island. As he strolled across the main street and along the row of stalls, the noise level dropped slightly in advance of his progress, falling silent as he entered each stall in turn, and ascending again once he was a few stalls past them, like a boat creating a wake in the sea.

He was doing his weekly rounds of informants, checking for unusual activity, gauging the impact the removal of Big G was having on the local criminal trade. Much to his chagrin, the impact had been minimal, locally at least. A few of the more connected and "active" vendors, with more feelers in the local underground enterprises, had noticed it was harder to find or procure certain items or that they took longer than usual to arrive, but other than that, not much in the way of news. He reasoned that this was likely because, at least here and in the western Caribbean, the market was largely his, not Big G's, so the disturbance had been minimal; as for him, it was business as usual.

One particularly older gentleman in a stall selling hand-carved instruments at the end of the row did have a small tidbit that made him pause. His name was Jefferson, no first name, and Jefferson had been around the islands for over half a century, in a variety of jobs, before coming to his current position of stall owner. He had been a smuggler, a rum runner, a pirate of sorts, hijacking personal watercraft from wealthy yacht owners, an antiquities dealer, fake of course, and had picked up spot work as a cook, a steward, and other odd jobs on cruise ships and in hotels when he felt the need for a more steady and reliable income. He also knew how to keep his ears open, how to eavesdrop on conversations without being noticed, and how to value the information he learned based on the recipient. He had proved quite valuable to DeGroot in the past, and DeGroot respected his talents and valued his information highly as both reliable and accurate.

Today, Jefferson had a small tidbit, little more than an island rumor, a rumbling in the underground community. It was rumored that one of DeGroot's inner circle, a top man in his organization, had gone missing and had been snatched or killed—it was unclear which—in Greece.

DeGroot showed no outward emotion upon hearing this news and acted as if he discounted it altogether, chiding Jefferson good naturedly for believing island gossip like an old woman. Inwardly, however, alarm bells were going off in DeGroot's head. He hadn't heard from Akbar in forty-eight hours, not unusual in and of itself, but coupled with the lack of other news, like that of the death of his subordinates, or their remains being found in a obvious place as a message to others, he started wonder if there wasn't a grain of truth to the rumor.

DeGroot continued his journey to the end of the row, bought an orange soda at the refreshment stand, and turned and headed back to his blessedly air-conditioned office to ponder this new piece of intelligence, possibly make a few calls to investigate further, and plan his next move.

Lentas, Crete

Aboard the *Lady Elena*, the boat's namesake was a little frazzled. Not only was she dealing with her own business at the boutique long-distance on a daily basis, but was trying to keep up a good front on her father's business as well. The managers at his various offices had been trained well and put up a good façade—"Mr. Papadapoulos is traveling. We expect him back in touch any day now…" But her father's closer colleagues and customers had his direct and cell numbers, and refused to be brushed off so easily.

Elena was versed enough in her father's legitimate dealings, after a quick perusal of the contents of the filing cabinets in his office, to answer routine questions about order status, pricing, and the like. But there were often more detailed and more urgent and disturbing calls that she was not equipped to deal with directly, and those were the toughest to handle. The callers, often with heavy accents or in languages in which she wasn't fluent, asking questions about certain individuals or purchases about which there were no files, no notes, no references, even the callers' names were not known or noted anywhere, and she didn't recognize them as being in her father's inner circle as she knew it. Clearly, there was a side to his business that he'd kept from her, and she wasn't sure whether to be angry at him for keeping secrets or grateful to him for protecting her. Her ambivalence shifted toward the grateful side after one particularly disturbing call from an arrogant, gravel-voiced man with a heavy Czech accent who got increasingly agitated at her attempts to placate him regarding his shipment of missile guidance systems. She had no record of such a shipment, didn't know when her father would return, or anything about his delivery date or anything else. He threatened to come find her and "assist" her with the order, and she hastily hung up on him, shaking in frustration and fear at her father's desk.

After that, she decided that she needed to do a little deeper investigation into her father's business and his records, starting with those she could find aboard ship. She began with the drawers in the office and worked her way through to those in the storage hold, his bedroom, and on both his computers. She came away with little new information on her father's current business for the effort, but she did find out a few ancillary facts that could come in handy. She knew she was missing something vital, some clue as to the whereabouts of the key information she needed help find and rescue her father. Elena knew that Stark had searched the ship after the local police had finished and that his reputation was that of a very competent, thorough operative, according to sources she had located in her father's files. Maybe he knew more than he was letting on or had information whose importance he'd underestimated. She knew she'd have to find him and meet with him, maybe exchange information, and help each other in some way. She found herself looking forward to that meeting, for a variety of reasons.

Chapter 18

Arlington, Virginia

I walked into the lower level cell with the needle in my hand prominently displayed, set it carefully on a small table by the wall, well out of reach should Akbar, by some miracle, find a way to untether himself from the chair bolted to the floor. Akbar looked up, noted the needle, shook his head slowly, and closed his eyes and bowed his head again.

Without raising his head, he intoned slowly, "When are you Americans going to learn that drugs only weaken the already weak and give release to the strong among us?"

"I guess they might, if I knew what you were talking about," I replied. "Are you the strong and think drugs won't affect you?" I asked. "What makes your physiology any different than the next guy with respect to sodium amytal?"

"It's not the chemistry. It's the attitude that makes the difference," he said.

"So you're saying that if you have a sunny disposition, drugs don't affect you?" I scoffed.

"Drugs work in conjunction with the mind and the body to loosen the inhibitions and play on the fears of the patient. If you have no fear and are not inhibited to begin with, the drug's effects are greatly mitigated, and training can compensate for that by allowing those who are pure to overcome the residual effects," he replied ruefully.

"I don't think training or purity are going to help you in this case. There's nothing in that syringe," I offered.

"Pretty unusual tool to use when questioning a tourist," he retorted.

"I'm not buying the whole tourist thing, and we both know it. I know you have a solid background in inflicting pain and are supposedly impervious to it when it's inflicted on you. I tend to believe the former, but the latter, not so much.

"I need information about what you were up to, who hired you, and why, and I need it quickly. I don't have a lot of time for niceties," I said. "We're going to get right to this. Tell me what you were doing in Athens, start with the meeting at the Parthenon."

"I told you, I was simply touring the sites with a few friends," he said.

"With Mac 10s?" I replied in disbelief.

"Simple precaution, I have a few enemies, some of whom would like just such an opportunity to silence me for good."

"Who sent you to the Parthenon?"

"Nobody 'sent' me. I arranged a meeting there with some friends as a central location in Athens, so we could find each other easily," he said

"Okay, so who were the friends you were meeting? Let's start there," I agreed.

"Just some old acquaintances, from Saudi Arabia," he replied.

"Names, I need a few names, Akbar," I replied, adding a little edge to my voice.

"Their names are irrelevant," he shot back.

"I'll decide what's relevant," I replied more heatedly.

"What will happen to them if I tell you their names?" he asked.

"Not your concern, they are in custody as well, and we'll decide their value later," I replied curtly.

I was growing tired of this little dance already and could feel the clock ticking away Big G's time. I needed to get to the meat of things and get there quickly. Time to pull out the big guns. I reached over to the small table and retrieved the syringe. I stood over him, pulling the plunger out and pushing it back in slowly, almost lovingly, making sure he got a good look at the size of that glistening chrome 4" needle. His chest tightened slightly, a defensive maneuver that was useless based on his position and the bindings holding him tightly against the chair back. He must have thought I was just going to kill him by shooting an air embolus into his heart. I'd cracked the armor, and he'd shown some fear for his own life, no matter how slight or minor. Time to go to work.

"I'm under a bit of time pressure, Akbar, or I'd sit and chat further with you about your vacation plans. I need to know who you work for and what you were doing in Athens and why. There's no way out of here, no choice for you but to give me what I want. I'm good at this, and I won't give you the satisfaction of killing you before I get what I want. I'll ask you nicely one last time—who's your boss?"

"I don't know what you're talking about. I'm retired from the military," he replied.

"Nice try," I seethed and stepped over to him, pulled back the plunger of the syringe, and carefully inserted the tip of the needle into his left wrist just at the base of his thumb. I knew the needle itself hurt like hell, but he barely flinched. His breathing accelerated, however, and I knew he was having trouble keeping up the façade. I gave the needle a little shove by the barrel, and I felt his arm tighten in response, but not a sound came from his lips.

"Any idea who's paying you these days, Akbar?" I prompted.

Not a word.

I leaned over and whispered in his ear, "You can make this stop, or I can make it worse, your choice."

Still no response.

Slowly, carefully, I reached down and grabbed the barrel of the syringe in my fist, hooked the ball of my thumb on the top of the plunger, and gave it a gentle push, driving air into the joint in his wrist. Separating the small but heavily enervated bones, stretching the connective tissue, and tearing the tendons slightly with the pressure caused him excruciating pain. His hand started to spasm, fist closing and opening unbidden, quickly and violently. The tape on his wrists held his arm immobile, but his hand was hopping like a toad on a griddle. His face contorted into a fearsome grimace, eyes narrowing to small slits, spit flying from his lips as his breathing accelerated. Suddenly, he let out a blood-curdling scream as his reserve finally broke, and tears started to roll down his cheeks as he fought the pain.

I pushed the plunger a bit more, and he suddenly went slack, his face pale as he passed out from the intense pain. I left the syringe in place, but relieved a little pressure on the plunger, and hustled out to the anteroom and grabbed the half-empty bottle of water Stacks had left there. I doused Akbar in the face with the cool water and brought him around. He returned full to consciousness and gave me a glare that would cut concrete.

"If the next words out of your mouth are not the name of your employer, I will keep pushing that plunger like I'm blowing up a bicycle tire," I snarled slowly.

He nodded, tears still staining his face mixed with the water.

"His name is DeGroot," he hissed. "That's all I know."

"I strongly doubt that, and I'll show you how little I believe you," I replied. I reached over and thumped the back of the plunger on the syringe, sending a bolt of pain up his arm, causing it to spasm again.

"Okay, he's Dutch, has a place on Aruba, downtown."

"That's better—now we're doing business," I replied. "What did he have you do for him?"

"Mostly finding and removing his enemies," he replied in a broken voice.

"Was one of those enemies Big G Papadapoulos?" I asked.

"Yes!" he screamed, and he launched his body forward against the restraints, bending his head forward to stretch his neck down toward his chest and grabbed a shirt button with his teeth, tearing the button off with his incisors and swallowing it before I had a chance to intervene.

I yelled up the stairs for Stacks, and when I turned back to face him, I saw his eyes go slack, his breathing slow, and his head lolled forward gently to rest his chin on his chest.

Stacks burst into the cell, saw Akbar unconscious, cocked his head, and asked, "Nap time?"

"Sort of, he had a shirt button coated with something or made from something, some fast-acting poison. He kicked before I could get Big G's location out of him, damn it."

"Did you find out anything useful before he checked out?" he asked.

"I know the name of the guy behind all this. I know he snatched Big G, but I don't know why or where," I answered.

"Net gain," he replied. "Let's get him out of here and see if we can find his boss. Where do you suppose we might start looking?"

"Pack your trunks and fins. We're heading to Aruba," I answered.

Chapter 19

Mediterranean Sea

Big G had analyzed his situation, made a plan, and true to form, was executing after patiently waiting until the perfect time. He was currently halfway up the rope dangling from the lip of the hatch above him, with about forty feet left to go. After three days of being bound, eating minimally, and moving even less, he was incredibly stiff and sore, the pain shooting through his shoulders as he heaved his way as quietly as possible up the 2" thick hemp, slippery with marine grease and decaying sea creatures. He was making headway, but knew he had to be quick and quiet. He needed to get to the top undetected by the crew, who had been in the midst of lowering his latest meal when the supply ship had bumped into the hull, signaling the arrival of fresh food, cigarettes, magazines, and the like.

He knew from past deliveries that the crew would be occupied for about fifteen minutes, between tying up the launch, lowering the rope basket, pulling it back up, chatting with the launch captain, casting off the launch, and getting back to business after stowing the new supplies. He'd taken less than two of those to finish unbinding his hands, having rubbed his bindings against a sharp spot in a weld along a seam in the bulkhead. He took another two to work some feeling back into the hands and feet, and a few more working his way up the rope, after making sure it was secured to something substantial at the other end.

He made it to the top and poked his head over the lip of the hatch opening, slowly and cautiously.

Aboard the *Lady Elena*—Crete

Elena had been methodically and thoroughly searching through her father's papers, looking for some clue as to what his latest phone calls might have meant, and who and what might want him out of the way. She had a certain level of faith in Stark's ability to rescue her father, but knew also she couldn't just sit by and do nothing to help the cause. She needed to keep busy just to keep her mind off his situation, and helping in the search served both purposes.

She had just run across a file with a series of phone service invoices for wireless phones, ostensibly for his employees or crew, when she noticed something—the receipt was for over thirty different phones, each with a different number registered in a different location, with different area and country codes. Strange, she thought, if he was buying them for the crew, they would all be for the same service location, and if they were for office employees, they would be for at least locations where he had offices. These didn't seem to match any type of pattern, but all were placed and activated on the same day. That seemed strange to her as well; if they were for employees, they would have been spread out over several days, as people's schedule allowed them to get to a store or to a phone and take the twenty minutes to activate the number, set up the account, etc. Big G's employees were extremely loyal and motivated, and did his business on his time, and only his business—they didn't squander a lot of personal time while at work out of respect for him and his extreme work ethic.

She set the bill aside for her to ponder later; maybe she would find additional paperwork that would explain the phones. She continued to go through file after file, and a picture of an organized, focused, and powerful enterprise began to emerge. This was the strictly legitimate side of his business, the side with a strong paper trail, lots of banking records, invoices, bills of lading, shipping schedules, client account information, and more. It told the story of his slow, steady, almost relentless growth over a decade and a half.

She got to the last drawer in his file cupboard, a converted closet full of lateral file cabinets, the bottom drawer labeled "copies"—ostensibly back-up copies of items in a land-based file depository, in case of fire or for convenience when at sea. Several years ago Big G had joined the modern age and digitized all his records, backing up religiously and buying terabytes of online back-up storage space in a secure server farm to hold all the data generated by his far-flung enterprise, obviating the need for such a hard copy system. That should make these records both old and obsolete.

Being her father's daughter, however, thorough and meticulous, she explored the files anyway, and found some interesting notations.

Some of the files were as advertised, old records and back-up copies. However, she did find a few files that fit a different description. She found page after page of coded records, mostly numbers and short alpha notations, like ledger pages, including dates, weights, and other number combinations that were less obvious as to their meaning. A sailor courtesy of her seafaring father since childhood, she recognized geo coordinates, longitude and latitude, indicating locations on the globe. She set these files aside as well, with the phone bills, finished the cabinet and drawers of his desk, and moved on to the stateroom, finding nothing of additional interest.

Suddenly exhausted, she trudged up to the salon and poured herself a stiff gin and tonic, sitting back on the overstuffed sofa to ponder her discoveries. Half an hour later, the whine of a small motor approaching broke her out of her reverie. She could see the wake of a small craft approaching the yacht, and hear the rising note of the engine as it got closer. After a few moments and the craft got closer, she recognized one of the ship's own skiffs, the sky blue mid-stripe clearly visible, a white-clothed steward at the helm. The small boat coasted to a stop and gently bumped the hull of the larger craft, and the steward tossed a line over the rail. She jogged toward the bow to tie off the line to a cleat and drop the boarding ladder.

Once the steward was aboard, she noted his downtrodden yet determined demeanor and asked him what the trouble was, and why he was on the ship on his time off.

"I'm afraid I have some news, ma'am," he replied sheepishly. "I was approached by a stranger in the town pub, where I was having a drink with some of the other crewmembers. He said he had a message from Mr. G and that I should relay it to you immediately."

"Please, Giorgi, tell me quickly, is he all right?" she asked breathlessly.

"He apparently is still alive, but possibly not for long," he breathed.

"Please tell me quickly, what do you mean?"

"The stranger said that Mr. G would remain 'out of circulation' until such time as all his customers and deals had been transferred to the man's employer, who's identity would be revealed shortly and only to you. He said that if you told anyone in authority, called anyone, or refused to make the endorsements and transfers, Mr. G would be executed in a very public way," he cringed.

Her face went from one of anticipation, to uncertainty, to hardened, focused obstinance. She would not let a terrorist, blackmailer, and thief simply take away her father's legacy, his empire, his dream. Not one to take such things lying down, Elena was already mentally spinning through her options, testing and discarding plans of action as they reached their fatal flaw. She took stock of her resources, both human and financial, found considerable ammunition there, and kept exploring ways to put what she had to best possible use.

"Is there anything else?" she asked.

"Yes, ma'am, he said that if I didn't deliver this message and take back your answer, he would execute my little girl in twenty-four hours. He showed me one of her shoes—he knew her name and dress size..." his voice trembled.

"Please, Giorgi, I would never let that happen. I promise with every resource I have and every fiber of my being, your daughter will not be harmed," she assured him.

She dismissed the steward, telling him to deliver the following to the stranger in the pub: "I'll comply with his wishes, but will need to meet with him personally to execute some of the documents so that they would be accepted by some of the legitimate customers. Tell him to simply contact me at this number, and we can set a date and time for the transfers," she intoned smoothly. She made him recite the private cell number she gave him and saw him safely back on to the skiff and away toward the town. She knew that her agreement and subsequent conversation would buy her some time to craft a workable plan. She knew she needed help and thought she had a good idea where to turn.

She headed down the salon steps, entered her father's office, opened the safe, and reaching in and feeling along the back wall of the safe, found the tiny catch in the lower corner that released the false back panel. Behind the panel, she knew there was a sterile cell phone, a compact, flat black 9MM KelTec luger, spare magazines, and the name and phone number of a trusted friend of her father's who had been in the Yugoslavian special forces, a good customer and trusted friend of her father's whom he'd recommended that she contact in case of trouble. She put the small pistol in her pocket, folded the paper in half, and grabbed the sterile phone, heading up to the salon for a sure cell signal. She had two calls to make, one to the Slav and one to America.

Chapter 20

Eighteen Thousand Feet over the Atlantic Ocean

Stacks and I managed to hitch a ride on a small military transport plane, the military equivalent of a Gulfstream G3, used for ferrying three-stars and above to various meetings, based out of Andrews Air Force Base. While not as luxurious as the civilian version, it was nonetheless comfortable, fast, and reliable. I had called the whole team, set up a conference call, and brought them up to speed on the latest developments, leaving out a few of the more gory details. I spent a few minutes outlining a plan of action to locate Big G based on reaching the kidnapper and persuading him to divulge the holding location.

Stacks and I would handle onsite surveillance, ops planning, and initial incursion. BJ and Sam would act as back-up, arriving in Aruba on another transport through the civilian airport, posing as an American couple on their honeymoon. Sam managed to pull together a significant care package of comm equipment and some other odds and ends they might need, packed it up, and put it in the belly of an army transport plane that happened to be heading into the Caribbean for other reasons, but the pilot promised the attractive redhead that he would stop and drop it off at the Aruba airport while the plane got refueled. Tang would coordinate from Langley, providing intel support, analysis, comm monitoring, and tactical guidance based on satellite imagery, military comm intercepts, and other little sources he had access to on a clandestine basis.

We didn't have the local support for this one as we had in the Greek isles, so we had to plan tight, shop smart, execute well, and think on the fly. A simple smash and grab on a guy this well-protected wouldn't be easy. I'd taken the liberty of having Tang and Alan Sherman dig up everything they could find on DeGroot—a file about 2" thick, as it turned out that Alan had pulled together on short notice, and while we headed into Aruba, I reread it for the third time, trying to ferret out any little morsels of intel I could use not only to gain entry but to pry Big G's location out of him when we had him.

DeGroot's file read like a lesson in how to be a bad guy, but there was little that could be verified by more than one source, lots of rumors, indirect references, assumptions, and deductions. Not much hard fact to work with, except the early background section. DeGroot had been born to sketchy parents in a working-class neighborhood in Arnhem, a larger village in Gelderland. His father had been a carpenter by trade, a gambler by nature, and the family was not only chronically broke but moved frequently to stay one step ahead of the debt collectors and local moneylenders. His mother coped with this errant behavior as best she could, using a mixture of men and alcohol to dull her understanding and soothe her need for attention and affection. Between the semiconscious mother and absent father, young Koenraad found himself with a lot of unsupervised alone time on his hands. This and his hyperintelligence was a recipe for trouble, with no guidance and direction to channel his natural curiosity and drive. Naturally, he fell in with what is termed the world over as "the wrong crowd," a group of young thieves, pickpockets, vandals, and killers in the making, who chose to spend their time terrorizing the local merchants, breaking into some of the more upscale homes for the portable goods there, and keeping the local police busy chasing one or another of them for stolen cars, loud parties, and the like. He soon rose to some prominence in this endeavor, eventually leading the gang after locking the current leader in an old refrigerator at the trash dump with a water hose drilled through the top, slowly drowning the trapped gangleader in a matter of hours. His father eventually disappeared altogether, not quite a step ahead of the local organized crime shylock for bad gambling debts. His mother, destitute, alone, alcoholic, and directionless, eventually took her own life, leaving young Koenraad to find the result, now an orphan. Free to roam the world at sixteen, he stowed away on the next steamer leaving the coast, bound for wherever it landed. He eventually ended up in Marseille, crime capital of Europe, where everything was there for the taking. The variety of goods and other items illicitly coming thorough this small port town was astounding, and young Koenraad was immediately in his element, connecting with a motley collection of local smugglers and black marketeers. He started with small boatloads of cigarettes, moving untaxed cartons from the United States into European cities, and moved up to drugs, indentured sex slaves, and eventually found his niche in guns, running handguns stolen from around the area through the Marseille port out to locations in South America and Africa.

Eventually his reputation for technical knowledge and sharp dealing found its way to a legitimate arms manufacturer, H&K, who contacted him through a local retail outlet and made him a low-level salesman. DeGroot knew an opportunity when he saw it, and the H&K connection gained him the legitimacy he needed to put a veneer on his less-than-savory dealings and gave him an excuse to travel freely on an international basis on someone else's dime—he took the job immediately.

I thought I had spotted a tidbit or two in there that might be used to reach the criminal mastermind, where some pressure might be applied psychologically to get him to open up. Now, to tighten up the snatch plan. Surely DeGroot would have security to rival most world leaders, and a report on exactly that was in the back of the file, outlining the number of guards witnessed by an Aruban local contact, their behavior, the rough layout of the building and surrounding city, with a set of possible approaches Tang had thrown in to spark some new ideas by his boss. This was a do or die for Big G—if we didn't find him quickly and his captors got wise to our impending intrusion, he'd be dead in twenty-four hours. With the access points established, my team prepped and enroute, all I needed was a clever way to shift the guards' attention, locate DeGroot in this building, get to him undetected, disable him, find a way to extricate his huge, uncooperative carcass out of the building undetected, and get him to a remote location for some friendly questioning.

I got on the phone and called Tang at Langley and asked him to put together a special care package and get it on the next plane flying toward the Caribbean, gave him the items I wanted, and called Dick in his office on the fourth floor at the Agency to fill him in on what was happening and why. He was glad to hear from me, but didn't want details at this stage, just results. He knew the clock was ticking on Big G and didn't want to waste time with reports and red tape, just to accomplish the goal. I liked Dick at that moment for that reason—when things got sticky, he stepped back and let me do what I do best. He knew that was the best way to get the outcome he wanted and had become adept at cleaning up my "messes" afterward as a result. Me, operating in a non-NATO nation, with no official sanction, on a clandestine mission to correct a situation that shouldn't have occurred in the first place was a recipe for a mess. I'm sure he knew it going in, but his options were limited, and he knew I'd get the job done.

I finished with Dick, hung up, and sat back in my seat to think, turning over the plan in my mind trying to find holes, flaws, missteps and misjudgments, bad lines of sight or bad firing angles, escape routes, transportation needs, and timing, trying to make sure that we all got the job done quickly, quietly, and got out of there alive. After an hour, I felt pretty good about the plan—you can never be completely confident since something always goes awry, and the more complete and perfect it is, the more likely that you'll get locked in and can't correct. Better to leave things a bit loose and provide us some flexibility. I had a framework that provided some options, depending on what we found when we arrived, and proceeded to relate the outline to the team on a conference call just before touchdown in Aruba.

Somewhere in the Mediterranean Sea

Big G worked his way up to the top of the rope and cautiously popped his head over the rim of the hatch, just far enough to see where his guards were and whether they were sufficiently occupied to let him scoot to the gunwale and hop over the side undetected. His caution was well founded, because if they caught him, his time in the hold would be both limited and unpleasant. As it turned out, all the guards were busy ferrying supplies from the opposite rail to the internal companionway about twenty yards away. Each guard would take an armload and disappear down the stairs for between two to six minutes, before returning for another load. With four guards in cycle, he had an interval of maybe forty-five seconds when the deck was empty or the last guard's back was turned bringing up another load.

He watched for about ten minutes to make this determination and then waited for his opportunity. Still stiff and in pain from his incarceration, he didn't have much confidence in his speed or agility at this point, but he had few options, and this was his best opportunity to make something happen. He realized he was ill equipped for a long stint in the ocean as well, having only the clothes on his back and not even all of those. No food, no light, no shelter, no flotation device of any kind, he was at the mercy of the currents and his ability to stay afloat until fortune somehow smiled upon him, or he drowned from exhaustion. Even that was better than being at the mercy of his captors; at least he would die on his own terms, having taken every action available to him.

When the moment came, he tensed his muscles, pulled himself up and over the rim of the hatch, rolled quietly onto the deck, got himself upright, and sprinted as best he could to the starboard rail and leaped off into the sea. Just as his heel dropped below the railing on his way down, one of the guards turned around with his last load of supplies and caught the movement out of the corner of his eye. The guard dropped his supplies and ran to the starboard side and peered down into the water, but by the time he got there, Big G was deep in the water and swimming as quickly as possible back toward the ship, trying to cover his resurfacing with the minimal bobbing wake generated by the waves against the bow and hide in the small area below the curve of the hull until he could get his bearings and develop a plan. The boat was sitting at rest, but the current was still moving at about three knots, enough to tug at him, pulling him along the hull back toward the fantail. The buildup of barnacles and sea life on the hull was thick and razor sharp, tearing the skin off of him every time the current pushed him toward the hull. Slowly he worked his way back without too much damage or losing too much blood in the water. He got to the stern, where the single large screw was at idle, and cautiously poked his head out around the corner to get a bearing.

What he saw made his heart sink. They were far enough from land that there was nothing to see but open water. No landmarks, no land, no towers, lights, trees, nothing but blue water and sunshine. If he moved away from the boat, he would standout against the featureless background like a grain of rice on a jewelers black velvet pad, a sitting duck for the guards to shoot him, wound him, send the launch out, and pick him up. Patience had been his ally when he was biding his time in the hold of the ship, but now the clock was against him—he couldn't stay in the water in the lee of the hull forever.

He heard shouting from the deck above him, as by now several guards had gathered at the rail and were scanning the sea for him, having realized what had happened after a quick look to find the hold empty. They couldn't see him from where they were, but he had to show himself eventually. He would either be seen floating away from the ship, at which point he'd be a visible target, or he'd never be seen again, having drowned. Either way they seemed to be in no hurry, and he noticed they left two guards on watch, who settled in with fresh cigarettes to wait after finishing the supply unloading.

Time dragged as Big G grew more and more tired fighting the current, holding his body out from the hull to avoid injury. After nearly an hour, his energy was dangerously low. He only had so much left before he let go and floated away, powerless to do anything else but wait for the inevitable.

But fortune was with him. After nearly seventy minutes, he felt rather than heard the vibration of an approaching ship propeller. He turned in the direction from which the vibration was emanating and saw a small speck on the horizon, which resolved into a sizeable fishing trawler in just a few moments, heading back to port after a long day at work in the local waters. Big G had no idea what time it was precisely, but he'd been taking note of the angle of the sun and reasoned that it must be later in the afternoon. The trawler would be full of the day's catch and moving slowly, the crew tired and off guard, busy prepping the catch, cleaning up, stowing gear in preparation to unload and head into town for the evening. This was his chance. He could only hope that the trawler passed close enough to stir the water's surface to hide his movements, let him get into the passing ship's wake, and let the current take him far enough to be out of sight of the crew on deck above him.

As the trawler drew close, he realized that he would have the added benefit of the new ship drawing the attention of the freighter's crew, and when the two craft were about even, he pushed off the hull of the stern and angled himself toward the spinning screw of the trawler. As he had anticipated, the following wake propelled him on a parallel course to the passing ship, and he managed with his last bit of energy to fight his way across the wake to the opposite side of the fishing boat, using the boat's bulk to hide him from the freighter's crew as it pulled him along. The less-disciplined fishing crew had done an incomplete job of rigging their boat for the trip home, and some kind soul had left a line dangling below the water on the port side. Big G grabbed the line and held on for dear life. His escape effected, he now turned to his mind toward what to do once he reached port.

Chapter 21

Ten Minutes Out from Aruba

Once I was done with the team briefing, I headed back from the comm section to my seat, when my private cell phone chirped in my pocket—private travel had its perks after all, and cell phones did nothing to disrupt navigation equipment, a myth perpetrated by the airlines to keep customers contained, quiet, and pliable. The truth was that high in the air, the signal was difficult if not impossible to capture—the plane moving at some 400+ mph making the satellites and cell towers that normally coordinate quite easily, handing off signal from tower to tower as you drive, have trouble keeping up. But our speed had slowed considerably as we approached the airport, and the cell towers on Aruba had no trouble locking on and delivering the call. I answered to find, much to my surprise, Elena on the other end, speaking quickly, quietly, and somewhat angrily and adding Greek epithets liberally, making her difficult to understand.

Once I got her a bit calmer and she slowed down, she was able to relate the message from Big G's captors, their conditions that she keep the authorities out of it, and the pressure to comply at the risk of harm to her employee's family. She seemed resolved to do whatever was necessary to not only keep the family from harm, but to rescue her father, or die trying. Fortunately, with our plan in place to snatch the boss of Big G's captors, their threats rang somewhat hollow, and I was able to reassure her that these characters would be in no position to hurt anyone in just a few hours and that she had performed splendidly in buying us sufficient time to enact our plan to spring Big G and capture DeGroot.

When she heard his name, the Greek epithets started up again, and I knew I'd struck gold. Her distaste for the man was the extra fuel she needed to furnish the courage she would need to carry out her role in this little scenario. I needed her calm, focused, and motivated, and her hatred of her father's rival was just what the doctor ordered. Her part of the plan now fell into place, and mine shifted to one of the possible directions I'd anticipated in a fortunate way. I could now use Elena as bait to draw DeGroot out of his stronghold where we could get at him more easily. All she had to do was comply with his wish to transfer the accounts, files, and customer endorsements, agree to a meeting at a location of her choosing (at my direction), and show up ready to look willing and able, but not too willing. We would handle the rest.

I outlined what we knew so far, what our plan was, and she quickly and enthusiastically agreed to participate, wanting to be close to the action. By the time I had laid the whole thing out for her and the team, we had landed in Aruba.

Oranjestadt, Aruba

DeGroot had been confined to his office for the morning, sitting at the conference table with three cell phones lined up in front of him on the polished mahogany. He'd been in touch with his contacts and emissaries in various parts of the world and with his own operatives. He knew that his message had been delivered to Elena and had gotten back a response in the affirmative, on the condition of a face-to-face meeting. He felt he had nothing to fear from her and agreed to the meeting, contacting her using the number she had relayed to him, and setting a time at a location right here on his own turf. It couldn't have been easier, perhaps too easy, but his plan was coming together too neatly for him to pay any heed to such subtleties. All he knew was that he'd get what he wanted, be free of the constraints that Big G represented, and go on to virtually own the weapons market globally unchecked and unfettered.

He was still in touch with operatives in Greece, Washington, DC, and the Mediterranean, but had yet to hear from the crew of the ship holding Big G, hence the second cell phone. His apprehension grew with time at not hearing from the crew leader, but it was tempered by the reports from his DC contacts hired to follow any strange movements out of Dulles commercial air terminal. Those operatives indicated that no suspicious traffic had left in the last twenty-four hours, no last-minute flights added, no sudden changes in flight plan midtrip, no unusual cargo loading operations being performed. He felt reasonably certain that no official response to his missive to her had been launched.

She had respectfully requested twenty-four hours to arrange for her own transport to Aruba from Crete, and he had agreed. Therefore, he had some time to get it all arranged, get the details nailed down, and be prepared for her arrival. The location they'd agreed on was a warehouse DeGroot owned through a shell company on the outskirts of Oranjestadt, at the end of a dead-end street in a rather disheveled neighborhood. He would set up there well in advance, where his security could see anything approaching down the narrow, partially paved road, the only one connecting the warehouse to anything. He would keep her there, forcibly if necessary, until all his clients had been endorsed over to him, current shipments assigned to him, accounts payable assigned, and the business basically an empty shell. At that point, her usefulness to him, as well as Big G's, was at an end, and he would have his crew quietly dispatch them both, disposing of the bodies in an effective way so that they never resurfaced. The arms dealer and his only living relative would quietly disappear and never return to trouble him again. His heart warmed to the possibilities.

Queen Beatrix Airport, Aruba

My team had gathered at the airport, arriving in singles and pairs so as not to arouse suspicion, per standard operating procedure. We were fortunate to be able to use a small and mostly unused portion of the commercial air terminal reserved for the now nonexistent military presence in the island. We picked up our gear and packages from the civilian portion of the terminal as quietly as possible, camouflaging the shipments in a covered baggage carrier truck dressed as airport personnel, a simple matter of entering the employee locker room and liberating a couple of safety vests and headsets unobserved.

We quickly set up a makeshift base of operations in an unused hangar at the edge of the tarmac, unpacked the gear, and started going over intelligence and maps of the island, planning timelines and approaches coordinating the attack from three directions. The plan was fairly simple: Elena would approach from the road, as would be expected by DeGroot's security team. That would keep them focused on her for several minutes tracking her progress toward the building. She would mysteriously encounter engine trouble in her rental car about thirty yards up the road from the parking area, get out within sight of the building, raise the car's hood, make exasperated movements and sounds, and start walking toward the warehouse. That would buy sufficient time for team two, myself and Stacks, to approach from the rear unnoticed and set up a position about ten yards behind the building, in the surrounding forest. As we moved into position, the plan called for team three, BJ and Sam, to approach from the east and set up a position at the top of a large cliff facing the only side of the building with windows. Their position was above where the casual observer could see if they looked out the window, but gave them a good vantage point to see what was happening inside the building, thanks to some of Sam's fancy gadgets, like a thermal imaging camera and monitor, a parabolic mic that could hear a gnat at one hundred yards, and some other little toys that might prove useful.

That was the plan anyway. The holdup seemed to be getting Elena here, briefed, and ready in time to make the meet. She'd been delayed on a commercial flight by a storm and would land just an hour or so before the meet. We'd have to pick her up, transfer her to the "faulty" rental, get her headed in the right direction, get to our positions, and test the comm links in less than an hour—thank goodness Aruba was such a small island, or we'd have been cooked.

The warehouse, according to the intel that Tang had been able to put together in rapid fashion, was a simple square corrugated steel structure, approximately thirty feet on each side and twenty-five feet tall, thirty at the ridge of the steel roof, with one man-sized door, one loading door the size of a two-car garage but taller to accommodate semitrailers, one window, and a rotary fan roof vent. Inside several rows of pallets had been lined up creating islands and aisles, and a small office had been built in the rear on the upper floor to maximize floor space.

Stacks and I would create a door directly under that office using a plasma cutter Sam had thoughtfully provided. It was quick and relatively quiet, and with the distractions of Elena's approach and some added showbiz touches we'd planned, we would gain access to the building and the office in just a minute or so, right under the nose of the perimeter security. Sam and BJ would provide some additional distractions from their raised position, noisy enough to provide cover for our entry, and coordinate the team movements on the comm net, as they had the best observation vantage. A good plan, well-thought-out, and well-equipped teams with experienced, trained operatives, what could go wrong?

Chapter 22

Sixteen Thousand Feet over the Atlantic

Elena had caused a bit of a stir on the commercial flight on Olympic from Athens. Not only was she attracting the attention of every male passenger and crew member that passed her first-class seat, but the pilot and copilot both had come out of the cockpit to personally welcome her to the flight, ask if she needed anything, and chat with her while the plane was stuck on the tarmac waiting for the storm to clear so they could take off. Now, in the air, she was at liberty to move about the cabin and asked the flight attendant if she could chat with the pilot or the navigator at their convenience.

Elena had an idea, one that had occurred to her when the pilot came out of the cockpit and left the door to the cockpit open. She caught a glimpse of the navigation computer readout with its longitude and latitude indications, and it gave her an idea. She rooted through her bag and came up with the file containing the phone bills and the page with the odd numbers on it. They were formatted the same as those on the computer read out, and it dawned on her that they might be the same type of information. She would ask the pilot or the navigator if they could look up the numbers as locations and see where they were on the globe. Those locations might give some indication as to what they related to or what they were for.

The trip was a long one, from Crete to Athens to London and then to Queen Beatrix, and she was currently on the last and longest leg, with about three hours to kill left in the flight. That meant the pilot had little to occupy him beyond routine flight checks, communications, and monitoring, the plane on autopilot. He emerged from the cockpit, a smile on his face after receiving the message from the attendant, pleased that such an attractive passenger had requested an audience with him.

"Good evening, Captain" she purred.

"Good evening, ma'am, how has your flight been so far?" he asked politely.

"The flight has been fine, but I have a rather strange request that you might be able to help me with," she replied.

"I'll do my best to offer you any assistance you might require," he replied gallantly, drawing himself up to his full height.

"How wonderful! I have these numbers my husband left me, and I think they might be location coordinates. He's been kidnapped, you see, and I think the key to his release might be in these locations, if that's what they are. Could you or the engineer possibly use your navigation computer to give me a real-time map indicating where these coordinates connect to?" she said breathlessly.

"My goodness, kidnapped! Well, normally such a use of the computer would be strictly against airline policy, but under such extraordinary circumstances, I think we might be able to bend the rules just a bit and punch in a few numbers quickly, maybe give you some indication as to where they are on the globe. Please follow me," he intoned in a most officious tone of voice, realizing that it was the plane's gear she wanted, not his gear.

They entered the cockpit, breaking a score of FAA regulations, the two of them keyed the numbers from the page into the navigation terminal, and programmed a global Mercator projection with the coordinates indicated. They showed ports in France, Germany, Spain, all along the northern coast of South America, the coast of Africa, the Suez Canal, and about ten other strategic points on the globe, all at water locations. Elena had a pretty good handle on her father's business operation by then having dug through the files and studied them extensively. These locations didn't correlate exactly to his overseas operations offices, shipping points, or storage facilities. Strange. Some were actually in the water off the coast of the continents. She'd been sure they would form a pattern that would help her discern what they meant. They stared at the screen for a while, trying to memorize the locations, as there was no print facility from the in-air terminal. She got as much as she could locked in her memory, graciously thanked the pilot for his time and discretion, and quietly went back to her seat, immediately lost in thought. Why would her father have a list of cell phones located in ports and in water-based locations, probably ships of some sort, that he didn't own? She'd have to ask Stark in an oblique way so as not to reveal that she had the information; maybe he could shed some light on the possible solution.

She thought about Stark, too, while the plane continued toward Aruba. She hadn't expected to see him again so quickly after their last encounter and found herself a bit nervous about the coming meeting. Little flutters in her stomach and a generally warm sensation deep in her belly told her that her nervousness had nothing to do with the potential danger of the encounter with DeGroot, but with her anticipation of seeing Stark again. He was quite the character, and while his arrogance was initially annoying, decisiveness, focus, and competence virtually radiated from the man, and his strength made him attractive in his own way. She had had liaisons in the past, some with the seemingly endless rogue's gallery of her father's associates, especially early in his career when she was younger, and while they seemed tough and dangerous, they lacked an inner core of courage and seemed hollow and shallow, with no depth or worldliness to them. Initially drawn to this dangerous type, they all seemed to be commitment phobic, and her own feeling of their lack of direction assured that those relationships, while some were quite intense, were doomed to early failure.

Stark was different. He was self-assured, but in a quieter, more direct way. While he was successful, she could sense that he didn't need money and wasn't impressed by it, but was more concerned with the bigger picture, the outcome of the mission, doing a good job, treating his people with respect and pride their special skills deserved. She could also sense in him a bit of loneliness, of sadness, almost. Not a needy, helpless type by any means, but there was an empty spot there, she felt. Maybe some additional conversation would yield some clues. She'd try to arrange for some alone time for them after she took care of this heinous little chore for this fat ogre, and he was dispatched by Stark's team and taken away. She could look forward to that little chat to take her mind off the reason for the trip in the first place, her father and his captivity. She knew him to be tough as nails, but everyone had their breaking point, and it had been several days at this point since he was taken, with no contact from him. She hoped he was still alive.

Oranjestadt, Aruba

DeGroot sat in his little war room, a secure room off the back hallway designed for complete isolation, communication security, and physical safety. He's had the walls reinforced with thick aluminum plating specially designed with floating hardened steel rods that rolled if you tried to saw through the aluminum skin, making forced entry difficult. The door was 6" thick steel plate with a matching frame set into the surrounding masonry, the floor 8" of concrete with iron rebar, the ceiling 5" of concrete with a steel liner. The shielded communications lines, fax, high-speed broadband Internet fiber, telephone, and satellite all came in through one hardened point in the floor and were encased in ½" thick steel pipe all the way to the terminal at the street. If intruders were detected, the door automatically locked for twenty-four hours on an electromagnetic charge powered by a separate hardened 220-volt line direct from the local substation. Here he could reach out and communicate with his global empire even during the most expansive crisis, untouched by whatever was going on outside. Here, he felt entirely safe.

Of course, he'd had no intention of meeting Elena at the warehouse; he had minions and employees for such drudge work. It was simply a ruse to get her here to his own turf, to come to him on his terms. He would send Wesley Johnson to take care of this little task; he was bright enough to handle the paperwork adequately and would give the woman a sense of security in his local Aruban law enforcement uniform, ribbons and tassels, and braid shining in the sun.

He needed to move quickly to get the contracts and accounts signed over today before anyone but him realized that his crew on the containership had let Big G escape—he'd heard the disturbing news from the ship's captain minutes after two of the crew had noticed him jumping overboard. The heard the splash, but didn't see him surface and assumed he was drowned. For DeGroot, this wasn't quite the outcome he had envisioned, but this far into the plan, dead was as good as captured, so long as the secret stayed a secret until the paperwork was signed. He had wanted to inflict a bit more pain on his old adversary, but he'd have to settle for inflicting mental torture on his child, with no captive available. Flexibility was the key to good planning, and at this point in his life, DeGroot had learned this lesson the hard way to the level that this little glitch didn't even ruffle his demeanor a little. He took it in stride and moved forward in this thinking, six and seven moves ahead like the chess master that he was.

He heaved his bulk up out of the chair, headed out of the secure room, down the hall, and down the stairs to the kitchen to raid the fridge for some leftovers from his expansive dinner that the butler had left him. He fixed a snack, filled a snifter with Louis XIII cognac, and settled in his study for an evening of online chess, confident that by tomorrow all of Big G's business would be his, and he could move to the next phase of his plan without any opposition.

Chapter 23

Mediterranean Sea

Big G was glad that he was fond of the water and boats in particular, having grown up in a small fishing village where his father fished on weekends, but he knew most of the commercial fisherman on the docks, working there as a teenager to help support the family. He'd managed to pull himself up the rope and into the trawler that had covered his escape, make his way to the bridge, and take the captain by surprise. He'd quickly explained who he was, his bedraggled appearance, and the reason behind it and asked a stunned and amazed captain for a few favors.

The captain agreed immediately, and not only got him below into a berth, but found him some fresh clothes, a place to wash, and got some food in him. He agreed to take Big G with him to the closest port, and the captain went beyond the simple ride and insisted that Big G come home with him to meet his family and share a meal with them. After his long captivity, the thought of friendly people around him was especially welcome, and considering that no one knew where he was and no one in that town would recognize him, he felt fairly safe staying in the captain's home for a brief time.

The two men chatted amiably on the trip in to port, and Big G even took a part in preparing the boat for the night's docking, rolling lines, stowing gear, and such as he had years ago. He found these routine tasks soothing and comforting, and helped prepare him for the ordeal to come. He knew that his presence or lack thereof on the containership had been noticed, but didn't know if they had seen him attach himself to the other boat. He had to assume the worst and consider that they were looking for him with considerable resources, based on those spent to capture and hold him. Therefore, he had to inconspicuously make his way back to his ship in Lentas, discreetly contact his staff and security detail, and after dark set sail for the middle of the sea, where he would be safe.

Above all, he needed to get a hold of Elena, make sure she was safe, and fill her in on some rather delicate, complex plans to respond to DeGroot's assault. For now, finding a cell phone and a signal was the first order of business. The ship's captain had one his wife used, while he simply radioed in to a central dispatch operator or to the Greek Coast Guard in the event of trouble. The ship pulled into port just as night was falling. He'd only been out of circulation nine days, but it felt like a month. He needed food, water, and most of all some real, restful sleep. But there was work to be done, and he needed to create a strong relationship with his new host, as he sensed that it would come in handy in the days to come.

The two sailors walked down the pier to the dock, leaving the crew to finish putting the ship to bed, climbed into the captain's aging Toyota pick-up, and took a short ride to the captain's house on the outskirts of the town of Corfu. It turned out that "house" was kind of an understatement, more like a castle. The Ionian Islands were full of such castles, often Byzantine in origin, and this was no exception, the walls acting as part of a sixteenth-century fortification. The house itself was of considerable size, all built of native limestone, and sprawling over a four-acre lot surrounded by high crenellated stone walls at the top of a hill.

The captain, who introduced himself as Spiro Kathemaedes, walked through the grand entry gate with Big G in tow, whistled for his dogs, which came running at the familiar sound of their master returning home. If his wife heard the commotion, she gave no indication of it, and the reason became clear—the house was so large and rambling, she couldn't hear their approach until they were several rooms deep into the castle. The captain's wife, Sophia, greeted them as they entered the kitchen, showing no surprise whatsoever at the wretched creature her husband had brought home from his day's labors, like it happened every day. After the initial introductions, she surveyed the gaunt, dirty, and odiferous form that Big G presented, made a tsk sound, and reached out to take Big G's hand, leading him to a small suite of rooms off the kitchen, originally intended to house the downstairs kitchen staff. She told him in reassuring soft tones that he was welcome in their home, but would be more comfortable when he got cleaned up a bit. She pointed out the shower, milled French soap, fresh soft towels, and promised to find some suitable clothes, estimating his sizes with a shrewd eye for detail.

Big G, feeling more grateful than he had in years, stripped off the ill-fitting work clothes, stepped into the steaming hot water of the shower, and relaxed for the first time in the last nine days. By the time he had stood in the shower with the hot water pelting his back and shoulders, cleaned the week's filth off his body, and dried off, Sophia had found some underwear, slacks, a shirt, socks, and some used work boots, leaving them piled and folded neatly next to the bed in the attached bedroom. Big G quickly dressed and retraced his steps to the kitchen, from which delicious and enticing smells of traditional Greek island delicacies wafted. He realized that he was ravenous after nothing but leftover crew rations for nine days and felt light-headed at the smell of such heady dishes as home-made Moussaka, lamb shank, lemon drop soup, Dolmades and rice, and fresh crusty bread.

Sophia, noticing his pale countenance, helped him to a chair at the well-used wooden kitchen table. She brought him a cup of strong Greek coffee, admonishing him to sip it slowly, lest his stomach revolt. She sat across from him, studying him as he sipped his coffee, making small talk, and probing gently, trying to discover who and what her guest might be. Before long, Spiro rejoined them, having showered and changed into fresh clothes.

"I see you're treating our guest well, Sophia," he intoned cheerfully.

"Of course, Spiro, just like all the other 'strays' you bring home from the docks, although I suspect that this one is different," she replied with a slight smile.

"Yes, I feel you are correct. This one is not my typical new friend, but he has been through great misfortune and can use our help," he replied.

"Tell me all about your adventures, Georgi," she said, "but first, you eat."

They dug into the hearty, simple food, saying little, the two men enjoying significant portions and eating rapidly, as ex-military personnel are want to do, per their boot-camp training. When they were finished, the plates cleaned, coffee and dessert before them, Sophia cleared the table and tended to the dishes while the two men pushed back from the table and began to converse, and Big G unraveled his story of the kidnapping, his treatment, his revelation as to his captors, and finally the time leading up to his escape and latching on to Spiro's boat. He left out no details of the story itself, but held back some of the more gory details of the reasons for the kidnapping and what his business leading up to it involved.

"That is a fantastic story, Georgi," said Spiro, with a slight grin on his face. "What do you think, Sophia?"

"I think you are right, as you often are, about his needing our help," she replied, still slightly astonished at his amazing tale.

"What do you plan to do now?" Spiro asked. "Clearly you are a capable, resourceful man, likely of some means. That means you have tools, resources to call upon, to make things right with this DeGroot. How do you plan to do that?" he continued.

Big G sat quietly for a moment and finally responded, "I'm not entirely sure, but I have the outline of a plan. I know I need to regain my strength, to disappear for a bit, until I can fill out my plans and gather my resources to carry it out. The best place for me to do that is at sea, on my yacht. I would like you to take me there, in your fishing boat, to keep my presence a secret."

"Where is your yacht moored now?" Spiro asked.

"Off the coast of Crete, in Leyntas."

"Tomorrow is Saturday. I normally give the crew the day off. I'll be happy to do that, and more, to help you get your vengeance on this DeGroot," he replied. "Let me make a few calls, to some friends. I won't tell them who you are or why you're here, but they can help us. My boat is rigged to be operated by three crew, and a few extra hands, especially those skilled with a pistol, would be handy to have with us."

"That sounds like good thinking, my new friend," Big G said with great sincerity. "One other thing, before you call your friends, I'd like to contact my daughter, let her know I'm safe, give her some details so she can prepare for our arrival."

"Certainly, the phone is in a drawer in the kitchen, next to the sink—help yourself. We get good signal up here on the hill, no obstructions," he replied.

"Thank you very much for your generous hospitality, both of you. In the state I was in, few would have given me a second glance," he said.

"If I recall, you didn't give me much choice when we first met," Spiro chuckled.

"I'll make that call now," G said.

Spiro stood up, winked at Sophia, tilted his head, and turned to leave.

"For now, we'll give you some privacy, have a drink, and rest for a bit. Tomorrow may be a very taxing day," Sophia added, joining him as they moved to a large, richly furnished parlor adjacent to the kitchen.

Big G found the phone, a nearly new LG model he was familiar with, and dialed his daughter's number from memory. He made a connection quickly, as predicted, and the phone on the other end rang, two, three, four times, and went to voice mail, the familiar voice of Elena filling his ear, reminding him to leave a message at the tone.

This kind of news was not something you left on a voice mail, so he disconnected, folded the phone, and stood next to the sink, thinking for a moment. He couldn't call one of his offices; it was after hours, and if his staff found out he was alive and in good hands, the secret wouldn't be a secret for long. The yacht had any number of communications devices, but none were particularly secure, in terms of staff. He also suspected that the yacht might be compromised, either by police or by DeGroot's men, and if he wanted to move discreetly, he'd need to keep his current viable condition a secret. He could move more easily if everyone thought he was dead. Better to wait until Elena was available directly.

She wouldn't recognize this number on the caller ID, so he'd have to try back later.

He dropped the phone back in the drawer and headed to join his hosts in the living room, looking forward to human contact after nine days in a ship's hold.

Chapter 24

Island Jungle Warehouse, Aruba

Elena's flight finally landed in Aruba, and Stacks snatched her out of the arrivals line as she exited the plane, and shepherded her over to the hangar the team was using as a base. We got her comm gear installed and hidden in her clothes while they were briefing her on her role and bringing her up to speed on the new intelligence the team had gathered since landing. The new comm gear was a much newer vintage than what they had used in Greece, and the earpiece was so tiny as to be almost invisible even in her delicate ear. The small transmitter was equally sophisticated and wireless, about the size of a nine-volt battery but half as thick and heavy, which they hid in the lining of her fashionable jacket. It had a range of about sixty meters, adequate for the task without leaving a huge electronic footprint should DeGroot have any signal-sensing gear in place as part of his security system. It gave off about the same signature as a Citizen Ecco watch, which they gave her as well, just as a cover.

After a studied explanation of what we needed her to do, I took Elena aside for a brief private chat.

"Are you sure you're okay with this?" I asked, looking her right in the eye.

"I'm a little nervous. Your team looks and acts so committed to this, so professional. They are very, what's the word, 'solid" aren't they?" she asked.

"I trust them with my life all the time. You're in great hands with us, and I'll be right there with you, in your ear the whole time. I can hear what's going on around you as well, and it's very sensitive, so all you have to do is whisper if you feel things start to go badly," I reassured her.

"I feel so safe with you. I'm just nervous about doing my part believably. I hate this man DeGroot. He's kidnapped my father and used him as leverage to take my father's business and ruin him—the hardest part will be holding back enough not to try and kill him!" she responded in a sort of dangerous sounding growl. Her face was flushed, and she looked truly beautiful.

"I have faith in your abilities. You'll be fine, and I can coach you through it if things get sticky," I added. "I have an ulterior motive in wanting this to work out for the best. I'd like you to come back in one piece," I continued.

She looked at the floor and blushed even deeper, and then looked right into my eyes and said, "I'd like that, too."

"All you really have to do is get the meeting with DeGroot going, and then when I say, drop to the ground and stay out of the line of fire. We'll take it from there," I told her. "DeGroot's used your father as bait to get to you. We're turning the tables and using you the same way to get to him."

I left her with a few more operational details, loaded her into the rental car, and watched as she pulled away to wait in the local cantina for a signal from me that we were in place. The team loaded into the transport SUVs and headed into the jungle, to take up our positions ahead of the meeting, hoping we were early enough to avoid detection and beat DeGroot's advance team to the punch.

I rode with Stacks in the lead vehicle, and we found a small clearing about two kilometers from the warehouse. We parked the vehicles and unloaded our gear, gathered up some branches to camouflage the trucks, and faded into the jungle, comm gear on, moving toward our positions as silently as possible.

Aruba is a Caribbean island geographically, but it doesn't resemble most of the others that you see on the travel posters. There are wide, white beaches, but the interior is largely arid and rocky, not the lush jungle of many of the other central Caribbean islands. It is part of the "ABC" islands, the other two being Bonaire and Curacao, and they are actually closer to Africa than to the Caribbean. There are some stretches of forest, stocked with scrub pine, and some mangel and mangrove swamps, cori trees and other deciduous trees, but not the dense, damp rainforest that causes problems with moving smoothly and quickly, and above all, quietly through them.

The warehouse was located on the edge of the national forest preserve park and offered some fairly solid stands of trees and a varied topography, allowing us to move swiftly and nearly silently and unseen all the way to within about twenty meters of the front and rear of the building. We took up our respective positions, tested the comm and other gear, and settled in to wait.

Fortunately, we had indeed arrived ahead of DeGroot's team, and the warehouse and surrounding forest were almost completely silent. It remained so for approximately thirty minutes until I got a small buzz in my earpiece from Sam, who was positioned a bit to my right and above me on a sheer bluff.

"I'm getting movement in the trees below me slightly to your right about your three o'clock," she intoned.

"Thanks, Sam, any idea how many?" I replied.

"Sounds like maybe three, not much gear rattle, they're either really good or just packed light," she said back.

"Thanks, we'll be ready," I said.

I strained to hear any sort of movement in the forest, but unaided could discern nothing but birds and small rodents scuffling about in the leaves. Sam knew her business and had some terrific listening gear. I had no choice but to take her word for it. I started scanning in the indicated direction with the high-power binoculars and finally, after five minutes, caught a hint of movement off to my right, very low to the ground, just a shadow of an outline. I kept watching, and eventually out of the shadows I was able to resolve an image of all three of the opposing team, two larger and one smaller figures, sleek silhouettes only slightly broken by gear and belly crawling slowly just behind the ridge of a small hill. Sam had been right on both counts, not much gear, including no body armor, but carrying H&K MP5 machine pistols. Good weapons for close-up work, under twenty yards, when volume and mobility counted as much as accuracy. Our best strategy would be to take that advantage away from them, keep our distance, and make it hard for them to move by pinning them down from above and behind. They had underestimated our abilities and level of commitment—a bad mistake to make in anyone's book, and the last gang to do so paid for the mistake with their lives.

Before DeGroot's guys got too close, I buzzed Sam and BJ and instructed them to dispatch this advance team with the silenced sniper rifles at their first opportunity, quickly and quietly. No sense taking chances or leaving loose ends. A few moments later, I was able to detect the slightest movement in the trees and heard a small sound similar to a fist smacking a side of meat, three times in quick succession, less than two seconds apart. Then the forest was silent again and stayed that way. I got a quick buzz from Sam.

"I can hear a small motor vehicle approaching from the front. Timing's right for it to be Elena in the rental," she whispered.

"Thanks, keep your ears peeled—it should stop suddenly in just a moment."

"Yep, just quit with a sputter..."

"Keep me apprised..."

We didn't have to wait long. Figuring their rear was covered, the frontal guard made no secret of their presence, chatting to each other loud enough for us to hear on the other side of the building, and we could smell the smoke from their cigarettes as it wafted over the roof in the breeze.

"Guards approaching the rental and Elena down the road, moving steady, not stealthy," she cautioned.

"Thanks, sounds like they're not too worried about interference…" I replied.

Time to move. I got the plasma cutter out of my satchel and got it primed and ready, and Stacks covered my rear as we advanced toward the back of the warehouse, to a position about ten meters short of the treeline. We dropped down on the backside of a small hill and kept out of sight in case the perimeter patrols changed their pattern and came early. The plan included timing things so that the perimeter patrols passed in front of us from left to right, heading right at BJ and Sam, only to be eliminated as they rounded the corner of the building, before they could be seen by the front guard or through the windows on the off side of the building.

Sometimes things work out as you plan them. Here came the perimeter guards, two of them, strolling lazily along, smoking and chatting like they hadn't a care in the world. From our hidden position, we watched them go past without noticing us, continue, round the corner, and two more small smacking sounds followed by a muffled grunt told me that BJ was on the mark as expected.

Sam buzzed me.

"Sounds like they've got Elena in tow and are walking toward the front door down the road. Still no sign of DeGroot…" she whispered.

"Any new arrivals?"

"Not that I've been able to detect," she replied.

"Keep me informed, out."

With the perimeter guards gone, the rear echelon eliminated, and the front guards twenty yards down the road, now was the time to advance and get started on the new "rear door" with the plasma cutter. We crawled over the hill and humped it double time across the clearing to the rear of the building. I fired up the cutter and, carefully and quickly as I dared, started cutting a double-sized doorway about four feet across and seven high, in a swinging arc, but leaving the top of the arc still attached by a tiny piece of metal. I'd examined the building quickly as I was running up to it and, based on the rivet pattern, picked a spot between two reinforcing studs, meaning there was only thin corrugate between me and the meeting within. I got the cut done, and Stacks and I scampered back into the trees to wait for a signal from Sam. I didn't have to wait long.

A few moments later, Sam buzzed in. "Mid-sized SUV approaching down the front road, looks like three occupants, moving steadily," she noted in my ear.

"Size on the occupants?" I asked. I'd read the file on DeGroot and knew his weight was pushing four hundred and would cut a distinctive figure even with limited visibility through tinted windows.

"Two wearing 'boonie' hats, one a Fedora, head size appears normal," she replied.

I looked at Stacks, who just shrugged, knowing we were ready for just about anything, no matter what they threw at us.

"Three subjects exiting the SUV, all appear within 'normal' size range—doesn't look like DeGroot's here yet—standby, this might just be the advance team," she surmised.

"Standing by," I responded.

The SUV had passed the trio including Elena walking along the road without stopping. Now they were entering the building, calmly, in no particular hurry. Apparently, no one had missed their perimeter guards' presence, nor found the three rear guard bodies. Pretty confident in their mastery of the situation, the two new soldiers greeted the front guard pair with clear recognition, by name, as they escorted Elena inside and shoved her into a chair in front of a table in the middle of the room. Sam's bugs were working perfectly, and she had patched the audio into the comm network so we could hear what was going on inside. I could hear the scraping of chair legs against concrete as everyone settled in, the four guards boxing the compass in a circle around the table, the larger male on one side, Elena on the other.

The man seated at the table certainly cut an authoritative figure, roughly six feet tall, broad shouldered but with a full gut, encased in a quasimilitary type uniform, complete with gold braid at the shoulders and military-type ribbons pinned to his left chest above the breast pocket. Steel grey hair in a fringe around a bald pate, cut short and brushy, over a face that had seen a few things in life, with eyes that missed nothing and saw everything. He said nothing initially, content to sit and let Elena soak in his presence, let her apprehension build, a practiced technique often used on accused prisoners.

Elena did indeed soak all this in, but her apprehension didn't come from his presence or demeanor, or from any guilt on her part. When he didn't say anything for a few moments, Elena, a shrewd negotiator, skilled in such things based on working with suppliers in her clothing business, recognized the silent ploy and let the silent air expand on its own. She said nothing, simply taking him in, observing him directly, her gaze never wavering or diverting from his. After a few moments of this, he finally leaned back and broke her gaze.

"I suppose you're wondering who I am," the man across from her intoned. "I don't like to play guessing games, so I'll just tell you—it will save time. I'm Chief Police Inspector Wesley Johnson, head of the Oranjstadt Police Department here in the capital city. Mr. DeGroot is a staunch patron of local law enforcement and asked that I meet with you as a favor to him, as he was unavoidably detained on other business."

"I was told I would be dealing exclusively with Mr. DeGroot to secure the release of my father. How do I know you have the power to do that once we start the proceedings?" she shot back.

"Please rest assured, I enjoy the full confidence and authority of Mr. DeGroot in these dealings and have been fully authorized to make arrangements for release and transport of your father once the transactions are complete," he replied calmly.

"And if I refuse?" she asked directly.

"I am also authorized to make 'alternative' arrangements for your father's destination and disposition," he replied, with a trace of menace in his voice. "It is in everyone's best interest for you to work through these transfers with me, and if you're half as intelligent as I believe you to be, you will proceed in these dealings without further delay," he continued.

Upon hearing that DeGroot was a no-show, I got on the comm unit and made some last minute adjustments to the plan. I had a couple of choices: I could proceed as planned, storm the building, capture this Johnson character, try to pry a location for DeGroot out of him without going overboard and killing him right here. Or I could have BJ drop him with a shot through the window, or capture him and take him with us on the extraction route before any real business was transacted and hope he could lead us to Big G before DeGroot tumbled to the fact that he wasn't on the job any longer and he wouldn't be getting Big G's company. This DeGroot sounded like a bad actor, and based on his file, I was sure he had a few surprises up his sleeve. It might be best to come back for him after we were sure Big G and Elena were safely out of harm's way. That would cut collateral damage, complete the mission, and allow us to regroup, retool, draw up an effective plan, and execute it with minimal delay. Kidnapping it was.

I told Sam and BJ to approach cautiously to a closer vantage point, while Stacks and I popped up over the hill and humped it to the rear of the building in anticipation of using the new "back door" we had created. I pulled a flash-bang grenade out of my bag, courtesy of Sam and her terrific planning, and prepared to cut around the corner and throw it through the window on the end of the building closest to Sam's position. That way, if something unexpected came up, she could see me and cover me. Stacks would then wait four seconds and enter through the new door and, in the smoke and confusion, take down two of the guards standing around the table, while I'd take the other two. That would leave Johnson and Elena seated and vulnerable. BJ would pin Johnson to his chair with the red-dot laser sight while I explained the situation to him. At least that was the plan.

I crab-walked down the length of the building, after checking my other weapons and putting in a fresh clip, one with a small piece of colored tape on the bottom, in the Sig Saur 9 mm Sam had provided. I got everyone filled in on the comm unit as I went, and when I got to the end of the building, rounded the corner, and looked up, just catching the reflection of some movement inside the warehouse at the same time as I heard a slight shuffling sound from inside the warehouse. I froze and asked Sam for a sit-rep in a hoarse whisper.

"Looks like one of the guards has been dispatched to retrieve something from the truck. Johnson nodded or signaled him with a hand, which is why you didn't hear anything," she reported.

"I'll hold position and stand by. We need them all inside for this to work," I replied.

"Roger, I'll track his movements as best we can and give you the high sign when he's back inside," she said.

"Copy that, One, standing by," I heard Stacks acknowledge.

I couldn't see the SUV from my position crouched down below the window on the off-side of the building, but I trusted Sam to track him with the scope and give me some warning if something untoward occurred. After what seemed like an eternity, but was in reality about two minutes, the soldier exited the truck and came back inside and, after dropping something heavy with a thud on the table, shuffled back to his position at the northwest corner of the table.

"Guard 2 is back in position, all clear for go," Sam chirped in my ear.

"On my count, four, three, two, one."

Then I pulled the pin on the grenade, released the toggle, and tossed it hard enough to break through the window and travel into the middle of the warehouse. A second later, the grenade went off with a sharp bang and a blindingly bright flash, and started to release thick grey smoke, filling the interior of the warehouse. Just as the flash exploded and blinded all the occupants except Elena, who'd been instructed just as I threw the grenade to close her eyes and be ready to hit the ground, Stacks swung into action. With a huge crash, Stacks lowered his shoulder and hit the back wall of the warehouse full force with all his weight and momentum behind it, breaking the tiny piece of metal holding up the cut-away section and dropping a large section of the wall into the interior, adding to the confusion as sunlight hit the smoke and the sudden breeze stirred up more of it in huge swirls, blinding anyone who wasn't disabled already from the flash.

Right after I hurled the grenade, I'd taken off running and entered the new opening right behind Stacks and kept running until I tackled the nearest guard, knocking him into the one closest to the front door, dropping them both. I banged the head of the first on the concrete, knocking him unconscious, and popped the second in the face with the butt of my pistol, disabling him. Stacks had hit the other two in similar fashion, but with his added weight and technique, ended up travelling further into the interior and ending up directly behind Johnson, both guards laid out flat on their backs, unconscious and out of the game. I looked toward where Johnson was and noted a small red dot on his chest. He tried to rise out of the chair, but Stacks moved quickly up behind the chair and placed a huge hand on his shoulder, forcing the police chief back into the chair.

As the smoke was clearing, I walked up and helped Elena to her feet from where she had flattened herself on the floor, out of the line of fire that never came. She got up a bit slowly, slightly shaken but operable, and stood next to me with her arm around me.

"Stay put, Johnson, or this will end badly for you," I cracked at the policeman. "If you look down, you'll notice a little red dot on your pretty uniform. One move I don't like, that dot becomes a sizeable hole," I warned.

"Who are you, and what do you mean, barging in here and disrupting our business?" has asked, trying to retain some dignity and muster up some type of authority to regain control of a hopelessly out of control situation.

"Who we are is none of your business. As far as you're concerned, we're just here as support to help you unburden yourself of some information regarding the whereabouts of Big G," I replied.

"I don't know what you're talking about," he shot back.

"We'll see…" I replied quietly and motioned to Stacks, who grabbed Johnson's wrist and twisted his arm behind him, forcing his head down to the table with the other hand. He reached out with the other hand and grabbed the other wrist and brought them together, held them with one hand while whipping out a heavy nylon wire-tie from his belt, effectively handcuffing the policeman's hands behind him in a couple of smooth, swift motions. Stacks sat him back up in the chair, and the red dot reappeared, unwavering, on his chest.

I instructed BJ to climb down from his perch and join us, while Sam and her sniper rifle stayed put, trained on our new friend. Johnson just glared and didn't say a word. I escorted Elena out the door and walked her a few feet from the building, with her leaning heavily against me, clearly shaken and relieved her part was over.

"I can't believe that worked," she exclaimed breathlessly.

"I told you that you were in good hands. My team's the best there is," I reassured her.

"I'm so glad that's over, but we still don't know where my father is, or even if he's alive," she exclaimed.

"We're working on that now. Next step is to take Mr. Johnson with us someplace quiet and private, see if he can persuade him to lead us to your father, and we either dispose of him or use him as a bargaining chip, depending on what we can find out about him and estimate his value to DeGroot," I replied.

I knew we had to stay on the island, but we needed to find somewhere we could work in private on Johnson without being disturbed, and we needed a few supplies. We also needed to get Elena to someplace safe where she couldn't be found. Time to check in with Langley, see if we could get some logistical support from stateside.

I pulled out a sat phone and called Dick; luckily he picked up on the first ring.

"Dick, just a quick call to check in and ask a favor," I started, before he could interrupt me.

"Well, nice to finally hear from you. Dare I ask how things are going?"

"It's under control, but we need a little assistance with logistics. Can you find me a safe place to stash Big G's daughter on Aruba, preferably not somewhere that requires a credit card. We also need somewhere to do some private work, somewhere quiet and out of the way."

"How big a place do you need?"

"Not huge, but thick walls would be good, or underground, or well away from the neighbors," I replied.

"Let me check on local assets and get back to you in a few minutes—you in a place where an incoming call is appropriate?" he asked.

"Yeah, we'll be in a car out of earshot of most," I said.

"Back in ten," he said tersely.

"Yup."

I folded the phone and took Elena's arm, and we strolled over to a small patch of shade out of sight line of the door to the warehouse.

"We'll need to move you to someplace safe for this next portion. My people are searching for such a place right now, and we should have a destination in a few minutes," I told her lightly.

"I don't want you to leave me alone. I don't care where it is," she replied, the fear showing in her voice mixed with adrenalin.

"We've taken care of you so far—rest assured we'll continue to do so until this is over and we find your father and rescue him," I replied reassuringly.

"I'm so worried about him, I don't know what to do," she confided.

"I have every confidence we're closing in on his location, and from what I've heard, he's a pretty resourceful guy. If there's a chance for a rescue, I have no doubt he'll find a way to stay alive until we arrive," I said. "Stay here for a moment. I'll go brief the team and we can get out of here."

I walked toward the warehouse door trying to show as much confidence as I'd imparted to her, but it had been an eventful morning, and I was still not much closer to finding her father. I stuck my head in the door and motioned for the team to gather up near the doorway, out of earshot of the bound police captain. Just as they gathered, my phone buzzed in my pocket. The caller ID said "OUT OF AREA" with no number. I figured it was Dick getting back to me with a location.

"Dick, what have you got for me?"

"I found a couple of options on the safe house, depending on where on the island you want her. The other location, I have one I think might work," he replied without preamble.

"Give me the coordinates for the safe house closest to the southeast side of the island," I asked.

"I'll text you the numbers. Meantime, here's the dope on the second location. My staff here found an old abandoned Soviet air base, built in secret just before the Cuban missile crisis. Most of the actual operations spaces are underground, which is why we never picked up on it until much later, after they'd left. You may have to do some work to gain access, but as near as we can tell, no one's been there for years, no one's monitoring it, no security to speak of other than physically locking the place and chaining the outer gates," he replied.

"Sounds perfect," I said. "Text me those numbers as well. I'll call you when we've gained access."

"Talk to you soon, good luck—find Big G and get him back where he belongs. We're hearing a lot of rumblings in the lower echelon of the weapons trade that there is a shake-up in the offing. We can't keep this under wraps much longer," he reminded me.

As soon as I hung up, my phone chirped with the text message containing the two sets of GPS coordinates, which I handed to Stacks to feed into our onboard GPS in the larger SUV.

We got the police captain under control, unconscious and comfortable in the back of the larger of the vehicles, loaded up the rest of our gear, and the team mounted up and moved out. Under the circumstances, I felt it made more sense to stay together and armed, rather than split up and work more efficiently.

We rode most of the way in silence, each reviewing the recent action, seeking flaws in execution, errors in communication, and looking for ways we could have improved our performance. When you work with true professionals, there is little celebration after such an event until the assignment is truly over and everyone is safe, mission accomplished. The real pros are always looking to improve themselves; after all, it's your life that depends upon everyone being perfect. I really liked working with these guys, had found them to be the most well-trained, adaptable, flexible, intelligent, and capable professionals I'd ever worked with, in or out of the military in a dozen countries. We'd been together for a while and worked together like a well-oiled machine, which not only made us successful from a business standpoint, but also kept us safer than most such units. We continued out into the countryside, following the coordinates, planning our next move after we got Elena settled.

Chapter 25

Off the Coast of Corfu

Spiro and Sophia had proved to be excellent hosts, and the three had stayed up well into the night chatting and becoming friendlier before turning in for the night. Now, back aboard Spiro's medium-sized fishing vessel, the two men seemed like old friends. Spiro, true to his word, had rounded up a volunteer crew that would have given Captain Blackbeard pause. He had convinced six men ranging in age from twenty-two to fifty to join them—all of whom had decades of sea experience, were comfortable with firearms, and comfortable being on either side of the law, for the right price. Big G didn't know what they had been promised in return, but he suspected many of them had come along just for the possibility of some action. These were clearly not men who enjoyed sitting around whittling on the front porch.

The crew knew their business, went about getting the boat ready for departure, and shoved off in minimal time, heading out of the harbor as fast as the currents would allow without attracting attention. Once on the open water, they pointed the boat toward the eastern end of Crete and went about preparing for their next adventure. They broke down and cleaned a variety of weapons, checked engines, stowed gear, prepared a hearty midday meal, and in a few hours could see the eastern coast of the big island of Crete. They slowed and approached the island to a point where they couldn't be seen from shore, and hugged the coast around the southern shore toward Leyntas, where Big G's yacht awaited.

Without knowing what had transpired while he was being held captive in the hold of the ship, Big G decided to approach the yacht with extreme caution. Despite its antiquated and slovenly appearance, Spiro's ship was well equipped and well maintained. There was a brand new ship-to-shore radio, both down-looking sonar and forward-seeking radar with imaging equipment attached, even a small, unmanned remote-operated submersible, complete with audio and video telemetry, he'd bought online from a research center that had come upon hard times. This he used for checking deep nets for foreign debris, mines, and snags before sending a crew member down to free the net or make repairs. He also had satellite radio, satellite television, broadband Wi-Fi, and tucked in a drawer, an iPad.

As they approached the port of Leyntas, using powerful binoculars, they could see Big G's yacht, its white paint shining against the deep blue water of the harbor, the sun reflecting off its brightwork and polished gunwale rails like small stars. They dropped anchor, shut down the motor, and sat at anchor silently, the radar and sonar pinging like mad, searching for any activity above and below the water near the impressive ship. After an hour of quietly watching and listening, they came to the conclusion that the ship was unoccupied and that there was no one nearby watching. Time to make a move.

They fired the engine and slowly idled toward the big yacht, circling to the south to keep the yacht between the fishing vessel and the shoreline. At two hundred yards out, they stopped the twin screws, dropped the aft anchor, and lowered a small dinghy designed for four people into the water on the off side of the boat. Spiro handed out a couple of small two-way radios to two of the crew and hopped into the dingy, followed by Big G and two crewmen. He appointed one of the most experienced crew members, Spiro's brother-in-law, as interim captain, and instructed him to keep the radio channel open and wait for the all clear from him before sending the rest of the crew over in the other dingy. A burly fifty-year-old salt who had grown up in the same fishing village as Spiro, Yianni had an air of quiet confidence to his six-foot frame that would have intimidated all but the most hardened military veteran. Big G had no qualms about his acting as back-up for this little incursion, no matter what lay ahead.

They approached cautiously, searching for any movement on board, any sound that would signal an occupant, friend or foe. Nothing. Relaxed but alert, they reached the port bow rope, tied up the dingy, and tossed a hook up to snag the rope ladder to board the bigger ship. While Spiro clambered up the ladder, Big G struggled a bit, still weak after nine days of captivity.

He felt fine, but his muscles didn't respond as he wanted them to after little or no movement for over a week. He'd have to allow for that if things got sticky later on.

They dropped over the gunwale railing onto the teak deck as quietly as they could, fanning out fore and aft along the port gunwale, the sea at their backs. Big G headed straight for the wheelhouse, reviewed the control panel, and determined at a glance that the ship had been shut down properly and was at storage idle condition. Batteries were mostly charged, both fuel tanks full, and both anchors fully deployed. Clearly someone who knew the ship had carefully shut it down for the foreseeable future, not in the hurried panic condition that an intruder would have left it in. Big G immediately felt Elena's presence, knew his daughter had prepped the ship on her own, not under duress, and had left it ready for his return, right down to his favorite juice chilling the wheelhouse fridge.

The biggest mystery solved, Big G reverted to the position of captain of his own vessel, providing direction for the others to search the ship for stragglers hiding below, offering instructions as to the location of likely hiding places, firing the powerful engines to fully charge the batteries, and generally sliding back into his native element, gaining confidence by the moment as the new crew cleared the ship and made ready to get underway. The remaining four joined them aboard, save Yianni, and they proceeded away from Leyntas to open water to plan their next move.

Orandjestadt, Aruba

The big man sat in his darkened office, the only illumination a low-wattage desk lamp casting a cone of yellow translucence over a portion of his desk containing the phone. That phone had been strangely quiet, especially after he'd directed all his employees not to use any cellular communication to reach him and to rely on the constantly swept and encoded landline he'd had installed with the command center upgrades. His team at the warehouse was two hours late checking in, not typical at all, but not unusual enough to start panicking just yet. Not that he was prone to panic—the big man had seen enough come down the pike and had enough resources that panic had been removed from his emotional lexicon years ago. He knew eventually news would come; if that news was good, likely it would come from one of the team, whoever was left, and if it was bad news, it would come from other sources when one of the team was missed somewhere else. Either way, he knew that even the most carefully laid plans usually go awry on some level, and a couple of hours of flexibility was not indicative of a significant problem.

He worked on his second Louis XIII brandy, sipping and thinking of ways to retask his newfound client list to maximize profit. Taking Big G's business had been like taking candy from a baby, just reach out, grab the top dog, ransom the business from his loved ones, and then remove the top dog from the board. Simple. Things hadn't gone quite that way, but the results would be worth the deviation. With Big G dead, presumably, the contracts in hand were more of a formality, especially with his death not widely known. The daughter was now a loose end, albeit a small one, that would have to be attended to when the opportunity arose.

There were already rumblings, started by key individuals in his employ, that Big G wasn't going to be able to deliver a couple of his largest orders, and that kind of information could cause a cascade effect driving confidence downward among the buyers of the world. DeGroot knew he needed to get this transacted quickly to step into the void and instill confidence once again. Things were shaping up exactly as he intended, except for the pesky feeling creeping up in the back of his mind that something was amiss. The quiet phone was feeding that feeling, and his anxiety level was slowly rising as the clock hand swept into the third hour since he should have heard from Johnson.

He leaned back in his chair, sipped from the snifter, took a deep breath, exhaled through his nose noisily, and tried to calm himself. If he could just shake the feeling that something was coming after him. If only the phone would ring…

Chapter 26

Northeastern Edge of Aruba

My team had encountered little difficulty in finding the small suburban house owned by a shell company in the Azores owned by the CIA. Tidy, neat, occupied by an older couple of British ex-pats to keep it looking occupied and not abandoned, the house was empty of people when they arrived, but fully stocked with food, beverages, linens, toiletries, and assorted new clothing, enough to last a couple of weeks. It was a bit off the beaten path, and when we arrived, Elena took one look and relaxed. There were good sightlines out of all the windows, and you could hear any vehicle approaching from a long way off it was so quiet. That secure feeling only increased when the woman who lived there phoned and said that although they'd been on holiday in Spain, they were due back the next morning and would that be all right for them to be around. She explained that they could easily extend their vacation another week if need be. Elena was only too pleased to have them return to keep her company, and I felt better knowing that the couple would be around, especially the husband, who had been a colonel in the SAS.

Once she got settled in, we reloaded the vehicles and headed out for our new base of operations. As near as I could figure, the coordinates would lead us to a big open space on the northeast coast of the island. Once we got closer, I could tell that would be roughly correct, but that the problem was there was only one road in and out of this huge open undeveloped area. Good for our security, but if they closed off that road for any reason, as far as vehicular traffic, we'd be trapped. The surrounding terrain was pretty rugged, and I didn't give these SUVs much chance of surviving a high-speed chase over such terrain for any length of time before rocks, boulders, and ravines ripped out the undercarriages or tore the tires off the rims.

With this in mind, I had Stacks pull off the road and stop. Sam, in the other vehicle, got out, reconnoitered about a bit near the road, picked up a stout branch, and started poking the ground. Apparently satisfied, she opened the back of the truck, reached into her bag of tricks, and pulled out two small boxes. She dug around a bit further and found a small emergency trenching shovel as part of the emergency kit in the truck. BJ wandered over and helped her, and the two proceeded to dig two good-sized holes, one on either side of the road about two yards off the berm. They opened the boxes and took out a smaller, odd-shaped device about eight inches on a side, made of grey plastic with a small antenna of some kind sprouting off one side. They proceeded to bury these devices in the holes with just the tip of the antenna poking out of the ground per Sam's instructions.

They walked back to the vehicle, and Sam saw my curious look and raised eyebrows and sauntered over to me.

"Tough trap here, this road acts as a funnel going in, so it's pretty easily defensible, but if they block us in, we're screwed," she said quickly getting to the point.

"You read my mind, as usual," I replied. "So what's in the boxes?"

"Earthquake detectors, wireless," she replied nonchalantly, as is everyone carried such exotic hardware with them.

"Expecting a seismic event?" I quipped.

"Sort of. I set them to the maximum sensitivity, and when we get to the building we'll be using, I can set up the computer to act as the receiver and imager. We should get a graphic representation of any traffic coming down this road that weighs more than a bicycle," she informed me.

"From how far away?" I asked, intrigued.

"Roughly five miles, give or take," she replied.

"Perfect, we'll have about ten minutes warning if someone's coming down the road or parallel to it. How far off the road will these pick up? Is it sensitive enough to detect a crew of average size men walking?" I asked.

"They're pretty sophisticated. We should be able to pick up about twenty feet on either side of the road with vehicles. If it's men on foot, we'll have to have a bit more luck involved. If several of them let their feet fall together it should register—trained men know not to synch up on bridges, but this is rocks and scrub, and they may fall into step unconsciously," she replied.

"Excellent, we should be covered from this direction. How many of those do you have hiding in that little bag?" I asked.

"I have two more sets. We can cover approaches from 360 degrees if need be, especially if they're driving," she replied, closing the bag and hopping back into the SUV.

The little caravan proceeded along the road, still no runway in sight, but a large x-shaped brick building appeared on the left of the road, surrounded by a significant eight-foot fence, topped with razor wire, locked with a tow chain and a sizeable master lock.

Stacks glanced over at the entry gate as we passed, and sneered, "We had tougher security on our football field in high school, piece of cake."

"Good," I replied, "we'll likely need to get in there at some point, but for now I think Dick mentioned that most of the complex is underground, and the GPS is saying we're not at the coordinates yet."

We followed the road a little longer, and then the GPS indicated that we should head west five hundred yards. I didn't see anything of note, no buildings, no shacks or huts, nothing but arid, grayish brown rock and sand interspersed with scrub plants low to the ground. We stopped the convoy and got out of the vehicles to stretch and recon the area. No much to see. BJ wandered off to the west a few yards, then stopped suddenly, and motioned the rest of us over to where he was standing. Suddenly once we were closer to him, it became apparent why he had called us.

Carefully hidden in the sand and brush was a nine by nine foot steel plate with a large steel ring in the center, with Cyrillic lettering on it in red. BJ had felt the ground beneath his bulk flex when he walked over the door and noticed the ring on the ground; otherwise we'd have been walking around for an hour trying to locate it.

BJ and Stacks got on either side of the middle of the opening and cleared away the sand covering the edges. I jogged back to the lead truck and grabbed a tire iron with a crowbar on one end and double-timed it back to the door, wedged the narrow end underneath the center seam of the door adjacent to the ring, and heaved. It opened just enough for Stacks and BJ to get their fingers underneath the edge—they heaved on the count of three, and the door popped open. The dank, musty odor of wet concrete, earth, and decay wafted up from the opening. Clearly the place hadn't been used in a while. There was a long ladder bolted to the wall with rusty bolts leading into the opening, and even in broad daylight, you could only see about five rungs down into the hole before the darkness swallowed all visibility.

I told everybody to head back to the vehicles, and we rolled the three trucks into a rough circle around the opening. This provided a little cover and made unloading the gear easier. We grabbed some flashlights and headed down into the opening, BJ leading the way, his light swinging back and forth sweeping the floor at the bottom of the ladder to check for water, obstacles, booby traps, and other nasty surprises. The light showed nothing but dusty concrete floor with a drain in the center. We all regrouped at the bottom of the ladder. We found ourselves in a small square chamber with two tunnels leading away, one to the west, and one to the north, with full seven-foot ceiling height, block walls, and electrical conduit and light fixtures every twenty feet or so close to the ceiling.

"Flip a coin?" BJ quipped.

"Sam, you got any gadgets in your bag of tricks that will help us decide?" I asked.

"Not much. I feel a little breeze of moving air coming from that one to the north—it's got my vote for that reason alone," she replied.

"Fresh air it is," I commented, and we all headed north down the tunnel, following the movement of air about one hundred yards. Along the way, several doorways appeared on the left-hand side of the tunnel, none on the right. All were locked, and all had plain grey paint, peeling in places and no markings whatsoever, and the plates long ago removed to confuse intruders, in standard Soviet, scorched-earth fashion. At the end of the tunnel the space seemed to widen and broaden, and the flashlights revealed a large, open room, with a tiled floor and higher ceiling.

"Stay here for a few minutes. I'll follow this conduit down the corridor further, see if I can find a power box, get a little light on the subject," BJ said lightly, heading off down the corridor.

In less than ten minutes, I heard a clacking sound, and the overhead fluorescent lights buzzed and popped on one at a time, revealing the whole room in sick, slightly tremulous pinkish light. It looked like a cafeteria, with a few steel tables and plain wooden chairs scattered about, and what at one time must have been a commercial food service line along the far wall. Much had been removed, but they had left a counter and tray rail, steam trays, and a few service utensils lying around randomly, like they had left in sort of a hurry and knew they weren't coming back.

BJ came sauntering back to join the group and announced he had powered up the whole complex, that the generator source was nuclear and still had plenty of life left in it. He also mentioned he had passed what looked like a series of administrative offices and maintenance offices on his way and that they might reveal something useful.

"Let's split up and start searching the maintenance offices—we're looking for plans of the facility and any keys or code books that we can find," I instructed everyone.

We set off down the corridor, each of us peeling off as we came to a doorway that was unlocked. I took the last one and entered a plain, spartan office with a grey metal desk, a couple of metal chairs, some lockers against one wall, and a couple of file cabinets against the other. After a few minutes of rooting around, I came across something of interest, a set of blueprints showing the plumbing and ventilation systems in the complex.

I don't read Russian well, but the drawing itself was clear enough.

The whole complex was laid out in a giant square with the corridor we'd entered through forming the perimeter surrounding the entire complex. There were three other entrance tunnels like the one we'd come down, and there were ventilation shafts feeding each one from the surface, and a large central fan and CO_2 scrubbers in the middle of the complex to move and refresh the air below.

I had to hand it to Dick; if there was a perfect place to set up a base of operations, interrogate a suspect in private, and stage an assault, this was it. It had everything we needed. According to the blueprints I had found, everything you could ask for to stage a military operation was here, including living quarters, work rooms, maintenance shops, energy, water sources, waste disposal, transportation, we even found a small pen filled with what looked like golf carts for moving up and down the corridors quickly. A full food prep and dining facility was shown, as well as weapons magazine, laundry facilities, all military and industrial grade. With enough food, we could have moved in a stayed for a year. It even had a brig, which is just what I needed in the immediate term, to contain our little prisoner.

I briefed everyone quickly and delegated various tasks involved in setting up a small command center, and the team when about its business like the machine I knew it would be. Stacks and I transported our prisoner down the hall to the brig on one of the carts, locked him in a cell, and left him there to sleep off the powerful sedative. I left a radio, switched to a little used frequency, the mike key taped open, sitting on the guard desk outside the cell to act as a baby monitor, so I would know when our prisoner started to come around. I wanted him groggy but conscious for the next phase of the operation.

We then returned to the main dining area, which we were using for a common and ready room. BJ had found the weapons locker and had distributed its contents to the team, giving us some additional firepower in case we needed it. Sam had set up comms. for everyone including figuring out the Russian phone system for the complex. We got in touch with Tang back in Langley on a scrambled, secure line, let him know we were in and getting set up, and to thank Dick for the use of the facility. Now it was time to create the plan.

But first, I needed information. I grabbed Stacks after a quick review of everything and headed down the hall to the brig. I'd heard stirrings from the open radio channel and needed to check in on the police captain and see if I could get him to tell me where his boss might be hiding.

We entered the cell area, and I signaled for Stacks to stay behind in the anteroom, out of sight of the prisoner, so he'd bond with me and not feel that there was anyone else around, either to pressure him or to give him hope. I needed him to pin his hopes of survival on me and me alone. I moved into the block of cells proper and unlocked his carefully. We'd left him bound securely, but you never knew.

"Welcome back, Captain," I intoned cheerfully.

"Where am I, and what do you want with me?" he snarled, but without venom.

"Two good questions to start with, but I want to make one point abundantly clear to you. Under these circumstances, I'll be the one asking questions, and you'll be the one answering," I instructed. "Now, because I want us to get off on the right foot, I'll answer one of them for you right away. You are still on the island of Aruba, in a place you may not even know exists," I responded. "Now it's my turn. I want to know where I can find DeGroot. The sooner you tell me truthfully where he's hiding, the faster you can return to taking petty bribes and fixing parking tickets."

"I don't know where he is."

"Perhaps I wasn't clear. I need to know where he is, and if I don't find out, you'll never see the light of day again," I whispered. "Is that more clear?"

"I still don't know," he repeated.

"Is there a reason you don't know? If you're worried about what he'll do to you for revealing this information, don't. Worry about what I'll do to you if you don't tell me," I hissed.

"I don't particularly fear either of you, and I completely believe you when you threaten me. I've seen your work," he replied. "I just can't tell you because I don't know for sure."

"You're a policeman—surely you can make some educated guesses, use deductive reasoning, piece together clues about his whereabouts?" I intoned.

"I can tell you where he lives, but you can get that from the local phone book. His current and immediate whereabouts are unknown to me," he said.

"Let's start with where he lives and what kind of security is there—criminals don't usually list their locations in the local white pages," I replied sarcastically.

"You must understand, DeGroot is a local hero to the poor people of this island. He contributes to their welfare, offers them jobs, owns the restaurants, hotels, and stores where they work. They worship him," he whined. "They will protect him. They will hide him if necessary, but he doesn't see himself as a *master criminal* and sees no reason to hide as a result. His habits and needs make him easy to find…"

"What kind of habits?" I asked.

"DeGroot enjoys the finer things in life, especially food and drink," he explained. "He buys gourmet food from specialty shops. High-end wines and spirits are shipped in specifically at his request. Unusual foods and spices are shipped direct, but the post office is notified of their contents so that he is called promptly to come pick them up."

"How does he place these orders, and how are they received?" I asked, sensing an idea forming in the back of my mind.

"He orders off the Internet, a gourmet supply site, and when they arrive at the post office, he has standing orders to be called at his estate immediately, and he sends his driver to retrieve the packages," the captain replied.

"How do you know this, but don't know his whereabouts at the moment—sounds like you're in close contact with him?" I asked.

"DeGroot is very secretive, but still must function normally to maintain the veneer of a local businessman. I know his public persona, but his private affairs are exactly that. He has many real estate holdings. Officially he has a building downtown where it appears he lives and works, as well as other private dwellings on the island. I have been to his real residence twice. Both times I was blindfolded on the way in and the way out, but can tell you that the ride took a little over twenty minutes from my office at the government center building," he offered.

"Now you're getting the idea. Your cooperation is greatly appreciated," I quipped. "Now, what's the address of that more public residence?"

"He lives in a private building just off the main square, above a café. He owns the whole thing, including the garage underneath. Few buildings on the island have basements or underground spaces of any kind, due to the shallow water table," he told me.

"Very informative, all of a sudden you're Bob Vila—why the change of heart?" I asked.

"I have nothing to lose by telling you things you could easily learn, given enough time. I have no great love for DeGroot, only that I respect his ability to remove me from the planet never to be found were he to discover that I told you anything. I'm simply speeding along the inevitable..." His voice trailed off, and he looked off into the middle distance.

"I'm glad you worked through that, but if there's any removing from the planet to be done, it will be performed by me," I replied. "Let's talk about your visits to the residence. When you left downtown, could you tell what direction you headed for your twenty-minute ride?"

"It was late at night, no way to orient myself using the sun or wind, with the windows in the car up and the air-conditioning at full capacity. I do recall the car vibrating slightly at one point, possibly a metal bridge. And I remember the crunch of gravel in the driveway when we arrived. Beyond that, most of our roads meander a bit and are well paved, so directions would be guesses only," he recalled.

"It just keeps getting better. As the police captain, you don't know this island like the back of your hand? Come on, Captain, make a guess as to the location—based on what you just told me, my operatives could find that in about twenty minutes with a map, a car, and a radio. Save me the trouble—as you know, your life is not the only one at stake here," I barked.

That seemed to snap him back to the reality of his situation, and his mouth opened to respond but no sound came out. I let the understood threat sink in for a few moments, and turned and left him alone as I headed out the door and closed it behind me. Stacks was waiting patiently on the other side, and he looked up, noticed the grin on my face, and understood that we had enough if we needed to go now. I pulled him aside and gave him the lowdown.

"Our friend here is more cooperative than I would have expected. It's almost too easy. We now know it's a residence within twenty minutes of downtown, across a bridge with a gravel driveway. Head back to the mess hall, grab Sam, and sit down with an island map and Google Earth and see if you can find it based on that. I'll try and pin him down on some of the security details, see if I can find an obvious weak spot to gain access to him before he knows we're there."

"Sure thing, boss, back in a flash," he grinned and headed down the corridor.

I turned and walked back into the cell block, still trying to decide if a frontal assault on the residence I knew they'd find was better than a quick street-snatch at the downtown post office. If I could get an idea of what the house contained, what we'd be up against, I could decide, go get this scumbag, and get Big G back where he belonged.

Chapter 27

Off Leyntas, Crete

Aboard the *Lady Elena*, Big G and his new "crew" were settling in, and Big G and Spiro were sitting in the lounge, having finished a rudimentary but satisfying meal of hard sausage, cheese, and some bread he'd scrounged from the freezer and heated in the galley, along with some local wine. They sat facing the large panorama windows toward the stern, cocktail in hand, discussing their next move to find his captors and exact his revenge. Big G had grown to like Spiro more and more as their time together lengthened, and he found the sea captain to be insightful, practical, and competent in a range of matters not pertaining to the sea and fishing. Moreover, Big G had come to trust Spiro, and as a result, had decided to offer him some information as part of their plan that he never would have shared with his other associates.

"Believe it or not, I have elements of a plan in place against just such an occurrence as the one that has transpired," he started. "When I had been in business a few years, and I mean the black market arms business, not the legitimate enterprises, I knew that my competitors would stop at nothing to either remove me or steal my business or destroy me in one form or another. I took pains to deal as directly and honestly as I was able even in this illegal endeavor, to reduce the risk from competitors and customers. I delivered on my promises, no matter how challenging, and met or exceeded delivery deadlines and overcame logistical and financial challenges, to meet customer expectations. But this only went so far. I needed some insurance, something I could use as leverage to arrange for my own safety, release, or prevent my execution.

"In my dealings with the American government agencies—and please understand they were a good but small client compared to other governments in the developed and undeveloped world—I came across a supply of a new explosive device that they were testing, but had put into limited production due to the extreme power and simplicity of the device. They feared if they built and produced a quantity of these for military use and distribution, the 'wrong' people would get their hands on them, back engineer them, and use them against the United States in strategic target removal. These devices were extremely powerful in a relatively compact package and could be assembled from a wide range of readily available, legal, and untraceable materials. Virtually anyone with any knowledge of chemistry or physics could, with a few simple ingredients, assemble one, and use it with devastating effect on strategic targets. They can be remotely detonated, and a package the size of a dorm refrigerator could level a city block.

"I purchased twenty such devices from an inside contact at a warehouse in rural Virginia, who knew that the program that had created them had lost its funding, and that no one would miss them. I do business all over the world, most of it involving shipping and transport from port to port, moving weapons from their sellers to their buyers. I use ships a great deal, am familiar with them and the ports they sail to. I distributed these devices hidden in shipping containers on a series of ships that have disbursed themselves all over the globe. With two phone calls, I can retask the ship nearest the target, direct it to the port I need to destroy, and with the second call, detonate the device remotely from anywhere in the world via cellular phone detonator. This would work with other ships at sea as well as docked and port targets. All I need is a set of GPS coordinates, and the destruction of virtually any ship or port in the world is assured.

"The other wrinkle is that the detonators need periodic updates and calls from me to keep them from self-initiating. If I don't call those numbers every two weeks, they start going off by themselves, as my extra insurance against something like what happened to me last week. Fortunately, once I got to your house after you fished me out of the water, I was able to initiate an update call and reset the clocks just in time to prevent a catastrophe.

"Once we find the one I suspect is behind my abduction, we simply retask a ship to the nearest port to him, lure him to the dock to receive his 'merchandise,' and make a phone call from anywhere in the world, removing him permanently."

Spiro's face showed only mild surprise and no righteous indignation one might have suspected after hearing such a soliloquy from a man of Big G's stature. He looked slightly impressed, stood, and raised his scotch glass to connect with Big G's in salute.

"Good for you—everyone should have such a plan in your business!" he intoned. "Where do you suppose this villain might be hiding?"

"I'm not sure where he might be currently, but once I get in touch with my daughter, I may be able to find out," he replied. "In the meantime, you and I and a couple of your crew will be putting together a plan to draw him to a port where I can place one of my 'special containers' nearby."

Secret Base, Aruba

My team had done an expert job and found not only the residence based on the info provided by the captain, but had tracked down ownership records, plat drawings, the name of the lawyer and real estate agent who enacted the transaction, the previous owner, and a set of construction plans for the building. With that information in hand, we no longer needed the captain, so now my dilemma was what to do with him. My relationship with the federal government gave me certain coverage for certain types of operations, but one of the reasons they use contractors like me is for deniability later if things go wrong or come to light after the fact. In this case, I couldn't just eliminate the police captain of the capital city of an allied island nation and walk away unscathed, not without some intricate planning and a lot of people knowing. I could only go so far in the name of national security, and I didn't think that would easily qualify.

I'd learned over the years, when in doubt, spread the blame. I called Dick, got his voice mail, left a cryptic message juicy enough to get him to call back as soon as he heard it, and hung up. I'd leave the captain in his cell for now and make him as comfortable as possible, and we'd deal with him later. He was in this up to his eyeballs, but I didn't want him to become a distraction or get in the way during the operation, even if it meant keeping him from becoming "collateral damage" and solving the problem for us.

I gathered the team around the table in the center of the room with the house plans spread out, courtesy of Sam and her computer magic. Turned out the complex had a small print shop, and she had found some operational if older equipment and got a good-sized printout of the file from the Internet via the central courthouse database file for deed recordation and permits. Apparently, some extensive construction had gone on at the property a few years ago. After comparing the two plans, before and after, it was clear we were not just going to walk in the front door and find DeGroot in his living room.

Virtually every door in the place had been enlarged to accommodate his bulk, and at the same time reinforced and strengthened with steel framing and equipped with multibolt electromagnetic locks. Based on the electrical permit application, there was a completely separate set of electrical service for just one room, including phones, fiber-optic lines, high-voltage power, and satellite feeds of various types. The permit specified a high-tensile strength conduit throughout, creating a hardened bunker with completely separate power, ventilation, HVAC, communications, and physical strengthening, including steel-reinforced concrete walls, floors, and ceiling, high-voltage electronic magnetic door controls, IR, and full-color daylight video surveillance cameras. The military should be so well equipped!

Rather than try a frontal assault on this fortress, I had to find another way. We didn't have anything like the weaponry needed to penetrate such a space effectively without bringing down the whole building and the surrounding buildings as well, and I didn't feel like having to ask Dick to call in an air strike on a friendly nation. We needed something to draw him out of his protected compound and onto more neutral, open ground. Suddenly it occurred to me that the captain could be of further use to us after all.

I took a quick inventory of our resources, including weapons, ammo, and supplies left behind by our absent hosts. We were as well equipped as we would ever be for such a mission, thanks to Sam and her expert planning and some party favors courtesy of the Soviet government. Now it was time to let the captain in on the plan.

I stalked back down the hall to the cellblock and found the captain right where we'd left him. This time I brought Stacks in with me, in case my explanation of what we needed caused him to hold out hope for escape. The sight of the imposing figure of my right-hand muscle had quelled uprisings single-handedly in third world countries before, and I had no doubt it would be as effective here. We entered the cell and laid down the plan for him, emphasizing his role and how if it was performed well, things would go much better for him later.

"Okay, here's the deal. With or without your help, we located the house, got the plans, and it's not going to be possible to take him out of there with the resources we have, except you," I started.

"Now you want my help…?" he asked sarcastically.

"We don't want it so much as need it," I replied.

"What's in it for me if I help you?" he asked immediately, recovering some of his original police swagger.

"That depends. Regardless, it's better than a tangle with my friend here, and certainly better than a .22 in the brainpan, which has been entertained recently," I replied.

"A valid point, my new friend. What do you need me to do? Truth be told, I never really liked DeGroot, but he paid so much better than the real job and asked practically nothing of me, physically or morally, that I wouldn't do anyway—it seemed too good to pass up."

"Simple. We'd like you to do what you should have done yesterday—call in and report that all went well, Elena signed the papers, and you've taken a day to secure your retreat before coming out to his place to deliver the contracts."

"I see where you're going with this, I believe, and it won't work. He'll send someone to me to pick up the paperwork, rather than giving me directions to his mansion, especially after having gone to the trouble of keeping it a secret from me in the past."

"What would you expect his response be if you told him she refused to sign without meeting him face-to-face and that you had Elena with you?" I asked.

"That would certainly carry more weight, I would think," he replied thoughtfully. "He'd likely send a team to pick her up as well, but you could follow them there and see if he comes out to greet them when they arrive."

"Not good enough. I need you to be convincing, persuade him that she needs to meet him somewhere she feels safe in order to get the paperwork done, that if you try to kidnap or harm her in any way she'll make it impossible to get them signed," I replied.

"I'd remind you that DeGroot is a man used to getting his own way, one way or another, and is not afraid to take a direct approach to such problems. He's not likely to give in to a woman like Elena, just to get her signature that could easily be obtained under duress," he cautioned. "I have a suggestion you might want to consider," he continued. "I could just as easily tell him that she had been inadvertently injured in the fracas by one of his guards at the warehouse before she had a chance to sign without him present. Considering those guards, who have yet to report in, by the way, are just hired help, he should buy it. I can tell him I was unable to get her to sign in her unconscious state, and that the guard, feeling guilty, took her to a local hospital to be treated anonymously. You could set up the hospital, staff it with your own people, and when he comes to get the signatures in her hospital room, snatch him. He only has a couple of sources in the hospital. I could neutralize them for you, in exchange for safe passage off the island, say…"

I mulled this over for a long minute, then raised an eyebrow at Stacks, and tilted my head toward the door, and we adjourned to the hallway for a brief private conference.

"What do you think? Can we make it work?" I asked.

"You're the boss—it's up to you. I think he's gonna have to sell it awfully hard to get DeGroot to leave his hole for some signatures, but he won't likely risk a scene at a public hospital, if for no other reason than it gets him more attention than he wants locally," he replied reasonably.

"I think you're right. Anything you can think of that might sweeten the pot, make it more likely that he'll have to see this through personally?" I asked.

"I have one idea. What if we had the captain in there tell him that she had mentioned a big deal, one that there is no paperwork for yet, but one that means millions to Big G, was his big nut, his retirement order. Is that a big enough piece of bait to catch this fish?" he asked.

"From what I know if DeGroot, short of killing him outright, DeGroot would like nothing better than to take Big G's biggest order from him," I replied. "That just might be a big enough enticement to bring him out of hiding."

"Okay, let's go sell it to the captain, see if he can pull it off. I'll go get the gang working on hospital disguises, get the transportation squared away."

"Sounds good. Once I get the captain on board, I'd better get in touch with Elena, set it up from that end, see if we can get him some specifics before he makes his call," I replied.

We reentered the cell and, in a few moments, outlined our plan to the captain. He agreed that such a large order just might be enough, especially if the order was specific, but the client's identity wasn't. Since the guards were all dead and DeGroot had no real idea what had actually happened at the meeting at the warehouse, there wasn't much need for me to offer the captain safe passage off the island. I was pretty confident that the cause of his departure would no longer be an issue after today, and he could return to work as normal after the weekend with no fear of reprisal from DeGroot.

I did tell him I'd put in a good word for him with the local government for his cooperation, which was a huge fabrication—we weren't even here officially, and nobody in government even knew we existed, let alone working covertly in their country in cooperation with a police captain. It did seem to ease his mind, however, and would make him sell it to DeGroot a little more effectively.

His willing cooperation secured, I locked the cell door behind me and headed down the hall as I reached for my sat phone to call Elena, just as it started to ring. Dick had gotten my message and needed info as quick as I could give it. I told him we'd worked out our issues, explained about the police captain, and told him the plan. Needless to say, he was none too thrilled that we would be involving the hospital in our little scheme, but he seemed resigned if it would mean returning Big G to business as usual and detain DeGroot in the process. He cautioned me to keep as low a profile as possible locally to prevent any blowback that could spark an international incident, and hung up abruptly.

My team was busy getting organized for the next and hopefully final phase of this operation, when my sat phone vibrated. I pulled the device out, checked the screen, but didn't recognize the number. I answered anyway; it was Elena. She had gotten a new phone after losing the old one in the forest outside the warehouse and wanted me to have the number in case I needed to contact her. She had called the old one and left a forwarding message, but the battery was only good for a few days and she wanted to be sure I got the new number. She seemed pleased to speak with me live, having planned to leave a message, and after a few pleasantries, we got right down to business.

"Elena, I know it's a lot to ask, especially since we put you into and then successfully removed you from a dangerous situation once already, but I have a favor to ask."

"Please, I owe you my life, as will my father if you are successful at finding and releasing him. What can I do?"

"I need you to get some rest in a hospital for the next day or so," I replied enigmatically.

Chapter 28

Aboard the *Lady Elena*

Big G had been dialing Elena's cell phone number for the last two days, always getting shunted to voice mail, although he left no message. He needed to hear her voice live and to tell her he was all right. Meantime, he and Spiro had been putting their heads together to devise a plan that would draw DeGroot to the port on the south side of Aruba.

He knew that DeGroot was behind his abduction, and he knew why it had occurred. He knew that by escaping he had foiled that plan, but didn't know what DeGroot's next move might be, but he had an idea— just another reason he needed to speak with Elena. If he couldn't contain him, he might go after Elena to get to him and use her as leverage. He couldn't allow that to happen; he had to warn her, tell her to go to ground and hide. He'd called her house, her office, no answer, or no one knew where she could be found.

He told Spiro all of this, inherently trusting the new friend, following his well-honed instinct for people. He needed a fresh analytical perspective, someone outside to look at the situation and give some input that might lead to a viable idea. In truth, he had little to lose by trusting this fisherman who had no visible connection to the rest of his life or to DeGroot. The way his crew interacted with him and the air of extreme competence that radiated from him told Big G all he needed to know—this was a man to whom loyalty was second nature and who could be trusted implicitly as long as that loyalty was returned.

Spiro was sitting in the fantail of the yacht, taking in the fine surroundings of the luxury vessel, comparing it to his own humble work boat, obviously happiest when at sea. He related to Big G an idea that occurred to him that might draw DeGroot to the port, but it involved making contact with DeGroot's network on Aruba, not difficult, and relaying a message about a certain shipment being held in customs.

Big G warmed to the idea immediately, and filled in the details as they talked. If they could convince a known DeGroot associate that a very large and valuable shipment for one of Big G's customers, who would remain anonymous, had arrived at a temporary berth in the port of Barcadera on its way elsewhere. Big G knew that a container of advanced guidance hardware and software for the latest attack helicopter, Sikorsky's X2 Raider, would certainly do the trick, both for the high value in dollars and the secrecy and rarity of the order. The story would go that Big G had arranged for this container to be diverted from its original destination having left Sikorsky's Connecticut assembly plant for Brazil on a secret shakedown test program for the U.S. Army's AAS unit. The idea was to use the helicopter to stealthily penetrate the jungles of Southeast Asia, China, Korea, and other equatorial nations, and Brazil had offered a readily accessible jungle with some support already in place, in the form of a mineral and land development company with a helicopter hangar and maintenance facilities.

The shipment of guidance parts was destined for this support base, and Big G had gotten wind of it and "adjusted" some paperwork to divert the shipment to Aruba to be redirected to a private buyer. That exchange would take place on board the containership, where DeGroot would be locked below decks and the ship directed out to sea and scuttled with one of Big G's devices. If they provided a narrow-enough window of time for the ship to be in port, it would force DeGroot and a small group of paid mercenaries to take over the ship to off-load the container before it left for its new destination.

The story had enough truth to it, aside from Big G's involvement and the diversion, to hold his interest and pass cursory scrutiny. Big G was counting on DeGroot being greedy and desperate enough to forgo a lot of the typical due diligence and, in light of the short time frame, simply put a team together and take the ship—even if they were wrong, there's nothing wrong with having an extra containership available for their use, so the downside was minimal even if the intelligence turned out to be in error. The bait was juicy enough to bring him out personally to assure success, especially in light of his recent missteps though subordinates.

After some deliberation and an hour or so of research and hashing out of the details, the two men agreed on the plan and set a course for Aruba. The first mission was to infiltrate DeGroot's network and send the message about the ship to bait the hook.

Russian Base, Aruba

My team had done their usual exemplary job of pulling together their newest mission details. After raiding the base's infirmary for scrubs, uniforms, materials, and props needed to turn them into a crack mobile medical team. The scenario would be that Elena had been injured and was showing unusual symptoms that required the services of a specialty support team. I would call ahead to the hospital administrator at the main hospital in Oranjestadt and let him believe I was a prominent trauma surgeon and needed to treat a special patient on an emergency basis. I would need a private room to shield my patient's identity, an exam room fully stocked, and an operating theater reserved in case I needed it. I would bring my own support team, but would need areas of the hospital evacuated to insure my patient's security, for her own safety. That should reduce collateral damage.

The Russians had left a few vehicles when they abandoned the base in an underground garage, a few military staff cars, a small reconnaissance plane, and an ambulance, on the off chance they needed to transport a soldier to the local island hospital. Stacks got the ambulance going, and we loaded up the other two SUVs with gear and my team and headed to the Dr.

Horacio Oduber Hospital to set up the highly secure private patient. Elena had agreed to meet us at the resort across the street so we could prep her and load her into the ambulance in private.

We pulled into the resort driveway after an hour on the road and saw Elena standing there under the portico. I got out of the back of the ambulance, and she ran into my arms. I was so shocked I didn't know how to react for a few seconds, and then understood how much the stress of her father's abduction and her own ordeals in assisting us had taken their toll. She was a wreck inside and had been covering effectively since we got her out of the warehouse. She'd had time to reflect and to notch up her anxiety while in the safe house, worrying about her father. She'd not slept more than a few hours over the last two days and had dark circles under her eyes; her skin, no longer radiantly glowing, was now pale and drawn, and her hair roughly combed and lackluster. I held her for a long moment and then gently pulled away to look at her more closely. She looked up into my eyes, saw the concern there, and looked away shyly—a remarkable change from the brash, confident woman who had stalked onto the deck of her father's yacht two weeks ago. All this worked in our favor and would help sell the deception of a wounded, nearly disabled patient in a hospital when DeGroot first set eyes on her after years of absence from her life.

We got her into the back of the ambulance, dressed in a borrowed hospital gown, and onto the wheeled gurney. We fired up the old ambulance, lights and sirens blasting, and pulled out of the resort and across the street to the ER entrance of the hospital. BJ hustled her out of the ambulance and exploded through the double doors into the ER, brushing aside administrative nurses and headed for the back of the ward, where the head administrator was waiting. A physician himself, he took it upon himself to attempt to examine Elena, but one look at her haggard face and pallid complexion convinced him there was a genuine need for their facilities. I took him aside, explained that the patient was the daughter of an unusually rich and powerful diplomat, and needed both privacy and security, as we'd spoken of on the phone. He agreed readily and directed us to the elevator. We wheeled her into the elevator and up to the third floor, which had been cleared of other patients, and directly to a large room at the end of the hall. I left the imposing Stacks and BJ in the elevator lobby to act as security detail, and Sam and I wheeled her into the room and got her situated in a bed. We hooked up a couple of realistic-looking IVs, without really piercing her skin, and gave her some privacy.

We'd dressed Captain Johnson as an orderly and had him call DeGroot and report in. He'd told the story that Elena had gotten knocked unconscious in the fracas and that the other guards were dead as a result of an ambush by attackers unknown sent to protect Elena. He had managed to escape unscathed and get to a remote, safe location to hide from the protection detail, but that they had taken Elena to the hospital for treatment. If he wanted to get the paperwork signed and learn about a rather large shipment of very profitable weapons equipment that Elena had mentioned under questioning at the warehouse, he had better get himself down to the hospital and speak with her.

DeGroot had been by turns relieved that Johnson had escaped, angry that the mission had been a failure, and excited about the prospect of an even bigger prize to be had. Johnson could hear him breathing heavily as he paced his office, his bulk moving about the room with surprising agility in his excited state. DeGroot had agreed to meet Elena at the hospital in two hours to get the transfer papers signed and hear about this mysterious shipment. The plan looked like it would work, but much could still go wrong despite all their planning. Now, settled in the hospital room, we only had to wait for DeGroot.

We were chatting quietly, going through the motions of an exam in case a curious staffer should stick his or her head in the room despite signage not to, when Elena's cell phone tinkled. Every eye turned toward the bed as we waited to see who might be calling at this critical point.

Chapter 29

Aboard the *Lady Elena*

Big G had tried Elena's cell phone number for what seemed like the twentieth time.

The ship had been cruising at full speed, about twenty-five knots, heading through the straits of Tangier and out into the open south Atlantic toward Aruba for four days. He had retasked the containership closest to Aruba to the port of Barcadera and told the captain to wait for further instructions after docking. He was to tell the dock master that they were experiencing engine trouble and needed to be towed in to port to effect repairs. The fix would only take a couple of days depending on the availability of parts and that the crew and the cargo would not be coming ashore at all, so there would be no need for a customs, agriculture, or immigration inspection. Beyond that, the captain was instructed to say nothing to anyone, to lock down the ship, and evacuate all but a skeleton crew to elsewhere on the island before making the docking radio call.

He dialed again, and when he heard it go to voice mail after two rings, he almost hung up, but the message sounded different this time, so he listened. When he heard her voice imparting a new number where she could be contacted, the smile on his face spread from ear to ear, half joy mixed with relief, mixed with hope that he could finally get in touch with her and explain what had happened. He jotted down the number and immediately dialed. She picked up on the third ring.

DeGroot Mansion, Aruba

DeGroot had been waiting for the phone to ring, but when a call came from Johnson with the tale of failure and promised redemption, he wasn't sure what to think. His anger with Johnson for not completing his mission was tempered by his interest in his tale of an even greater reward for simply talking to his nemesis's daughter, who posed no threat whatsoever from a hospital bed. Could this be any easier? The only fly in the ointment was that she had insisted that he personally appear to be told directly about the new shipment. At this phase of his plan, he didn't want to venture out of his stronghold for any reason, but the promise of such easy riches was just too much for him to resist. If this order was as good as he suspected it might be, and based on Johnson's description, it had to be that big, final, retirement-sized order. Taking that away would be the end of Big G, free or not, put the final nail in the coffin of his business, while enriching DeGroot's own fortunes to a degree unimagined previously.

While normally a careful, calculating, cautious person by nature, his own greed at the prospect of such riches ready for the taking overwhelmed his natural caution, obfuscating the possibility that this might be "too easy" and was indeed a trap. After hanging up the phone with Johnson, his mind was racing, making plans to quickly gather an escort team of three and transport the group to the hospital in as inconspicuous fashion as possible. He would have to eliminate Johnson as a loose end at some point soon, if for no other reason than he knew some of the details of the last thirty-six hours and about the big order Elena had hinted at, and DeGroot couldn't afford any loose ends at this stage of the game.

After a few phone calls, the arrangements were made, and DeGroot, with an hour to spend before leaving, decided to treat himself in celebration of the upcoming success with a full gourmet meal. He called his chef and gave him explicit instructions to craft a few of his favorite dishes.

Chapter 30

Hospital, Aruba

Everyone stood still in the private room, and all eyes turned to the phone ringing in Elena's small purse. I looked at Elena, question marks all over my face. She looked just as surprised as the rest of us, mixed with a hint of trepidation at answering for fear of what she would hear at the other end. By the third ring, she had broken out of her paralysis and answered.

"Hello?"

"Elena, my sweet child, is that you?".

"Pappa?" she whispered. "Is it really you? Are you all right? My God what you must have been through, are you okay? Where are you?" she gushed, questions flying in disbelief.

"Yes, my dear Elena, it's me. I'm all right, still a little weak of body, but strong of spirit."

"Pappa, where are you? Are you free?"

"Yes, I managed to escape from those lazy buffoons DeGroot hired to kidnap and hold me," he replied wryly. "I've been trying to get a hold of you for several days, but your phone was turned off and your colleagues didn't know where you were or how to contact you."

"I'm so sorry, Pappa. I lost my phone and had to replace it with a new one and a new number, which you obviously found on my message. Oh, Pappa, where are you? Can I come get you? Do you need help?" she sobbed.

"Elena, please, I missed you terribly, but right now we have work to do. I'm fine, I'm on the *Lady Elena*, on my way to Aruba, nearly there in fact. Where are you?"

"Aruba, Pappa, how strange, that where I am, in a hospital on Aruba!" she exclaimed. "Why are you coming here?" she asked excitedly.

"Are you alone?" he asked.

"No, Pappa, there are a team of men here who have been looking for you, trying to free you."

"Who sent them? Who are they, and why are they involved?" he asked sharply.

"Oh, Pappa, they are very good men—the consulate sent them when they discovered you'd been kidnapped," she replied.

"Did you check them out? Do they know who kidnapped me? Have they found out who it was?" he asked.

"Of course, Pappa, your own people looked into them immediately after they arrived at the yacht after you were taken," she replied. "They have an excellent reputation, and from what I've seen, it's well deserved. They know who took you and are enacting a plan at the moment to draw him here and capture him to discover where he was keeping you."

"Who do they work for? Can I speak to the leader?" he asked, snapping back to business mode almost imperceptibly.

"Yes, you can speak with him. He's right here—his name is Stark," she replied, put it on "speaker" and handed the phone to me.

"Stark here, Big G, is that you?" I asked incredulously. "We've been searching for you for two weeks. Are you healthy and able to function?"

"Mr. Stark, who sent you to find me?" he replied a bit cagily, not fully answering the question.

"When you were kidnapped, my employers were contacted through the American embassy in Greece with an official request for assistance," I replied, parroting the official story.

"So you are all Americans?" he asked.

"Yes, I have a team of five, plus an entire government full of resources to call upon if necessary," I replied.

"Are they all there in the hospital with my daughter?" he asked.

"Four of us are here—a fifth is in the United States coordinating intelligence gathering and communication activities with other agencies around the world to coordinate your rescue," I replied.

"First off, I want to thank you for taking care of my daughter and for your efforts on my behalf. I'm certain they have been aggressive and extensive, and any misadventure you encountered on my behalf make me forever in your debt. Second, I have a plan of my own to capture my kidnapper. Yes, I surmised that it was DeGroot behind this. He's been trying to destroy me for years after I severed our relationship over some less than savory business practices."

"Thanks are not necessary, but I appreciate them nonetheless," I replied humbly. "Now, tell me about your plan, and I will tell you about ours, and we will see if we can box this character and get rid of him in some permanent way."

"My plan is simple and is already in play. I will send an emissary unknown in the underworld to seek out some of DeGroot's associates on the island's docks. He will masquerade as a drunken merchant marine who knows about a huge shipment of goods that is coming into port on forged papers. Word will filter back to DeGroot in short order, as he makes it his business to know of any and all contraband moving into and out of his territory," he explained.

"Once he knows of the shipment and the details of its berthing and schedule, he will surely assemble a small team and come to confiscate the ship. There is indeed a containership over which I have control docking in Aruba tomorrow morning. My compatriots and I will be aboard that ship shortly after it docks, lying in wait for DeGroot. When he comes aboard, we will subdue his team and imprison him below decks. At that point, I can dispose of him as I see fit," he continued. "I am currently three to four hours sailing time from Barcadera port and will rendezvous with the containership just over the horizon before it docks, staying below so that the harbor pilot has no clue as to my existence," he added. "Does this mesh with your strategy?"

"Wow, that's pretty ambitious for an arms dealer," I replied, a bit surprised. "But I must say, it meshes with our plan almost precisely. The phrase 'great minds think alike' comes to mind immediately. We intend to draw DeGroot to the hospital to have Elena provide him with essentially the same information on a shipment, but now we can add to the legend the portion about the high-tech helicopter parts that you 'diverted' before you were snatched, of huge value, big enough for you to retire once transacted. We needed something big enough to get him to leave his stronghold and personally retrieve the information, and now we have it. Rather than take him down here in a public hospital, we would simply shadow him, and when he heads for the docks, my team will take him down there. If you have a ship there already we can use, that simplifies things and keeps the action away from innocent bystanders," I explained. "How many of you are there onboard and, probably stupid questions but I have to ask, are you adequately armed to take on DeGroot's thugs?"

"I have a team of six, all competent and trustworthy, loyal to their leader, and he to me. We are indeed adequately armed for the task of effectively dealing with DeGroot and his minions. Is he still working with Akbar?" he asked.

"No, in our efforts to secure your location, Akbar has been eliminated with extreme prejudice," I replied.

"Then it will be an even easier day for all of us. He was the only serious threat in DeGroot's sphere, a truly dangerous character, not to be underestimated. You are to be congratulated, my friend, for eliminating him. Did you lose any men in the process?" he asked.

"One slightly wounded, but other than that, it was not difficult," I replied.

"You have my respect for that, and for taking care of your men as well," he intoned.

"I appreciate that, and reply in kind, after hearing of your escape from a difficult, dangerous situation," I offered. "Your reputation for resourcefulness is obviously well deserved. What do you plan to do with DeGroot once he's imprisoned on the ship?"

"I will deal with him summarily and in commensurate fashion with the grief he has caused me throughout my life," he replied firmly.

"I appreciate that. It appears that our plans work together and will dovetail at the docks. Would you like our assistance in that regard? I suggest my team come from behind DeGroot's mob and we can catch them in a cross fire as they attempt to board your containership. There should be good lines of fire at that point and little access for civilians, thus reducing collateral damage," I offered.

"Seems prudent, I will gladly accept your offer. How will I distinguish your operatives from DeGroot's?" he asked.

"Mine will be the professionals," I quipped. Big G laughed on the other end of the line, a strong appreciative sound that told me he would be an interesting character to meet at a social function.

"I understand, but such characteristics, while easily discerned by you and me, may be more difficult for my men to spot, especially when under fire," he deadpanned.

"My team will have on black paratrooper uniforms and military-grade body armor, although not as bulky as you might be used to seeing," I replied seriously.

"Ah, the new Carbon-Kevlar 'skinny suits'—I've heard of them but not seen any close-up yet. They have not been released for nonmilitary use. How did you get them?" he asked incredulously.

"I have my sources," I replied slyly.

"Perhaps when this is over, we can get together under more pleasant circumstances and discuss business," he replied.

"I'd like that a great deal," I said and meant it.

"Our plans are complete, then. The name of the containership is the *Orion*, and it will dock at Pier 12 at Barcadera at 5:15 a.m. tomorrow morning. I will be on it, along with my friends, and we will handle DeGroot with dispatch when he arrives. My emissary will include those details and the added detail of the helicopter parts in his tale in the dock's drinking establishments this evening, to verify what he hears from Elena this afternoon. Is there any way to remove her from the equation, keep her from harm?" he asked, sounding more like a father than a soldier.

"I promise no harm will come to her, but my guess is no matter how greedy DeGroot is, Elena is the only one that will be able to overcome his deeply ingrained cautiousness in order to act directly on the information. If an outsider told him, he'd take the time to verify it through his own sources, and there isn't time," I explained. "We will make her safety and well-being the top priority. You have my word as a gentleman and a soldier."

"Very well, we shall meet tomorrow morning. Until then, good luck, my new friend. Please put Elena back on the phone," he asked.

I handed the phone back to Elena, nodded my head toward the door out of the room, and Sam and I headed out to give her some privacy. We walked down the hall to brief BJ and Stacks on the new development, while I got a hold of Tang on the sat phone to let him know that our mission had changed but was almost complete. Once I explained the situation, I told Stacks and BJ after DeGroot was gone, to go back to the vehicles and get geared up to support Big G on the docks in the morning. Sam and I would follow along if needed, and we'd stay and take care of Elena now and bring her with us when we met Big G at the docks. Since the object was not to take DeGroot here, keeping the personnel to a minimum would help allay his fears and let him lower his guard, while preserving our cover identities. Once DeGroot was in the room, we'd try to make ourselves as nondescript as possible, but be within earshot in case he got rough with her. Based on what we'd learned of DeGroot, he himself wouldn't be much of a match in a physical confrontation; he paid people to do that for him. I was confident Sam and I could handle him if need be.

I headed back up the hallway to her room to find her sitting up in bed, tears in her eyes, but a smile on her face, relieved that her father was alive and well. When I walked in, she hopped off the bed and rushed over to me and hugged me hard, pressing her body against mine. This time I wasn't taken off guard and responded by hugging back, then pulled back slightly, and kissed her, softly at first, and then more urgently. She handled it with an equally urgent passionate response, and we kissed for a long moment before coming to our senses and remembering where we were. She pulled away, turned away shyly, and headed back to lie down on the hospital bed to wait for DeGroot to arrive.

We didn't have long to wait. After half an hour of small talk, my earpiece crackled, and BJ sang out that a Rolls Royce had pulled up in the front entrance portico and a huge man in a white suit and Panama hat had been assisted out of the back seat by the driver. At the pace he was moving, we had about five minutes before he walked in the door.

"BJ, how many guys has he got with him, and what do they look like?" I asked.

"Looks like just three, pretty unimpressive, locals likely," he replied.

"Four on three, I like those odds a lot. DeGroot himself isn't a factor," I shot back.

"Not even close," he replied. "This'll be a walk in the park, even if things get ugly in there," he added.

"Sit tight—let me know when he's past you," I replied.

We got Elena comfortable in the bed, made sure the IVs looked good, and checked Elena's appearance. She still showed the effects of the stress she'd endured over the last two weeks and looked like any other patient I'd ever seen; she should be pretty convincing.

My earpiece crackled again, and BJ whispered, "He's here."

We looked up, and DeGroot's bodyguard came through the open door and immediately sidestepped left and positioned himself just inside the doorway, leaning against the adjacent wall, relaxed but alert. DeGroot came through the doorway, turning slightly sideways to assure that his bulk would pass the door frame, his eyes fixed on Elena. He walked right up to the side of the bed without any hesitation and, in a surprisingly gentle movement, took her hand in his and held it. From the brief reaction that flashed across her face, it was all Elena could do not to pull her hand away in disgust.

"Little Elena, you've grown up since I last saw you," he intoned, his voice low and wheezy from the added strain on his heart and lungs from the trip down the hall.

"We've all changed in the last ten years, DeGroot," she replied icily.

"Please, accept my apologies. I had no desire to harm you, simply to transact business. My quarrel is with your father, not you. You were simply a means to an end," he oozed.

"Your men were a bit more aggressive than I expected for a simple business transaction, and my injuries are the result of that poor decision, one of many by the sound of things," she shot back, her venom showing for the first time.

"I regret their actions, as I said. I only hope your recovery is swift and complete," he replied. "Clearly, you need your rest, so I won't stay long. Shall we get directly down to business?"

"I have the documents you asked for. Once I sign them, you will release my father as promised?"

"Certainly, on one additional condition. You must tell me about the new, large shipment you discovered in your search of your father's papers," he breathed.

She played it perfectly.

"What shipment would that be?" she asked innocently.

"Please, let's be adults here and not play games with each other," he replied. "I spoke with Captain Johnson briefly before coming here. I know about the retirement shipment Big G set up, just not the docking and content details. A few simple pieces of information, and you will be reunited with your beloved father."

Her face crumpled in resignation, and she appeared to consider for a moment before speaking, this time with none of the previous fury.

"You're right. I simply want him back safe—he can always make more money. His life has no price. I will tell you what I know about the shipment," she said.

"Please, continue, you have my full attention," he replied softly.

"The shipment will be in the local port tomorrow morning. There is a container marked 'Machine Parts' loaded on the deck of a containership, which contains ten sets of guidance hardware and software for the new attack helicopter, the Sikorsky X2 Raider. The ship is called the *Orion*. It will dock at pier 12 after five thirty in the morning, ostensibly for repairs. They off-loaded the crew earlier, so there will only be a few engineers on board to care for the engines. That's all I know," she finished.

DeGroot sat quietly for a few moments, digesting this fantastic information. This was more than he could have imagined, worth millions on the black market. The advantage this technology provided the nation who owned it would change the face of warfare for a long time to come. The sky was virtually the limit on what certain US-hating nations would pay for this technology. With this technology at his disposal, Big G was a small speck on the horizon for DeGroot, of only minor concern.

He stood slowly, surveyed the room quickly, seemingly registering Sam's and my presence for the first time, and just as quickly dismissing them.

He turned back to Elena, released her hand, nodded politely, and said, "I shall make arrangements for your father's safe release. I will contact you with the details, once he is no longer a factor. We shall not meet face to face again. I plan to disappear once I have commandeered and sold this shipment, off the radar for the remainder of my life, to live quietly in a pleasant but remote spot, content to enjoy less rigorous pursuits and enjoy the balance of my life. I bid you adieu," he said and turned on his heel as best he could considering his size, and strode out the door, proceeded by the last bodyguard and followed by the initial one, as they ambled down the hall, past BJ and Stacks, and out of sight.

I looked at Elena and watched her burst into tears, her control clearly gone. What a masterful performance. She knew her father was already safe, but had made a deal for his release, knowing DeGroot was lying through his teeth. Now she shed tears of relief and stress, but appeared to gain strength after a few moments, some color returning to her face.

"I'm glad that slime is gone. Just picturing him on a beach enjoying what he thinks is my father's money was about to make me throw up on the floor!" she shrieked, grinning with victory.

"Now, let's go get this son of a bitch and make him disappear," she said ruefully, her passion and fire returning more steadily.

She sat up on the edge of the bed and asked that I step outside while she got dressed. I complied with a grin and headed out the door in time to see BJ and Stacks lumbering toward the elevator bay and off to prepare for tomorrow. They would take the ambulance and one of the SUVs, leaving the other for us across the street.

In a few moments, Elena and Sam emerged from the room. Elena looked much better, the stress drained from her face, her color high, an attractive dress and heels restoring her air of control, even a blush of make-up. I gave Sam a questioning look, and she just shrugged and looked admiringly at Elena as we headed down the hall.

Chapter 31

Mansion outside Oranjestadt, Aruba

DeGroot emerged from the back of the Rolls when its forward motion smoothly ceased in the circular drive, outside the front door of the mansion, his driver offering assistance to help heave his bulk out the huge doorway and into the house. He was clearly upbeat, chatting with the staff on his way to his office upstairs, even whistling a tuneless ditty as he climbed the stairs and entered his private sanctuary. He was elated to not only have the whole of Big G's business portfolio, but to have the knowledge that he could snatch the man's retirement right out from under him was supremely satisfying.

He called Johnson and gave him his walking papers, saying he had until the end of the month to find a replacement and vacate the position of police chief. He was officially retired, he told the career cop. Then he called one of his most loyal and capable lieutenants, an ex-Israeli Military captain and outlined the next mission to liberate the helicopter parts from the ship docking in the morning. DeGroot was no fool; he told his men to come heavily armed and well prepared for heavy resistance, including potential air support. He knew Big G had probably made provisions to protect a shipment of such value, but he didn't know the extent or magnitude of that protection. He had stayed alive by being properly prepared for all contingencies.

The two of them huddled over a computer terminal with a map of the pier and surrounding area and planned their approach to the pending ship hijacking. Also online were plans of the ship in question, the *Orion*, including deck layouts, armaments, hold arrangements, electrical layout, and schematics for other systems. The *Orion* didn't appear at first glance to be the pride of the fleet. Built in Norfolk, VA, in 1973, the containership had seen some hard miles in the last thirty-five-plus years, carrying cargo all over the world, from China to Dubai, to Singapore, to New York, to Iceland, and back. Under Libyan registry but owned ostensibly by a company in the Nederlands, it was one of the largest available, nearly four football fields long, almost 1,200 feet, and over 160 feet abeam, displaced 160,000 tons and was capable of cruising at nearly twenty-two knots. It was capable of carrying thirteen thousand standard containers and carried a crew of twelve, although there were accommodations for more.

What the plans didn't show and what DeGroot's research didn't show was that once Big G had purchased the ship, through a holding company and several intermediaries, he had refitted the ship to add a few extras. There was additional plating to armor the sides and external bulkheads of the superstructure, and the engines had been upgraded to provide additional speed and efficiency in response to the need to evade Somali pirates. The *Orion* could give as well as it received, as a 10mm Gatling gun, complete with protective shroud had been added, just aft of the three-story superstructure, along with a fifty-caliber machine gun mounted forward. On board in the storage lockers were modern weapons, including twelve-gauge Mossburg pump shotguns, American M-16 and AR-15 automatic assault rifles, and in the security lockers could be found shaped satchel charges, timers, detonators, and three MK-32 handheld rocket launchers, capable of piercing light armor, destroying tanks, and sinking the small Somali attack boats in less than thirty seconds. To the casual observer, with the exterior weapons dismounted, the ship looked no different than hundreds of other smaller containerships that plied their trade on a daily basis the world over. But after four attempted pirate attacks in the last two years, there was no one left alive to tell the tale of its modifications.

Of course, the most special feature on this particular ship was the powerful explosive device buried deep in its hull cargo hold. The device, a fuel-air bomb of significant proportion and powerful enough to virtually vaporize this mighty containership and its contents, lay hidden in a rusty half-sized container amidships on the lower level. One phone call from Big G would signal the detonator and ignite the primer, exploding the device in a tenth of a second, creating an instant hole in the ocean half a mile across.

DeGroot specified a team of five men, surely adequate to keep the ship's captain and a few deck hands under control, and help man the loading crane to off-load the prized container full of Raider parts. He arranged for a container-equipped flatbed truck to arrive shortly before the rest of the team and be left next to the dock, keys in the ignition. He arranged for a two SUVs to transport him and his team and their gear to the docks in the morning, sent his team leader to select and brief the rest of the mercenaries on the plan they had devised, and ordered dinner from the kitchen. DeGroot finished his meal two hours later, sat back in his favorite chair, enjoyed a rare cigar and a glass of port, and went to bed, falling asleep almost immediately, secure in the knowledge that his future was assured.

Barcadera, Pier 12

BJ and Stacks kept the pedal to the metal all the way back across the island to the Russian base. They wanted maximum time to prepare for the next day's mission and still get in some sleep before their predawn departure time. The plan was for them to collect their weapons and gear, including Carbon-Kevlar "skinny suits" with ceramic inserts battle tested in Afghanistan, and get an early start, to be back at the dock to meet the incoming containership when it docked at approximately 5:30 a.m.

Having participated in Akbar's abduction and seen the level of training, discipline, and firepower that DeGroot's teams brought with them, the two professionals knew what they were up against, and had no illusions about the difficulty level and danger that they faced the following morning. As experienced soldiers, they knew that the best remedy for bad odds was good preparation, so they planned their incursion with great care. They prepped and cleaned their weapons, loading them with anonymous commercially available rounds using gloves, to limit the back trail to them by the authorities after the fact. The one weapon they couldn't disguise well was the Russian RPG launcher they found in the weapons store. The pair had both seen these used in battle firsthand and knew how effective they could be in the right hands. Both had been trained on a wide variety of weapons and tactics over the years, and at this point, they had been working together for long enough that they could practically complete each other's sentences. They spoke in a reference-laden shorthand, reminding each other of past actions, what had worked well and what had not, as they sketched out a plan to defend the containership and take DeGroot alive, only to get him on to the ship's hold.

By 10:00 p.m. they had a solid plan put together, had communicated their plan to Big G aboard the *Lady Elena*, had their gear prepped and stowed, and hit the sack for some sleep, setting alarms for 3:00 a.m.

By 3:30 a.m. they had double-checked the base, removing any trace of their presence, secured the outer doors, and got the loaded SUV down the road on the way to the dock. The air was surprisingly fresh, the humidity low, and the air filled with the typical smells of the island desert, filled with the warm bite of creosote bush and salt. They arrived at four thirty, found an older, shabby-looking warehouse building not far away, and ditched the truck after unloading all the gear and packing it in their packs for easy transport. They headed for the dock at Pier 12 on foot, under cover of darkness, found the places they had seen on the recon photos, and got set up for the impending arrival of DeGroot and his men.

They assembled their weapons, double-checked lines of fire, glassed the area for signs of not only their own presence left behind, footprints and other evidence, but also signs of any previous visits by DeGroot's team recently. They saw no traces of DeGroot's team, and they had covered their own tracks well as a matter of course, according to their training and experience. Now, plan firmly in mind, they sat down to wait.

Chapter 32

Aboard the Orion

The captain of the *Orion*, Hamish Sinclair, was an experienced commander, former British Navy commander who had retired in the 90s at sixty, but grown restless and joined the Merchant Marine several years ago so he could return to the sea full-time. He'd seen action both in the Falklands and as part of a British detachment aboard an American naval destroyer in Desert Storm and Shield I and II. An experienced sailor and battle tactician, he alone knew what resided in his cargo hold. Big G had met him in a tavern in Amsterdam years ago during his naval service and had kept in touch over the years. When the holding company that owned the containership was seeking a new captain to replace the retiring commander, Big G recommended Sinclair for the job. Now, Sinclair figured it was time to return the favor and was as diligent as ever in boarding the harbor pilot, getting him situated, and reviewing his paperwork swiftly, all in order as required.

He had briefed his small crew the night before they arrived in the Aruban port, and they had a rough idea of what to expect. All weapons systems, engines, and other gear had been carefully checked and were ready to do battle. The crew at first had difficulty adjusting their actions under the captain's direction, because the orders were so foreign to what they were used to doing. Even hardened battleship crews had a specific prebattle mindset, one that prepared them for the endless waiting and sudden engagement of sea battle. In this particular case, the crew was very experienced, but the plan was different from anything they had encountered. Ship crews think in terms of direction, speed, maneuvers, target locations, and firing solutions. This plan was more like a defensive siege of a castle, as the ship would be docked and anchored during the mission. They had to think in terms of repelling boarders, defending the ship's gunnels from incoming invaders, and targeting the enemy one at a time from hidden locations, just as merchant ships in the sixteenth century had. After a few minutes of discussion the night before, they had warmed to the idea and were even enthusiastic about this new challenge.

Now, all his men were in position for Phase One of the operation, appearing that all was normal, but that repairs were needed. The ship's engineer had gummed up a cylinder and detached a steering mechanism, making the ship difficult to maneuver and slow, so that the harbor pilot had to concentrate heavily on his work to get the giant ship snugged up against the huge Pier 12.

After a seemingly interminable fifteen-minute ordeal, the harbor pilot finally called full stop into the interphone and disengaged the electronic controls on the bridge, and the deck hands cast the large lines to the fore and aft cleats, securing the ship to the dock. He headed down the gangway off the ship and walked down to the harbormaster's shack several blocks inland from Pier 12 and disappeared into the building.

What the harbor pilot had not seen while on board the *Orion* was the group of odd-looking mercenaries Big G and Spiro had assembled, as they were tucked into a container below decks for the short duration of his stay. The *Lady Elena* had rendezvoused with the *Orion* the night before, at a predetermined location fifty miles off shore, and Big G, Spiro, and his crew of eight men had boarded in two trips in a small inflatable boat between the two ships. Even Big G had been impressed when he saw the huge containership. In reality, Big G owned the Dutch holding company that technically owned the huge ship, as it did all the others in his "retribution fleet," but he had not been aboard the ship itself since its purchase. He had left Sinclair on his own to retrofit the new modifications into the craft, trusting his friend to know his business. The *Orion* dwarfed the smaller yacht when pulled alongside at a distance of two hundred feet, the rust-streaked bulkheads looming over the sparkling white craft like canyon walls. Even in the dark, the containership's presence was clearly felt by all aboard the *Lady Elena*, as its displacement quelled the small swells in the water between the ships, calming the waters to a glassy smooth lake.

Sinclair had insisted for safety that most of the ship's crew be off-loaded and kept out of harm's way, so once Big G and his team were aboard the *Orion*, the already sparse crew of twenty was off-loaded and ferried across to the *Lady Elena*, where they made themselves comfortable below decks out of sight. Only the toughest, battle-hardened crew of eight volunteers stayed back to help in the operation. The *Orion* had been rigged specifically to be operated by a small crew in emergency situations, and the remaining eight would plan their activities to make it look to the harbor pilot like there were more of them than there actually were, giving the appearance of normal operation aboard. Each of the eight were trained on the ship's modified armaments and were experienced ex-military veterans, calm, competent, dependable, and ready for action after long slack times at sea.

Once aboard, and after a brief tour where Sinclair proudly showed his owner and friend his modifications, Big G and Spiro gathered their team, briefed them on their mission, and gave them identifying information about Stark's team to prevent any accidental injury to their allies. They seemed impressed by the credentials attached to Stark's team members, the captain even commenting positively on their past military service, especially Stacks and BJ, who had been in the thick of things in the Falkland's as well. Once briefed, the team retired below to the now abandoned crew quarters.

The plan was this: With Stark's initial advance team positioned in the buildings a block back from the waterfront, DeGroot's group would enter and park close to the pier, anticipating that they would be off-loading the container onto the truck using the ship's crane. With nothing but open water facing the starboard side of the ship, it didn't offer an attack angle and was ignored. Some of DeGroot's team would be forced to make a direct frontal assault, either up the gangplank or over the gunwales pirate-style, climbing access ropes thrown from the docks over the gunwale rails. The balance would fire from ground positions on the pier to try to remove any crew members who showed themselves on deck and disable the communications antennae at the top of the superstructure to prevent mayday calls from being issued. These had been relocated below decks and dummy units placed in their place for effect. Once DeGroot's teams committed themselves, Stark's team would swing in behind them and trap them between the ship and their weapons, making the giant hull the backdrop in a giant shooting gallery and catching them in crossfire between Stark's team and Big G's team aboard the ship. At this point, the plan was for Big G and his team to drop over the side and disarm DeGroot's team, while Big G and Stacks grabbed DeGroot and marched him onboard the *Orion* to the holding cell below. The balance of the plan Big G had elected to keep to himself, and once they were assured that Big G would be left intact after the action, Stacks and BJ had relented, allowing him to keep his own counsel on the fate of DeGroot.

Now all the team below decks had to do was wait for their cue from the captain on the bridge.

Safe house, Aruba

Knowing that the assault team was well briefed and better prepared and that they would be receiving help from Big G and his team, I felt confident enough to concentrate on my job, which was to secure Elena in our safe house Dick had found us here on Aruba. Sam and I got her into the SUV after leaving the hospital, having "healed" her miraculously for the hospital staff, removing her IVs and bandages, removing the make-up and getting her dressed more appropriately for the coming day. She would not participate directly in the action, but would wait at the safe house for her father, whom we would deliver once DeGroot was secure. She was still a little shaken after her encounter with DeGroot, but was regaining strength and courage by the minute. She was more than eloquent in her praise and generous in her appreciation of our efforts in all of this and seemed to be more focused on me and my future than appropriate at the time. She had combed out her hair, and Sam had helped her get dressed and applied some make-up, and by the time we reached the safe house, she had regained a lot of that inner glow she had shown me previously, her smoky green eyes radiating intensity as she focused on me.

We went inside, and just as the three of us got settled in the small living room, my sat phone chirped, the display indicating a blocked number with a Virginia area code. I answered as I walked out into the kitchen. It was Tang from Langley. One of the researchers in Crypto section had figured out the codes in the ledger book I had taken from the *Lady Elena*. It had taken longer than expected because the book pages had gotten dropped off by a new courier who was unfamiliar with the office mail delivery scheme at CIA and had put them in the wrong inbox, that belonging to another researcher who was on vacation. The package had surfaced upon his return, and after just a few moments, they had backtracked the first few numbers, entered them into a tracking program to triangulate their signal source location, and discovered the same thing Elena had from the airline pilot—that they were cell phone numbers located on board ships centered in various ports around the world.

The research staff at Langley had taken that knowledge a step further than Elena had and overlaid the locations on a list of known weapons shipments, but none of them matched. The only pattern that emerged was that the numbers were all originated within a few days of each other and that there had been very regular call activity into each of the numbers at regular, patterned intervals. The break came when one of the older researchers, recently moved over from the terrorist desk, recognized this type of behavior from analyzing Al Qaida terrorist cell phone records. He'd seen this type of activity when the terrorists had promised bombing activity more than two weeks into the future, when they had to call remotely triggered explosive devices to reset timers and check battery charge in the detonator.

This information gave me pause, but I could start to see pieces of the puzzle coming together. Big G had set up a defensive perimeter with these ships and had installed some sort of device on each to not only keep track of them, but to be able to reach out to each and trigger the device remotely anywhere in the world. I had to admire the planning, logic, and vision behind such a plan. He could broadcast force and direct resources anywhere in the world with just a few days' notice, and if the device was an explosive, detonate it remotely, providing both safety and an alibi for Big G. Suddenly it clicked that one of these devices was likely aboard the *Orion* and that Big G planned to kill DeGroot in spectacular fashion by loading him aboard the containership and vaporizing it from afar.

I went back in the living room, and I guess Elena could read the change in my face.

"What's wrong, Stark?"

"Elena, did you know about your father's business activities?"

"Of course, he is a broker for international trade," she replied, giving the stock answer.

"No, I mean his *real* business," I replied.

She blanched a bit and admitted, "Yes, I know what he does and who he does it with," she said quietly.

"Did you know about the ships?"

"Ships? He ships most of his orders one way or another," she answered.

"No, I mean the armada of explosive ships he has arrayed around the globe," I shot back.

"I didn't know about them specifically, but since this kidnapping happened, I've come across bits of information about a series of port locations that are linked together by cell phone," she volunteered.

"Did you have any idea what they might have meant?" I asked incredulously.

"No, but I had my suspicions based on the data I found." She explained about the book codes and about the helpful Olympic pilot who plotted a few of the points, but aside from a few of the locations being close to port cities, she said she didn't discern a pattern to the locations and thought she'd ask her father about it once they found and rescued him.

I sat her down and explained what I had deduced from the data Langley had generated, and her eyes grew wide and her jaw opened wide, clearly surprised by the information.

I told her about the plan to vaporize DeGroot, and her jaw set and her frown rose into a sneer, and she found her voice again.

"Well, I can't think of a nicer person to meet such a fate. He kidnapped my father and tried to take his business, and now is trying to take what he thinks is his legacy deal. Good for my father for thinking up such a plan and having the fortitude to execute it, given what he's been through and the resources he had. You have to admire the simplicity..." she raged.

"Maybe it's that simple for you, but for us this presents a dilemma," I replied. "Our mission is to put your father back in his place at the top of the arms dealer pyramid. Any other side missions are beyond our sanction, and the moral issue is 'can we stand by and watch him eliminate a rival?'" I told her.

"There have been several deaths associated with this kidnapping, including several of DeGroot's men. Did they present any dilemma?" she asked.

"Not at the time, but paid mercenaries work under the premise that death may be a consequence of their job," I reminded her. "DeGroot himself, while despicable by most standards, is hardly a physical threat. At this point, we could easily subdue him and turn him over to Interpol for prosecution. I'm sure their investigators are looking for a reason to close his jacket."

"You are a good man, to even consider sparing DeGroot's life after all we've been through," she said softly, looking into my eyes.

"I just want to keep my job and wrap this up nice and neat without losing any of my own people," I responded.

"So what will you do?" she asked.

"I'll have to think about it a bit. In the meantime, we have to get some sleep, a very early and busy day ahead tomorrow. See if they have some food in this place for dinner, Sam, and I'll make sure things are secure," I said.

The girls disappeared into the small kitchen to put together a meal, while I scouted the perimeter for signs of unusual activity. Seeing nothing after a full sweep of the neighborhood masquerading as an evening stroll, I returned to the house to the wonderful smell of roasting lamb and rice with fresh sautéed vegetables and warm rolls, courtesy of Dick's local contacts, that the girls had located in the freezer and put together. I stood in the doorway and watched without the women knowing I had returned. They were getting along famously, working together and chatting about everyday mundane things. I marveled at their resiliency, especially Elena's. Any other woman who had been through what she had in the last month—including the kidnapping of her father, the waiting for a ransom, the travel, the meeting in the warehouse, the masquerade at the hospital—would have been a shattered wreck. Here she was, cooking a delicious meal and acting as if it was a day like any other. Amazing.

"How long have you been working for Stark?" she asked Sam.

"I met Stark during my time in the navy as a communications officer. We were supporting the evacuation efforts in Grenada, and Stark's team was working security. A band of guerillas had taken a small platoon of men prisoner, and his team was not only able to liberate them with any getting harmed, but rounded up all of the guerrilla forces, questioned them, and made them give up their commander, and then removed the commander and dispelled the remains of the guerilla movement after the main military force was gone. I'd never seen a commander build and execute a plan so completely and thoroughly, with so little risk or bloodshed to anyone. He attracted a lot of attention for that little escapade, and I knew if I got the chance I'd like to work with him again. When I got out of the navy, he somehow found me and recruited me on to the team. It didn't take much convincing—he's amazing to work with and really takes good care of us, as employees and friends," she volunteered.

"Did you ever, you know, see him socially?" she asked coyly.

"No, but if he ever asked me, I wouldn't hesitate, except that I have a strict policy about dating people from work," she replied.

"In your job, that doesn't leave many choices, does it?" Elena teased.

"You're right about that. I don't date guys who know what I do, and I can't tell the others what I do because of security concerns—our work is all highly classified," she replied wistfully.

I cleared my throat, just to let them know I was back, and walked into the kitchen.

"Smell's delicious, what's for dinner?" I asked comically, like an ad executive home after a day at the office.

"Just a little something we whipped up," Sam replied, grinning and a little embarrassed. "Elena did most of the work. She's a great cook."

"There wasn't much to work with, but I think it will be edible," Elena chimed in, removing the rolls from the oven and taking the last of the food to the table.

"Come, sit, and tell me about your adventures while we eat," Elena invited, playing the perfect host.

And we did, finishing the meal after an hour or so and telling stories, sanitized for public consumption of course, for another couple of hours before turning in. I put the girls in each of the small bedrooms upstairs, and I took first watch on the couch. At midnight, I woke Sam and we traded places for a couple of hours until it was time to get ready. I didn't really sleep, so much as rest and plan for tomorrow.

At about 3:00 a.m., I got up and started inventorying gear, cleaning and loading guns and magazines, gathering maps, and reviewing in my mind what was needed. I'd called Dick earlier and asked about some support gear, but hadn't heard back from him, partially due to the time change, partially due to it being Saturday, with a skeleton crew at Langley. Usually with any mission on active status, Dick would have stayed at the office 24/7 until it was over, but the years had caught up with him, and his stamina wasn't what it once was. In the age of modern technology, he figured forwarding all calls to his cell phone was good enough, as he only lived a few miles from the office, and his home office was connected to the office's sector server through a secure link.

The ship was due to dock in a couple of hours, and I needed to be there for my team to make sure everything went as planned. The SUV we had arrived in was pretty shot, not terribly reliable, and not very fast. It also didn't offer any advantage, as the docks were flat and unobstructed, and they could see me coming for a mile or more. All they had to do was wait at the head of the access road and strafe me upon arrival. No odds there for us. Sam and I needed to get in there quickly, with some surprise, and be in a position to lend critical support if needed, and that meant speed and firepower.

A plane might work, but most on the island weren't equipped with any armaments, and those who were belonged to the military at another location. The civilian airport was nearby, but unless someone had a machine gun mounted on their Cessna, a plane wasn't likely the answer. Besides, an airplane was noisy and could only go so slowly, and once you passed the correct firing angle, provided you had something to fire with, you had to make a fairly large circle to realign the shot—so much for surprise. I didn't have many choices, but I thought a quick detour to the local airport might bear some fruit.

We let Elena get some much-needed sleep and loaded up in the ailing truck and headed a few miles west to the airport, toward the commercial aviation terminal. At this hour, the only security provided was an overweight private guard at the entry booth, an aging ex-cop who was asleep when we pulled up. I killed the engine a few yards away and hopped out to investigate. It didn't take long for me to find another spot in the fence that wasn't complete or protected. A repair van had been restringing some of the barbed wire that ran along the top of the perimeter fence, and they had removed a section of fence and left their truck in the hole left by the missing section.

I returned to the truck and retrieved Sam and our gear, and we set off on foot, leaving the truck there with the keys in it, just in case we needed a quick getaway vehicle for emergencies. We worked our way around the perimeter fence to the hole I had discovered and just walked right through unchallenged. We headed over to the commercial aviation service hangar, just to check things out. At that hour, nobody was in evidence, and security was lax at best. I popped the door to the hangar, and we stepped inside and closed the door behind us quickly, trying not to make any unnecessary noise. It was a fairly large hangar, with shelves of spare parts and work benches around the outside walls and small planes parked inside in various states of disassembly. Most were not terribly suited for our purposes today, including the G4 near the middle of the aisle. However, I thought I might have found what we needed down at the other end of the building.

I caught a swatch of color out of the corner of my eye and headed toward the far wall of the building. Tucked away in the far back corner of the building was a Schweizer 269C helicopter, a small two-seater often converted to use as a crop duster. This particular one had the doors removed for new Perspex to be installed, and the sprayer booms had been removed to get it in the hangar doors and to make more room in the repair shop. It was also equipped with a spray applicator on a winched cable dangling from the main cabin, a throwback to the early days of crop-dusting that allowed for water bombing for stray brush fires, a common problem in this arid environment.

That fertilizer bucket gave me an idea. I hunted around the hangar for a few moments and discovered a locked cabinet with a skull and crossbones sticker on the side—just what I needed, the chemical lock up.

"Sam, have a look at that little helicopter over there, see if it looks like it's all there and can fly. I think the keys are in that little cabinet over there near the office. See if it's got any fuel, if the parts are still intact, and if it has a radio. I have an idea," I told her.

"Will do, boss," she responded quietly, immediately recognizing the keys in the small cabinet on the wall nearest the office and taking them over to the little copter, looking over the electronics and avionics, checking systems and gauges.

"You know what you're doing in one of these?" she asked over her shoulder.

"Spent a few hundred hours in one similar in military trim, running recon over the desert, ground-hugging before it was popular and computerized. We'll have to stay low to keep below the local airport radar," I replied vaguely.

I grabbed a small hammer and popped the padlock on the chemical storage cabinet, rooted around in there for a few minutes, and came up with what I needed. I grabbed the jugs of chemicals, snatched a small instrument battery from a workbench and a full roll of bell wire, some wire nuts and tape and an ignition switch I found lying on the floor, and headed over to the copter to help Sam.

"What have you got up your sleeve with all that stuff?" she asked incredulously.

"Just a little surprise for our friends on the pier," I responded cryptically.

I piled all the materials in the back of the copter and hopped in. I hit the battery switch, checked the fuel pressure, oil pressure, prewarmer for the turbine, choke, fuel settings, and pump switches, and hit the rotor starter, holding my breath. The engine caught, and the rotors started to gain speed quickly. I breathed a sigh of relief and shut the rotors down, but let the motor idle to warm up, now that I knew everything was in working order. For ease of movement around the hangar, the copter sat on a small set of dolly wheels.

"Sam, could you open the large hangar door on the end, then come back here and help me push this little beauty outside?" I asked.

She headed over to the door, got the chain wheel going, and slowly the door started to rise. She got it up far enough to let the copter exit without hitting the rotor shaft cap and stopped. She headed back to the copter and grabbed a landing spar on the off side opposite me, and we rolled the little copter out the door.

I hopped into the small rear compartment and went to work with the battery, chemicals, and switches, and fashioned a crude explosive out of one of the chemical jugs. The idea was to turn the sprayer bucket into an aerial bomb. I added some airplane fuel to one of the empty jugs and wrapped up a small lump of dry sodium in an old party balloon I'd found in a drawer. I suspended the balloon in the jug full of gasoline and attached the bell wire bare ends to the top of the balloon. I punched a hole through the lid of the jug and ran the wire through the hole twice leaving the two bare ends wrapped around the neck of the balloon. I connected one end of the cut loop to the battery and the switch, taped the battery to the outside of the bucket, and left the other end of the wire trailing free, and dropped the jug in the metal bucket at the end of the winch cable. Now, all I had to do was lower the bucket with the jug in it and let the wire reel stay in the cabin, paying out wire as the bucket dropped. When I got to the end of the wire, I would strip the end and attach it to the other side of the switch. When I hit the switch, the wire wrapped around the neck of the balloon would heat up, melting the balloon, dropping it and its contents into the high-octane fuel. Sodium explodes when it hits water or oxygenated liquids, and the resulting explosion, fueled by the av-gas, would be extremely powerful and happen almost instantaneously, sending metal bucket shrapnel outward in all directions. The cable extended over five hundred feet, which should keep the impact on the copter to a minimum, but be able to take out critical targets on the ground if timed accurately. Not great, but the best I could do under the circumstances. Sam climbed into the passenger seat and turned around to inspect my work.

"Not bad for improvisation, boss, pretty crafty—Martha Stewart would be proud," she teased.

"So long as it works, that's all we need. It'll be tough to aim, but the bucket has a cable release. If we can hit the switch and then cut the bucket loose, we should get some throw and some range before the explosion," I replied.

"We only get one shot with that," she replied, instantly grasping the strategy needed to make the bomb effective.

"Guess we'd better make it count, then, huh?" I replied. "Buckle your harness, we'd better get moving, the team should be ready for action by now," I said, looking at my watch. It was five fifteen, and the dock was about twenty minutes by air, just enough time. I spun up the rotors and grabbed the collective, raising the tail first and then the nose as I got a feel for the controls. We lifted off and turned southeast toward the dock.

Chapter 33

Barcadera Pier 12

As if on cue, as the harbor pilot disappeared into the harbormaster's shack, a large truck, followed a moment later by two Toyota Tundra trucks pulled up to the parking area adjacent to the length of the pier. The flatbed truck pulled close to the edge of the dock and parked, the driver exiting and walking down to the harbormaster shack and disappearing inside, as the inhabitants of the SUVs exited and spread out in a defensive perimeter. The last to exit was DeGroot, his bulk wedged into the rear seat door frame of the truck momentarily until one of the soldiers gave him some assistance. The sun had risen by now, and DeGroot squinted in the bright light as his eyes adjusted from the relative darkness inside the heavily tinted SUV cabin. DeGroot gave a couple of brief orders to the soldiers surrounding him, and they split into two squads of four, one squad heading toward the end of the pier and the gangplank, the other fanning out along the ramshackle buildings and retaining wall adjacent to the pier, twenty yards from the ship.

The group at the gangplank got to the base of the walkway and stopped, waiting for DeGroot to catch up.

They stood there, tense, shifting from foot to foot, guns up and waving this way and that, not sure what they were going to face but eager to get started. Maybe too eager.

Big G and Spiro were holed up in the top level of the superstructure in a navigational antennae repair space, in a little alcove open to the weather but protected on all sides by steel plating, the perfect lookout point high above the pier. Spiro's men were arranged on the lower walkways of the superstructure, with a couple sprinkled below decks to act as funnels and escorts as they drove DeGroot deeper into the ship. All were armed with Mossburg pump shotguns loaded with deer slugs, and sidearms of various types.

From somewhere in the general area of the dock, just as DeGroot reached the base of the gangplank, a pistol shot rang out, the slug whanging off the steel hull. Instantly, the four thugs surrounding DeGroot fell to the deck, one of them reaching out to grab DeGroot's arm and taking him down with them. The four at the back of the pier dropped to a prone position and started scrambling for cover. There wasn't much to be found, and Big G and Spiro had a view much like that in an arcade. From their vantage point, they could easily pick off the protectors near the back of the buildings one by one. Moving targets made it harder, but Big G managed to drop one almost immediately as he stood up to run around the corner of a building, the huge lead slug catching him in the left shoulder, nearly tearing his arm off and spinning him around and dropping him to the ground screaming in agony.

Upon hearing their comrade fire and scream, the rest of the support group started firing wildly at the ship, rounds of 7.62 millimeter NATO ripping through the air like angry wasps on a mission. Most didn't find a target worth mentioning, but a couple of wild rounds found their way up near Spiro, who was standing in the little inspection space, popping away with the shotgun like he was hunting quail on the ground. He felt a round whiz past his ear, close enough to remind him to duck behind the steel bulkhead.

Meanwhile, Big G was making his way down the gangway ladders on the off side of the superstructure to lower levels for a better angle of fire. The height had helped when the soldiers across the pier were the target, but they couldn't depress their aim far enough to see the other group at the base of the gangplank since they were standing underneath the curvature of the hull. The gangplank group had recovered their senses and had split in two, a pair taking DeGroot snug against the hull backward toward the aft fantail, the other pair heading toward the bow railing and mooring ropes.

Having heard the initial shot, Stacks and BJ took that as a cue to enter the fray, popped around the far corner of the warehouse they had been crouched behind, and saw what had transpired. They saw DeGroot go down and the thug in front and to their right go down, and broke cover briefly, heading toward a stack of tractor tires used as pier bumpers, twenty yards to their left, and slightly behind the three remaining support men. Stacks held a Russian version of the Mk 11 Marine sniper rifle known as the Dragunov, accurate to six hundred yards that fired a big 7.62x54R round that he'd scrounged from the old Russian base's armory. He'd found a few extra magazines for it as well and had them secured on his web belt. He popped up from behind the pile of tires and sighted toward the support group now scrambling across the ground seeking cover from Big G. In a classic cross fire setup, Stacks dropped one of the mercs as he stood up to make some time toward a stack of fuel barrels next to the building. He never made it to the barrels, the heavy slug dropping him like a sack of wheat.

BJ took that as a challenge, saw it as "in for a penny, in for a pound," and swung around the other side of the tire pile and picked off another of DeGroot's support troops, firing the smaller AR-15 left-handed from the hip, sending three double bursts of lethal lead toward him, raking his body from hip to shoulder and spinning him around as it nearly cut him in half. That left only one of the rear guard left, and he had managed to make it into one of the decrepit buildings behind him.

By this time, the forward pair that had moved to the front of the containership had come up with some sort of coordination and were firing toward BJ and Stacks's tires, effectively pinning them down. Big G and Spiro were of no help, as the two were still too high to get a good firing angle on the front pair who were tucked underneath the curve of the hull.

One of the rear pair protecting DeGroot had found some sense of the situation and lobbed a antipersonnel grenade up and over the gunwale railing, where it landed and rolled along the deck and exploded a second later, taking out teak decking, and a small chunk of the lower corner of the superstructure where it met the deck. Big G was on the other side of that wall, inside the cabin housed by the superstructure bulkhead, and the explosion must have rattled his teeth, the effect like being inside the Liberty Bell and setting off a firecracker.

Otherwise unharmed, he recovered quickly and yelled in Greek for Spiro to concentrate on the rear pair but not to hit DeGroot, while he moved forward below decks and took care of the front pair. Suddenly, a loud whoosh came from one of the buildings across the street, and Big G, Stacks, and BJ all looked up toward the source of the sound while dropping down instinctively at the same time, just in time to see a flash of light and smoke fly by headed toward the superstructure of the ship. The remaining support trooper had been carrying an RPG slung over his shoulder and had fired the powerful weapon at the ship in the vain hope of taking out all resistance to open the way for the rear pair to take DeGroot aboard to capture the ship.

The RPG round flew straight and true and struck the antennae repair well that only moments before had protected Big G and Spiro, blowing the top off the superstructure and taking the radio antennae, radar mast, and associated broadcast equipment with it, scattering metal shrapnel and debris out over the water. It also had the effect of keeping everyone pinned to the ground for a moment.

A minute later, Stacks and BJ had regrouped behind their tire stack and were huddled, likely preparing a plan to take out the front pair of thugs when the whooping of rotor blades came from behind them from the ocean side of the ship. They looked up at the small copter, which juked side to side quickly, a signal used in the military that meant the cavalry had arrived.

Chapter 34

On Board the Helicopter

I had managed to point the copter toward the docks and keep the machine flying on target and low enough to avoid detection by the civilian radar at the airport. It was still early morning on island time, and there was no real activity expected by the single traffic controller on overnight duty at this hour. On the way, I had told Sam to strip the free end of the bell wire and connect it to the other side of the switch. I hit the winch release and allowed the bucket and the reel of bailing wire to unspool as the cable lowered the bucket a few hundred feet, and then reeled the whole affair back in together back on to the winch spool, ready for action should I need it.

As we approached the dock, I could see the huge container tied up to the pier, but the ship blocked my view at that altitude of the pier itself, but also blocked anyone standing on the pier from seeing me as well. I used this cover to my advantage to get close before popping up over the forward deck of the ship. I had seen smoke rising from the top of the ship's tower as we approached, an ominous sign, but held course until I got close enough to see what the situation might be. What I saw looked strange, a group of men all lying flat on the ground in various positions not moving. I thought we were too late, that the mission had been a huge failure, that everyone had been slaughtered in an ambush. The blood rushed out of my head, my ears started to buzz, and my vision narrowed. I managed to swivel my head over and catch a look at Sam, who had been watching me and appeared horrified at what she saw.

"Hey, boss, you okay?" she asked quietly.

"Look down, I think we're too late," I managed to mumble.

She looked down through the lower Perspex window, and her eyes widened a bit.

"Maybe not. I think we might be right on time," she cried.

Below her, Stacks and BJ had stood up behind their tire stack, pumped fists in the air, and started gesturing toward the buildings behind them, waving us off. For some reason, the comm gear wasn't working. Sam realized it as well and started fiddling with the copter's radio. Suddenly static filled the cabin, and she punched a couple of buttons, the result being the loud voices of Stacks and BJ. They told us to steer clear of the middle building in the row of storage shacks behind the pier, and I thought I heard the words "RPG" through the static, but couldn't be sure. Close enough for me, I swung the copter away from the pier toward the water and over the ship, surveying the damage below as I passed over the top of the superstructure. The smoking twisted metal of the conning tower told the story well enough; an explosive weapon of some type had hit the top and removed a good bit of it, bits of wire and plastic dangling over the edges of a small central well, the tops of a metal ladder still visible.

Time to provide some support to my team. I figured the RPG was the biggest weapon a guy like DeGroot would ever think he'd need on a simple hijacking, that there wasn't anything more powerful or dangerous than that lurking below or my guys would have alerted me to it. So the middle shack just became the primary target. Once I had pushed the little copter out over the open water, I hit the winch release and started lowering the deadly bucket bomb below me. When two hundred feet of cable had been released, I swung the chopper around quickly, creating a whip effect down the long cable as the bucket lagged behind like a pendulum slung from its moorings. I headed the chopper back toward the little building, lining up the cable on the second floor window, and hit the brakes, raising the nose and slowing the chopper drastically. The bucket started its forward swing, and I hit the ignition switch attached to the battery. Two seconds later I hit the bucket release switch, hoping my timing was right. With the nose of the chopper facing the sky, I was working blind, but could feel the weight of the bucket shifting the balance of the little chopper through the seat.

The bucket let go just as it reached to top of its forward swing, lobbing the bucket toward the roof of the building. I righted the chopper and hit the winch return switch to bring the cable back in so it wouldn't snag on anything. I watched as the bucket arced toward the building, landing squarely in the middle of the roof. Instantly, two bright flashes occurred, and the building evaporated in a huge fireball. All in a day's work, or so I thought.

On the Pier

Stacks and BJ had been trying to raise the copter on their comm gear, but the moisture of the air near the pier must have infiltrated the circuitry as the humidity started to rise, and there was a lot of static and noise on the connection, their ears buzzing from gun fire, RPG explosions, and static. Finally they resorted to hand signals, trying to wave off the tiny chopper from the deadly RPG sniper hidden in the small storage building. They saw the copter change directions, and relieved that their boss got the message and was out of danger for the moment, focused their efforts on removing the remaining threat of the mercs in the foredeck and aft fantail of the ship.

Stacks popped up over the top of the tire stack and started popping those big rounds toward the pair at the front, providing cover while BJ ran crouched toward the rear of the ship and the gangplank. He hit the ground and rolled coming up firing from behind a stack of crates waiting to be loaded, hitting one of the rear pair in the gut, silencing his pistol instantly. He swung the weapon left a few degrees and kept firing, hitting the remaining rearward merc in the thigh, causing him to fall, his body covering DeGroot in a last-ditch effort to protect his paymaster.

Big G had managed to get below decks to the forward porthole and it appeared he had pushed the barrel of his shotgun out the opening, pointing it toward the remaining pair at the front of the ship. The size of the porthole didn't allow him to stick his head and shoulders fully through the opening, so he had to fire blind based on where he had last seen the two assailants. Caught between the hail of lead from both Big G and Stacks, the two forward mercs didn't stand a chance. The first had fired his weapon dry, and one of Big G's deer slugs caught him, taking the top of his head off leaving a pink spray and bloody pulp blasted onto the hull of the giant ship. One of Stacks's sniper rounds caught the other in the chest seconds later, dropping him where he stood. Both professionals knew better than to celebrate just yet, but Spiro popped up over the forward Gunwale rail where he had been crouched and pumped his fist in the air in victory. He looked up just in time to see the bucket release from the bottom of the small copter and land on the building behind the pier, see the monstrous explosion, and feel the heat of the ensuing fireball rising toward the sky, the concussive wave knocking him down, along with everyone else left on the pier.

Stacks and BJ recovered in time to look up and see the RPG round streaking toward the helicopter. They started screaming into the comm gear for Stark to drop the chopper. The last thug had fired the round a split second before the building vaporized, sending the grenade on its deadly path toward the chopper before its operator evaporated.

Chapter 35

In the Helicopter

I felt and heard the explosion as the bucket did its deadly job, and the pressure wave rocked the little chopper, pushing the nose down and the whole craft backward ahead of it. I grabbed the cyclic and righted the craft, looked out the forward bubble windows, and found myself staring at the front of an RPG round heading directly for my windscreen. Instantly, I dumped the collective the small chopper dropping like a stone, punching my stomach up into my throat. I wasn't quite quick enough, and the flying grenade round sailed overhead, just clipping the tip of one of the rotor blades, shattering it, but not doing enough damage to set off the grenade until after it had passed beyond the little airship. Alarms started sounding, and buzzers started going off creating a cacophony in the cabin, added to by Sam yelling at me to kill the engines and autorotate to try to save the remaining rotors. My brain kicked back into gear, and I killed the fuel to the engine and reversed the shaft direction, killing any forward momentum and releasing the craft from the rotor spin. We hung like that for a full second before starting to fall. I reengaged the remaining rotor blades, and we started to autorotate, dropping quicker than I was happy with toward the water one hundred feet below.

I worked valiantly to try and control our descent, to no avail. The little craft was crippled and sinking like a flat stone, the choppy water rushing up to meet us at a furious pace. We both buckled up and tightened our seatbelts, preparing for impact. In seconds, we hit the water with a loud crunch and a splash, as the front of the little machine hit the cementlike water and disintegrated. The impact drove my head forward into the center window support and drove the collective stick into my chest, cracking my sternum. With no doors to provide structural support for the Perspex bubble, it cracked and fragmented, cold water rushing in through the door opening, the weight dragging us down coupled with the weight of the engines pushing us under. I worked at releasing the safety harness and saw Sam struggling with her release handles, which must have jammed on impact.

I managed to get my release to work and wriggled out of the harness, pushing myself over the center console to help free Sam. The pain in my chest was staggering, but I needed to get her free so she could help get us to the surface before we drowned. I slowly calmed her down and signaled to her that if she just leaned backward I could get to her release and set her free. She looked into my eyes, got the message, leaned back, and I hit the release handle, freeing her from the seat. She started to get her bearings, worked out from under the harness, and headed out the door opening, oriented properly to start scissoring toward the surface. I leaned backward out the other door and headed up, my lungs screaming for air and chest throbbing in pain. As my head broke the surface and I sucked in a huge gulp of air, my chest muscles spasmed, and I cried out in pain. Sam heard me, paddled over to support my head, and started dead manning back toward the ship with me in tow as the darkness caved in on me.

On the Pier

Stacks and BJ had seen the helicopter and the grenade cross paths, but couldn't see whether the little craft had been hit. They saw the grenade explode behind the copter, and it moved out of their line of sight behind the remains of the superstructure of the ship. Figuring their boss had cheated death again, they hustled over to try to take DeGroot before he had a chance to escape. He had managed to worm his way out from under the body of his fallen bodyguard and was trying to stand up when the building explosion had knocked him back down. By the time Stacks and BJ arrived, he was on his knees and struggling to stand for a second time.

Stacks got there first and leaped through the air, launching himself at the big target much as he had years ago on the football field going after a quarterback. He hit the big man center mass, pushing him back to the ground. Stacks recovered and rolled to his feet with a big grin on his face, reached into a thigh pocket of his BDOs, and pulled out a set of zip cuffs. He pulled

DeGroot's hands behind his back, cuffed his hands, and rolled him on his back like a beached whale. Stacks stood there next to the DeGroot's prone form like a trophy hunter who had just dropped his first elephant, as BJ hustled over to his side.

Big G was just emerging from below decks and saw the tackle. He leaped in the air in triumph. Spiro, too, had seen the helicopter go down on the other side of the ship. He quickly found the interior gangway and headed down the ladder and subsequent passage toward the gangplank at top speed to tell the two warriors about their boss's unfortunate demise.

He arrived at the bottom of the gangplank out of breath and unable to speak, nearly bowling over the two soldiers with his arrival. He managed to catch his breath eventually and was able to grab BJ by the arm and pull him in the direction of rear of the ship, so he could see around the end of the fantail and arrived in time to see the tip of the tail rotor sink beneath the choppy water. Spiro's wild gestures and shouting were quickly translated, and BJ understood his boss's chopper had hit the water and gone down. His head swiveled around, seeking signs of a life raft, floating debris, or other indication that his boss had gotten out alive. He saw nothing but a small oil slick on the surface of the water.

Then he heard shouting from above him. Big G was standing on the deck waving his arms and pointing toward the water on the off side of the ship. Quickly surmising that Big G could see something he could not, he sprinted up the gangplank to the companionway and from there to the deck and across to the opposite gunwale rail. He looked directly down and sighed with relief, seeing his boss being towed by their communications officer toward the massive hull, apparently unconscious but alive.

Big G was already moving quickly and had climbed into the cabin of the deck crane. He fired up the engine of the giant spiderlike beast and expertly swung the boom over the off side of the ship, lowering the hook and cable toward the water. Based on hand signals from BJ, he dropped the hook into the water within ten feet of the pair in the water and let the current carry it toward them slowly and gently. When the big steel hook got close enough, Sam was prepared to reach out and grab the cable to control the approach speed.

She worked the hook under the belt of Stark's BDO pants and grabbed the cable above him, wrapping her legs around his chest gently for support and securing the two of them to the hook. She looked up and made a thumbs-up gesture, and Big G started the hoist, reeling in the cable slowly, lifting the two out of the water, and swinging the boom around to deposit them gently on the deck of the giant ship, where they collapsed in a heap.

BJ hurried over to the two wet forms on the deck, and he and Sam got Stark unhooked, laid him out face up on the deck, and then rolled him partially over, to let him expel the water from his lungs as he appeared to miraculously return to life. He coughed and sputtered for a few moments, then opened his eyes, and sat up, momentarily disoriented.

As his senses returned and he started to remember the events leading up to his loss of consciousness, his eyes narrowed and he yelled, "Did we get DeGroot?"

"Stacks has him cuffed on the pier, and all our guys are safe," BJ replied.

"How'd I get up here?" he asked.

Big G looked over at him, grinning.

"I plucked you from the water like a big fish!" he exclaimed. "I worked on the docks unloading ships as a teenager. I guess the crane is just like riding a bike—you never forget," he continued.

"I owe you both my life," Stark pronounced, "and I'm not likely to forget that, ever."

Stark motioned for Sam to come closer for a private conversation. She leaned over him and he whispered in her ear, "Get Degroot out of here, put him in a holding cell in the airport main terminal security office, keep him away from Big G."

Sam looked puzzled for a moment, then his real intentions dawned on her and she smiled admiringly at Stark and nodded.

Meantime, Stacks had stood guard over DeGroot, who was hurling curses at the giant soldier, exhorting him to let him go, he had done nothing wrong, to release him immediately. Stacks just stood there, grinning, until BJ and the rest of the team managed to get down the companionway, down the gangplank, and join him on the pier. They had left Stark on deck until they could rig a stretcher to get Stark off the ship safely without exacerbating his injuries, which included a fractured left wrist, cracked ribs and sternum, bruised heart, slight concussion, and some bumps and bruises.

Sam pulled the team aside at the base of the companionway and held a quick briefing conference to let everyone know what their next moves were. BJ and Stacks managed to get the huge arms dealer to his feet, and as instructed by Stark, put him in the back of one of the remaining SUVs, and drove him to the airport main terminal 20 minutes away. They accompanied him still cuffed to the security office and after a brief conversation, had the local security officer tuck him into the small holding cell at the back of the office.

"Comfortable?" Stacks asked sarcastically, pulling up a small stool in front of the arms dealer and settling in.

"You know better. Why am I being held here?"

"You're certainly more comfortable than Big G was in the hold of your ship for over a week, you fat piece of shit," he snarled. "You're being held here so that we can turn you over to the proper authorities for your recent activities. Who knows what they'll find in their investigations . . . ," he continued. "Your own greed and envy put you in here, and your arrogance and avarice lead you to that ship. I just don't have much patience left for you and don't want to endanger anyone else."

"You don't have the guts to kill me face to face. I knew it…" he snarled back.

"I have all the guts I need, to do what needs to be done. But the authorities will eventually unravel all of this, and my presence here will be incongruous with any available evidence. In short, I wasn't here and won't be here when you disappear. I'll be a thousand miles from here, with an iron-clad alibi," he replied.

"Sounds like you've thought it all through. How do you know my men won't come after you when I'm gone? They owe me their lives and will gladly die for me," he shot back.

"I have the distinct feeling that their loyalty will be easily redirected. I doubt any of them will miss you," Stacks explained.

"Akbar will come after you with righteous vengeance," he whispered.

"Oh, you didn't hear? Akbar took his own life at the prospect of spending the balance of his life in an American prison. He won't be taking vengeance on anyone except the seventy virgins he was promised," Big G quipped.

DeGroot's face changed expression for a brief second, but he recovered quickly, the bland look of self-assured boredom returning quickly to his oversized face. Stacks stood in the doorway to the back office, and waited for DeGroot to realize he wasn't going to be going anywhere for a while. He had lied a moment ago when he told DeGroot he didn't have the patience for him—Stacks had all the patience in the world knowing that DeGroot's life was beyond his control at this point and that his fate was in someone else's hands.

"How much is it worth to you to release me? We could work together and have it all… a partnership to conquer the arms world. With your skills and my connections, we'd be unstoppable," DeGroot surmised.

"Don't bother trying to bargain or negotiate—it's far too late for that. The moment you decided your life would be better without Big G in it, the moment you brought his daughter into your little sick, twisted world, that made it personal, it made you an extortionist, it made you a terrorist, and I don't negotiate with terrorists," Stacks hissed.

Stacks turned on his heel, and walked out of the security office and out into the morning sunshine. BJ fell into step alongside of him and the two headed back to join the others in the hangar base across the tarmac.

Back on the pier, Sam, having retrieved a stretcher from the ship's sick bay and with the help of a couple of Spiro's men, carried the injured Stark down the gangplank to the pier and set him down near the group of vehicles DeGroot's men had arrived in. With none of DeGroot's men left alive after the firefight, they would need to remove them in a hurry, taking the best in which to make their own way out of the area and leaving the rest behind for the local authorities to sort out. Knowing that the police captain of the local force was on their side in all this and that he had been recently fired, leaving the force in somewhat disarray, they weren't worried about official backlash. By the time they sorted out the bodies, put out the fire in the warehouse from the bomb Stark had launched, and figured out what had happened, Stark and his team would be long gone, and Big G and Spiro would be sipping Ouzo on the fantail of his yacht as they cruised across the Aegean Sea.

As they loaded Stark and Sam into the back of the largest van, they could hear sirens approaching as the first responders followed the rising pall of smoke from the demolished warehouse building. Spiro and Big G mounted up in the other truck, leaving Spiro's men to ditch the rest of the vehicles at their convenience, and they all headed toward the airport. It was mid-morning by now, and the commercial aviation area where Stark and Sam had liberated the helicopter was in full swing. The vehicles pulled up to the gate where they had started the morning, to find a new guard replacing the sleeper they had disabled, where Sam flashed her U.S. Government contractor ID and was waved through. They parked in the back of the lot while Sam made a few calls, one to Dick to arrange for a flight home and to have him dispatch some private medical help for Stark prior to loading him on the flight home.

The *Orion*'s captain and balance of his crew headed back to the ship, having gotten their orders to head toward open water and their next assignment. Spiro's men hopped into the remaining vehicles and headed for the nearest tavern for a celebratory drink before chartering a boat of their own and heading back to Corfu.

Once medical help arrived, in the form of an ambulance of similar vintage to the one they had stolen from the Russian base the day before and two Aruban EMTs, Stark's group including Stacks and BJ headed for the commercial terminal to wait for their return flight. Sam had the presence of mind to give the safe house a call and let Elena know that all was well, her father was fine, and they could be found at the airport for the next few hours. She arranged for a local car service recommended by the local airport concierge to pick her up and bring her to the airport. Elena, Big G and Spiro would use the car to go across the island to the other port where the *Lady Elena* was moored, and then head back to Leyntas and points unknown at their leisure.

Once Elena arrived, the group found a small private lounge near the terminal, ordered a round of drinks, and toasted Stark's health. Just as they were raising their glasses, the door to the lounge banged open and in came Stark, in a wheelchair, his face bruised and lacerated from the crash, his movements stiff from the pain in his chest at every breath.

"Rumors of my death are greatly exaggerated!" he shouted to his friends. "I may be beat up, but I can still toast to a successful mission," he added cheerfully.

"Well, I for one am glad your 'mission' is over and that I have my father back," Elena responded, her face lit by a big smile at the prospect of seeing Stark again.

"I have to concur, Mr. Stark. I applaud your expertise and am glad your mission included saving my life and reestablishing my business position. I am forever in your debt, but will find a way to repay you the favor, I promise. But I have to ask, how did you know about my abduction so quickly, and what was the U.S. Government's interest in what for all intents was a local matter?" Big G asked.

"Let's just say your interests and those of the US government happened to coincide and take a mutually beneficial direction," he replied.

The rest of the team smiled knowingly but didn't say a word, and returned to their conversations around the table. Elena had put herself nearest to Stark's chair, and they were chatting intimately. Big G and Spiro were replaying their involvement in the recent firefight, still running on adrenalin. BJ and Stacks, more accustomed to the "cool down" period after a successful mission, were trading stories of past actions back and forth as Sam looked on, keeping an eye on Stark, monitoring his health. She had called Tang in Virginia and filled him in on the mission, but not on the final disposition of DeGroot, and then put him on speaker so he could join in on the banter with the team.

The door to the club squeaked open, and a uniformed maintenance worker from the airport walked in and over toward Stark. Immediately, five hands went toward weapons they all still carried, unsure of the threat this new arrival might pose. The startled worker, not knowing what he had walked into, stopped in his tracks and put his hands up in a universal gesture of surrender, and he started babbling.

"Please, don't hurt me. I just bring a message to Mista Stark," he blurted out.

"A message?" Stark asked. "From whom?"

"I have a phone call for you from the States, waiting at the terminal office," he replied quickly.

Their hands relaxed, realizing that he wasn't anything to worry about.

"Sorry to break up the party, but I fear that's from Dick, wondering when we'll be back in Virginia," Stark announced. "I'll take it, if one of you could push me across the street."

"Hold our table, we'll all go with you," Sam said.

Indeed, when they all arrived back at the small commercial terminal, he took a call from Dick, which was short and sweet, with the understanding that the phone was not scrambled or encrypted in any way.

"Stark, what's your condition, been trying to reach you on your sat phone, no response?" he asked, with no hesitation or pleasantries.

"I'm alive, hurting a bit, but we got it done. Big G's here with us in Aruba, but his ship's on the other side of the island. He and Elena are heading back to Greece on a long cruise to reconnect and get his business back on track from a safe place," he explained. "Only casualty was the phone, which I suspect is lying in the bottom of the harbor."

"And the abductor?" he asked hesitantly.

"He's under control and tucked safely away," Stark replied vaguely.

"Put Sam on the phone," he ordered.

Stark handed Sam the phone and wheeled himself over to the rest of the team across the small terminal waiting room.

"Sam here, sir," she purred.

"Don't try that with me. How is Stark really?" he asked.

"He'll live, sir, but could use some skilled help to get his chest and head checked out," she replied.

"As I suspected, he's being the hero again, isn't he? Is Big G's daughter there?" he asked.

"Yes, sir, to both, but he saved my life this morning, so I think he's earned it," she replied respectfully.

"Okay, tell him I'll send a second plane for him properly equipped to care for him, should be there in a few hours. You stay with him to look after him, get him loaded, handle paperwork, etcetera. The rest of the team, get on the plane I sent for you, which should be landing any moment, and we'll see you when you arrive back here. I'll have you met at Dulles and ferried back to Langley for a debriefing," he instructed.

"Yes, sir, I'll handle it and tell the rest of the team," she replied softly.

"Oh, and Sam? By the way, what's this little adventure going to cost me, do you suppose?" he asked, and Sam could almost see him wincing as he waited for her answer.

"Sir, if I had to guess, somewhere in the Somali Pirate range," she replied, referring to a previous mission with a successful conclusion but a moderately high price tag.

"Well, I guess we can talk about it when you all get here," he replied, sounding a bit relieved.

He hung up without another word, and Sam went over and joined the group, relaying the newest instructions to the team. Stark motioned for Big G to join him back across the street for a drink, including Spiro and Elena in the invitation. As they headed over, Sam pushing him across the tarmac with Big G strolling alongside, Stark motioned for Big G to bend down. Stark whispered in his ear so that the rest of the team couldn't hear.

"Don't you have a few phone calls to make?" he asked with a conspiratorial air. Big G's considerable eyebrows rose up his forehead in surprise, and Stark chuckled. "I figured out what the code numbers mean, and those numbers haven't been called in a while. They probably need reset about now," he added.

"I had planned to take care of that once we were back on the *Lady Elena*," he replied cautiously. "I have twenty-four hours safety built into the programming, just in case," he continued.

"We'll talk about that at more length later, but I'm glad you're as responsible as I had assumed you'd be," he whispered back.

"For your own safety, the less you know, the better. Rest assured there are adequate safeguards and stop points built into my plan. I've learned it's better to be flexible and be prepared," he added.

"I couldn't have said it better myself, Big G," I replied.

We got settled in the tavern at a table in the back, and I noticed that Elena managed to pick the chair right next to where they parked mine, facing the door. She had experienced a tearful reunion with her father at the airport and was more relaxed and under control than I'd seen her since we met on the yacht. She'd put on a pair of 4" red heels, a revealingly short red dress, and dabbed on some make-up, and looked fantastic.

I was pretty heavily medicated at this point, to make breathing less painful. My left wrist was tightly wrapped, and I had a bit of double vision, but beyond that I wasn't much the worse for wear, at least functionally. Drinking alcohol was definitely out of the question for now. I ordered a soda for me and Ouzo for the rest of the table, in celebration of a job well done and to new friends.

When all the toasting and celebrating had settled down, Elena leaned over and said, "I know you have to go back to the US. When can I see you again?"

"That's the tough part of this job. I never know where I'm going to be. I should be in Virginia for the next few weeks or a couple of months healing up after this. I could use some company to make the time pass faster, if you're interested," I replied.

"I have so much to thank you for—I don't know how I can ever repay you for your courage and help in rescuing my father," she continued.

"Well, I'd love to take credit for that, but your father actually rescued himself, to be honest. I just pursued the guys that took him and moved them out of the way for him," I said.

"I've only been to America a couple of times, briefly, several years ago on business. Maybe you could show me around Washington if I came to visit you?" she asked breathlessly.

"I'd be proud to show you off in Washington, Elena. Come anytime it's convenient. I'll show you the sights, take good care of you," I replied gallantly.

She leaned down and kissed me, passionately and slowly, then stood up and smiled, and took her father by the arm. The two of them headed toward the door, once the hooting and catcalls died down from Spiro and the rest of the tavern patrons. I just sat in my wheelchair like I'd been clubbed with a sledgehammer. Spiro got up and headed out behind them, looked back, and gave me a wink before he ambled out into the morning sunshine on his way to rejoin his crew for their trip back to Corfu.

Sam and I sat quietly at the table, chatting about logistics for getting all the gear back to the office, speculating about how the debrief might be handled later on today, waiting for our flight.

But Elena and Big G weren't done here quite yet. Big G had a few final words for DeGroot, now that he was safely tucked away in a cell. The pair headed back to the public terminal and ducked into the security office. While Elena chatted with the desk sergeant and every head in the room was turned toward her, Big G headed quickly and quietly toward the rear of the office where the cells were. He saw that the local security officers were standing near the door of the cell and there were two healthy-looking and suitably sized Aruban Government policemen, standing by to transport the big arms dealer to the larger prison in the capitol for further interrogation and arraignment. The local airport cops had printed DeGroot, done a cursory search of his voluminous person, put real steel cuffs on his wrists, taken his belt and shoelaces, bagged and tagged his personal items, and were walking him forward a few steps to hand him over to the government authorities for transport. There were six men plus DeGroot clustered in the small area at the end of a hallway leading to the door of the cell.

Suddenly there was some confusion in the knot of policemen. DeGroot had spotted Big G at the other end of the hallway, and had used his bulk to his advantage. While the officers were focused on their paperwork, he had shoved his hip into the nearest security officer, knocking him off balance, and swung his hands around and snatched the officer's pistol out of his holster. With a wild look in his eye, he aimed the .38 service revolver at Big G, firing once. The sound of the revolver was exceptionally loud in the confined space deafening the officers around him and partially masking another shot from further down the hall.

Suddenly, DeGroot's head seemed to vaporize before their eyes, and the big man sunk to the ground like a sack of sand, dragging several of the officers to the floor with him. Elena had seen DeGroot's maneuver from behind her father further down the hall, and sensing what was happening, reached into her purse and retrieved one of Stark's Sig .45 pistols, leveled it at the big man's head and fired. The big slug had nearly removed the back of DeGroot's head, spattering blood and grey matter all over the rear of the cell and the surrounding officers. His shot had gone wide, missing Big G by a few millimeters and careening off the doorway behind him.

Pandmonium ensued, as everyone in the room hit the ground at the sound of the first shot, the trained officers pulling out their service revolvers as they ducked behind office furniture and partitions, prepared to return fire on the now dead target.

Elena raised her hands, dropping the heavy weapon to the floor in the process. In a few seconds, the lead Government official had taken control of the situation, and directed one of the security officers to arrest Elena and Big G. Big G's face still registered a combination of shock, surprise and pride as he watched his daughter calmly cuffed and taken to a nearby desk for questioning.

After a long afternoon of questioning by government officials, the tale of the past three weeks had come out, edited of course for police consumption. Big G did a good job of relating the story, relating the events convincingly enough for the government officers to release them pending an investigation. He told them if their story checked out, he would agree to work with the Aruban prosecutor not to press charges against either one of them. After four hours and a little haggling, the father and daughter pair waslked out of the security office, out of the airport terminal, and into the dazzling sunlight of the Aruban afternoon.

Chapter 36

Later, On the *Lady Elena*

Big G and Elena sat in the salon sharing a bottle of wine from the galley, quietly thinking about the last few days' events. Big G had been holed up in his below-deck office for about three hours, reviewing contracts, contacting customers, and making other phone calls. He had a lot of reassuring to do, but surprisingly, his customers were not only happy to hear from him, but several either increased existing orders or originated new ones. Things were going well, but he had one more series of phone calls to make.

He and Elena had discussed his little phone-in plan on the way across the island to reach the yacht, and she understood why he had set it up and how it worked. She was neither surprised nor ashamed of her father for hatching such a scheme. Based on recent events, she had no trouble with that at all.

* * *

Epilogue

So now I was all healed up from my excursion to Aruba and heading toward the director's office for a debriefing and reassignment. This really was just a formality; my team had been debriefed individually two weeks ago, and I had filed my report along with theirs from the hospital. Dick had come to see me personally, and he'd heard the high points, obviously trying to estimate how much trouble he was in and how much carnage and collateral damage I'd left behind while completing the mission.

In the intervening two weeks, I'd lain in a hospital bed recuperating from broken ribs, a cracked sternum, which they'd had to wire back together much like an open heart surgery patient, a wrist broken in three places that they'd pinned back together, a number of deep lacerations, a bullet crease, and some shrapnel wounds that I'd received from flying pieces of the helicopter water bucket when it exploded. It hurt to breathe, and I couldn't draw a big enough breath to muster up even a moderately loud voice until late last week.

After we'd gotten out of Aruba on the planes Dick had arranged, the local police had assembled at the docks and tried to sort out the mess. With no leadership from their captain, who had made a hasty exit to the south of France, where he bought a little villa and spends his days tending a nice garden and making wine, the police department was a little less efficient than a well-oiled machine. They were having trouble reconstructing the kind of action that would have resulted in eight dead mercenaries, the burned and scattered remains of a warehouse, a small oil slick on the harbor, a containership that wasn't there but for which there was no record of it ever leaving, and a collection of shell casings and bullet fragments from eleven different weapons, some of which were Russian in origin and quite old to boot. The pieces didn't fit together well for them, and with DeGroot dead and our team out of there and beyond their reach, it would take them a while to pull the pieces together in a credible way.

They did notice a marked drop in petty crime on the island, and the new police captain had started an internal investigation into some of Captain Johnson's more nefarious activities, resulting in the removal of some nine other officers complicit in a range of crimes, graft, and corruption of various types. He'd rededicated his police force, hired a slew of new recruits, and was making a great run at reforming the department into something a bit more effective, hoping to spark some additional tourism after word of our little escapade leaked to the local press and was picked up by the wire services. Between that and the Natalie Holloway incident, revenue from visitation to the island was down considerably, and they needed to clean up their act to help get it back.

The locals never found the Russian base either, and I suspect Dick would keep that one in his hip pocket as well until he needed it again. We'd done a good enough job buttoning things up before we left to keep the place hidden from all but the most resourcefully curious, and the large radiation warning signs left covering the ventilator opening on our way out should keep even the nosiest tourist at bay for a while.

Spiro and his band of fishermen warriors made it back to Corfu just fine, and he still runs a fishing trawler every day and at night tells stories of the biggest one that didn't get away.

About the Author

Dave Poulos is an entrepreneur, marketer and business consultant, speaker, and author. He's written over twenty published articles on marketing-related topics and serves a host of business clients nationwide as a marketing consultant. Previously, after graduating from a large university in the Northeast, he was a contractor to federal government agencies with three initials, offering a variety of "information" services. He was raised in Northern Virginia, inside the Beltway, and currently lives with his wife and family in Maryland.

Special Thanks

Many people are owed a debt of gratitude for helping me create this book. Special thanks go to my readers, Tony Shockley, Dr. Stephen Flannelly, Lori Adams, and especially Dr. Edwin Sapp, professor at University of Maryland, without whom this story would have been much different.

www.ingramcontent.com/pod-product-compliance
Lightning Source LLC
Chambersburg PA
CBHW051311300726
48976CB00002B/359